R0200390706

07/2019

PRAISE FOR ANNE D. LeC

The Halo Effect

"Anne LeClaire's new novel *The Halo Effect* takes us into the life, the grief, the anguish, and the ultimate redemption of a man who has endured the excruciating loss of his only child through murder. It makes an eloquent statement about the curative power of the creative act and the leap of faith it takes to choose living and loving when the black peace of death seems so seductive. It's beautifully done."

—Elizabeth George, *New York Times* bestselling author

"The terms 'literary' and 'page-turner' dovetail beautifully in Anne D. LeClaire's new novel. *The Halo Effect* is a must-read for LeClaire's faithful fans and a sit-up-and-take-notice book for those who have yet to discover this talented, truth-seeking storyteller who asks the big questions as she observes the small but intricate details that make us human."

—Wally Lamb, *New York Times* bestselling author

"*The Halo Effect* will keep you turning pages, and fast. But it is that rarest of page turners, a novel that illuminates our frailties and the depths of grief while also managing to be hopeful and wholly human. Anne D. LeClaire has written a bighearted book that will leave you breathless."

—Ann Hood, author of *The Knitting Circle* and
The Book That Matters Most

"*The Halo Effect* is a wonderful hybrid: a compelling murder mystery and a thou   was fascinated by the book's

—   *he Sandcastle Girls*

PALM BEACH COUNTY
LIBRARY SYSTEM
3650 Summit Boulevard
West Palm Beach, FL 33406-4198

P9-EIE-551

"Profoundly moving and deeply satisfying."
—Margot Livesey, *New York Times* bestselling author

"I wasn't ready for this one. As a fan of Anne LeClaire's work I knew her writing would be its usual excellence, watchful, luminous, and moving, but in *The Halo Effect* she has also drawn a New England community in its exact contours by placing it under the revealing pressure of tragedy. The result is a mystery at once literate, intimate, and almost intolerably suspenseful—reminiscent of Louise Penny at her best."
—Charles Finch, *New York Times* bestselling author of the Charles Lenox series

"Prepare yourself for one of the most important books of the year."
—*Fresh Fiction*

"Anne LeClaire has a genuine knack for writing deftly created characters and embedding them in inherently fascinating, unpredictable narrative-driven story lines. *The Halo Effect* is a riveting read from cover to cover."
—*Midwest Book Reviews*

"I love this book. It is a master class in voice and character."
—Hallie Ephron, *New York Times* bestselling author

Listening Below the Noise:
The Transformative Power of Silence

"Luminous."
—*PBS NewsHour*

"Eloquent and moving . . . Although technically a memoir, this book moves beyond that genre into spirituality and philosophy. LeClaire's reputation as a novelist may draw readers to this lovely book, which should also have crossover appeal to spiritual seekers of any religion and no religion."

—*Booklist*

The Lavender Hour

"LeClaire packs this winning novel with resounding life lessons and a resonating set of romantic relationships."

—*Kirkus Reviews*

Entering Normal

"Exquisite . . . A beauty . . . If you love the feel of Anne Tyler's novels, then this has your name all over it."

Daily Mirror (London)

"In rich and limpid prose, LeClaire shifts the point of view . . . focusing on the small acts that get us through the day, or the night, or not. A woman's book in the best possible sense, this will leave readers warm and satisfied."

—*Booklist*

"An emotional wallop comparable to that produced by Sue Miller's *The Good Mother* or Jane Hamilton's *A Map of the World*."

—*Publishers Weekly*

"A gentle, spirited novel about friendship and survival."

—*USA Today*

Leaving Eden

"A light, breezy novel about serious subjects. It's eventful, with a lingering death, a murder, a secret revealed, to say nothing of a makeover."

—*Boston Globe*

"Artfully crafted characters resonate within this emotional novel detailing one girl's ability to face the hardships of her life."

—*Romantic Times*

The Law of Bound Hearts

"Recommended . . . LeClaire has crafted authentic characters and successfully portrays the power of forgiveness."

—*Library Journal*

"A gripping, emotional intensity and depth of feeling highlight this poignant and lyrical novel, which illustrates how precious life is."

—*Romantic Times*

the orchid sister

ALSO BY ANNE D. LECLAIRE

Fiction

The Halo Effect
The Lavender Hour
Entering Normal
Leaving Eden
The Law of Bound Hearts
Land's End
Grace Point
Every Mother's Son
Sideshow

Nonfiction

Listening Below the Noise: The Transformative Power of Silence

Children's Fiction

Kaylee Finds a Friend

the
orchid
sister

Anne D. LeClaire

LAKE UNION
PUBLISHING

This is a work of fiction. Names, characters, organizations, places, events, and incidents are either products of the author's imagination or are used fictitiously. Any resemblance to actual persons, living or dead, or actual events is purely coincidental.

Text copyright © 2019 by Anne D. LeClaire
All rights reserved.

No part of this book may be reproduced, or stored in a retrieval system, or transmitted in any form or by any means, electronic, mechanical, photocopying, recording, or otherwise, without express written permission of the publisher.

Published by Lake Union Publishing, Seattle

www.apub.com

Amazon, the Amazon logo, and Lake Union Publishing are trademarks of Amazon.com, Inc., or its affiliates.

ISBN-13: 9781503903272
ISBN-10: 1503903273

Cover design by Faceout Studio, Tim Green

Printed in the United States of America

Dedicated with gratitude to my tribe:
You know who you are.
Thanks for always having my back.

There was Pantagruel told by the keeper of the fountain that it was his wont to recast old women, so making them again young and by his art to become like to the young wenches there present whom he had that very day recast— and altogether restored to that same beauty, form, size, elegance and disposition of limbs as they had displayed at the age of fifteen or sixteen years . . .

—*Rabelais*

. . . and the mask is torn off, reality remains.

—*Lucretius*

ON THE NATURE OF THINGS

Tia Clara woke at dawn from a restless night troubled by a dream of lost girls and a much-scarred woman of many masks. A crescent-shaped shadow obscured the eastern sun. Despite this sign—or perhaps because of it—she was mindful to begin the day as usual, dressing in her worn cotton blouse and dark skirt, the hem of which brushed against her swollen ankles. She tied the strings of her old apron around her waist. She undid and replaited her thick braid of white hair with fingers so practiced she required no mirror. Her nose was thin and curved, her skin as weathered and wrinkled as that of a sea turtle. Like the sea turtle, she, too, had a reptilian dip to her neck so that her head jutted forward, a result of a spine curved not only by the decades but by years spent watching. Listening. Finally, although it was still early for the tourists, she gathered her things—small folding chair and table, embroidered cloth, umbrella to ward off the heat of the sun, collapsible wooden frame, small carton of her wares, and, lastly, the canary cage—and set them in the two-wheeled cart. As she pushed the cart over the uneven *calle* leading to the village square, the burden of knowledge weighed heavily on her. She carried inside her the truths of Playa del Pedro, stories sung to her by the ancestors, confided by the sea, whispered to her by the wind. In this way, she had learned the past and foreseen the future of the village, all that had been and that which was to come.

A stranger watching as she unfolded the legs of her table and set it on a patch of sidewalk would detect no indication of the disquiet that lingered in her heart—unrest caused by the sleepless night and troubling dreams, the penumbral sunrise, and the knowledge she held. Taking care, she shook out the ecru linen that had once belonged to her *madre* and her *abuela* before that. The edges were adorned with silken threads of green and blue, yellow and orange. She smoothed the folds with gnarled fingers grown thick at the knuckles and spread the linen over the table.

Muttering imprecations, she lifted her chair from the cart and, as she did every day, set it behind the table. She had selected this spot years ago, a favorable site across from the taxi stand and next to Solano's bakery. She watched as the daily life of the village awoke around her. In contrast to the dark visions of the previous night and the omen of the shrouded dawn sun, all appeared almost festive. Music boomed from the speakers in the square; the trill of young laughter floated from a nearby *calle*; satisfying aromas wafted her way from the bakery. In a few minutes, Juan Solano would send his son over with a cup of *atole* for her and, for the bird, crumbs of day-old bread.

She watched as Jesús Rodríguez chose a seat in front of the bakery. Soon Aldo Ventura would join him, and the two would position stones on a backgammon board, its red and black points faded to shades so dull as to be almost indistinguishable. They would agree, as they did every morning, that the loser would pay for the coffee. This would be Rodríguez. Not because he was the poorer player, but because Aldo cheated. She turned her attention away. These toothless old men were of little concern.

On Avenida Cinco, two *federales* patrolled the waterfront. She could remember a time when there were no *federales* in Playa, no Hotel Molcas. No *norteamericanos*. And little crime. She could remember when the park was only a rough field where the men who worked on the coconut plantation played ball. She studied the air around the soldiers and saw the shimmer of red, the vibration of the fire serpent. The younger of the two strutted with the self-importance of a rooster. A whistle from the pier signaling the morning boat from the island brought Tia Clara back to the business of the day. She opened the cardboard box and took out string hammocks, woven shawls, and a selection of belts, which she hung from the dowels of the hinged wooden frame. Vanilla blossoms and dragonflies were carved into the wood. Felipe the carpenter had made the frame for her after she had cured his infant son, who had suffered from ill winds during the first weeks after his birth.

Once the carton was empty, Tia Clara opened her umbrella and screwed its small clamp onto one end of the table's edge, throwing half the surface into shade. In the shadowed section she set down the wood and wire cage. Pieces of broken mirror, affixed to the wires with red and yellow yarn, caught the sun's reflection, causing them to dance around the sidewalk and square. Her shawls and hammocks were well made, as good as any shop in Playa, but it was the bird that drew the tourists. *"Adivinación?"* Tia Clara called when they passed. A sign on the table informed passersby: FORTUNES FOR SIX PESOS. At first they would keep their distance, reluctant to be drawn in, but they always stepped closer once she opened the cage and took out the canary. It was not yellow but green, which she knew was the most successful color for canaries. Head cocked, the bird would consider the cards, pluck one from the spread. Holding the card in its beak, it would cross to her hand, perch on her wrist, and drop it into her open palm. By now, Tia Clara would have chosen a single tourist to receive the card—most often a woman, as women were more open to this kind of thing—and give a brief reading. If it was the first reading of the morning, she would wave away the offered pesos. It brought bad luck to charge for the day's first fortune.

In the beginning she had used an ancient deck, but she soon realized that the tourists did not like it. They wanted to know about money and love—always love—and they did not want to see images foretelling illness or sorrow, loss and regret that waited on the horizon, confirming what Tia Clara had learned long ago: it took a sturdy heart to bear the weight of truth. Now she spread out small pink cards printed with words like *Love*, *Fortune*, *Happiness*, and *Health*.

The ferry whistle sounded again. Tia Clara took her medicine pouch from the pocket of her apron and sifted dried chia onto her palm, then sprinkled it on the table at the four directions for the creatures that held up the sky. Armadillo, Snail, Turtle, and Crab. Even for the *gringos*, things had to be properly done. Then, moving quickly, furtively, she tossed an extra pinch into the air, a gesture to placate old ghosts and quiet new fears.

"*Buenos días*, Tia Clara." Paco, the baker's son, held out a cup of the thick chocolate *atole*, sweetened with honey, scented with vanilla. He placed a small saucer of dried crumbs on the table.

"*Gracias,*" she said. Recently, because he was in love with María, the middle daughter of Eduardo Linones, the wispy second shell that she could see enfolding Paco's body was a shade of rose, dusted with gold.

She finished with the chia, pulled tight the drawstrings of the pouch, and thrust it back in her pocket. She dumped the crumbs on the floor of the wire cage and returned the bird to its perch.

Now prepared, she gathered the folds of her skirt between her knees and waited for the passengers to disembark from the ferry. She sipped the drink Paco had brought, felt its warmth spread through her, and cast her eyes across the street, where Jorge Portillo slept in the rear seat of his ancient Pontiac with its ragged pockets of rust in the rocker panels and doors. The dark visions of the night clouded her sight. Three weeks had passed since Jorge had driven a tourist to the airport at Cancún or the ruins of Coba and Uxmal. Even with her poor hearing, Tia Clara could catch the jagged cadence of his snores. From the near distance, she saw Inez Portillo approach. Inez walked past the taxi stand where Jorge slept, not sparing a glance at her husband. Before she passed Tia Clara's table, she crossed to the other side of the *calle*, heading for the chapel in the center of the square. Sorrow lay on the woman's shoulders like a cloak. The shell that surrounded her pulsated a brilliant, silvery white. This, Tia Clara knew, was the true color of grief. A dark hole pierced the vapor above Inez's heart.

Three weeks ago, Graciela Portillo had disappeared. Every day since, morning and evening, Inez went to kneel before the Virgin, to light candles and pray for the return of her eldest daughter. *Go home, Tia Clara could have told her. There is nothing that prayers can do for Graciela now. And the father of your little ones drinks all night and sleeps his days away in the back seat of his car. These children need you now. Go home.* Tia Clara did not say these things. Inez would continue to light candles. Jorge would continue to drink. The young ones would survive. And when she was ready, Inez would come to Tia Clara, who would cast the black and white corn. And then? This question haunted Tia Clara. Would she tell Inez what she had seen, what the sea had whispered to her? Would she reveal that Graciela had been with child when she left Playa del Pedro? That the infant, a boy who would have been Inez's first grandchild, was to die unborn? And finally, even knowing that it would deepen the darkness in the shell above Inez Portillo's heart, would she reveal the rest? Would she tell Inez that the daughter, as she had known her, was lost? That already the ancestors wept for the child she had been? Tia Clara, too, grieved for Graciela, a child she knew possessed a great gift, but she did not waste tears. Long ago, she had learned that tears changed nothing.

Behind shut lips, Tia Clara muttered to herself, her mouth moving as if she were chewing prayers. She reached again into her apron pocket and withdrew a coil of red twine. With agile movements despite swollen fingers, she formed and knotted the string in three loops. She bent over and set the twine on the ground and then took a wooden match from her pocket. She struck the head on the surface of the sidewalk and watched it jump to life. If it were possible, she would have touched the flame to the past, burning memory. Instead, she ignited the bright coil of thread. The twine twisted and curled until each knot was consumed by the flame. She watched the smoke as it spiraled upward. A clockwise direction. That was good. Still, she feared it was too late to protect Graciela or the others who were in the dark place.

She listened to the murmur of the sea. The events unfolding now were inevitable, rooted in her past and that of others, in actions born of love and of passion, feelings twisted and deformed. Her time of reckoning was coming. She understood that past, present, and future were as irrevocably connected as the three knots of red twine that smoldered at her feet. But this morning, as she readied for the tourists and performed her rituals, Tia Clara was unprepared for what was to come and for the scarred woman of many masks.

MADISON

After the accident, everything changed. The most visible of the transformations was the slight limp, which remained even now despite the doctors' hopes that with therapy it would be corrected. And, of course, the scars. Some of those would fade, she'd been told, and, if she elected for more surgery, would become smoother, less vivid. At that time, the last thing in creation Maddie wanted to think about was undergoing more operations, and after the first five years had passed, she no longer considered it. The scars had become such a part of her that some mornings when she stood before the mirror, they hardly registered.

The other wounds were less visible. Her personality, once gregarious and fun-loving, even rebellious, was more subdued now. Early on, when she had returned home from rehab, she had begun to avoid calls from friends and well-intentioned acquaintances who offered more of the sympathy she did not want and counsel she had no desire to hear again. *Give it time,* they advised. *What you're feeling is to be expected. You've been through a huge ordeal.*

You have no idea, she wanted to tell them. How could they? If they had been burned, lost the two people they loved most, did they think they could expect time to make the pain and grief fade? *Burn.* A soft-sounding word. But in fire, the skin did not burn. It melted. No one wanted to hear that.

Even visitors to the burn unit, witnesses to her suffering, had only glimpses of what it was like. Pain so encompassing that even her grief had to be put on hold. The only person who really understood was Kat. Throughout the first months—in fact, for most of the first year—her sister had taken a sabbatical from her job at the magazine and had practically moved into the hospital with her. She'd been there for the procedures that went so far beyond pain that Maddie thought there were no words to describe it. "Agony" was the closest she could come. And even now, fifteen years later, she couldn't remember the worst of it. It had been explained to her that the morphine drip masked the pain and sedated her, and the Versed prescribed to quell anxiety had induced a kind of amnesia, making it unlikely she would ever completely recall all details of the accident or the days in the hospital that immediately followed. What she did remember later had brought on nightmares. Kat, whose career depended on using language, agreed with her that there were some things that defied description. One night, Maddie had awoken to see her sister sitting by the bed, silently weeping.

"Oh, Kat. Kat, don't cry," she had whispered.

"I hate that this happened to you," Kat had said. "If I could, I would change places with you if it meant you didn't have to go through this."

Maddie didn't for one second doubt the truth of this. Kat was twenty-nine at the time of the accident, nearly ten years older than Maddie, and had long been her protector. Unable to guard her from the plane crash that had killed their parents and nearly killed Maddie, Kat did everything else for her. She learned from the staff how to change the dressings and cover the scars twice a day with a special salve and later, at the rehabilitation center, how to assist with the physical therapy. Maddie had fretted that Carl, Kat's husband, would resent the weeks and weeks she spent at her side, but her sister tossed this concern aside. "He knows this is where I want to be. And you know lawyers. Always busy with work. He probably barely notices I'm gone." But later, after

Carl told Kat he wanted a divorce, Maddie wondered if perhaps he had minded very much indeed and added that to the list of things she had to feel guilty about.

But years passed and life went on, as it always does. Kat returned to DC and Maddie buried herself in her work, both achieving a measure of success in their fields, focusing on the present and knowing there was no way to prepare for a future held in the capricious hands of fate. Only much later would Maddie look back and see how much of their past was covered by the steely blueness of irony.

KATHERINE

Kat woke in a narrow and unfamiliar box of a room. Her brain, her mouth, even her body felt dull, cotton-swathed, and she concentrated on trying to pull up some memory of how she had come here. She lay listening, but only the faintest of sounds penetrated the walls. She lifted her head, fought against a wave of vertigo, and looked around. She remembered falling asleep in her elegant room at the spa, and this place was far removed from that. Cinder block walls instead of polished wood. A short chest of drawers next to the single bed where she lay. No rug or art on the walls. A simple globe lamp hung from one corner of the ceiling. There were two doors, one shut, the other open to an adjoining lavatory no larger than a closet. Smaller, in fact, than her closet at home. She saw a toilet and sink, a tiny open shower. A flicker of green along the floor by the closed door startled her. A gecko. Harmless.

She returned to her survey of the room. There were no mirrors. No clocks. Nothing for her to differentiate night from day except the small square of blue above the single skylight. Pale light fell onto the walls, the faded candescence of either dawn or dusk. The air smelled of fresh paint and another slightly earthy aroma.

She propped herself up on her elbows and swallowed against the threat of nausea. She wore pale blue pajamas. Three words were embroidered on the pocket flap in a darker blue. The sight triggered a slice of memory. So she was still at the spa in Mexico. But what was she doing in this cell? Another wisp of memory floated just beyond her reach, and with it came a fluttery fear. She swung her feet to the floor, felt the cool tiles beneath her toes, then rose and walked to the door, bewildered at the unsteadiness of her legs. She twisted the knob, pulled, but the door didn't budge. "Hello," she called, her voice weak. "*Hola?* Is anyone there?" She twisted the knob and pulled harder, but the door still did not give. The flutter grew to a steady pulse. Where the hell was she?

"*Hola?*" she called again. She tried to concentrate, to piece things together, to remember how she had come to be in this space, but her brain was too foggy to process anything, and she could only remember going to sleep on the soft mattress in a beautiful room. The short walk to the door had left her spent. She made it back to the bed, and although she struggled to resist, again sleep claimed her.

She woke to her name.

"Katherine?"

She opened her eyes, saw, in the shadow of the light cast by the globe fixture, a man. Recognition surfaced. Dr. Verner. She searched his face for reassurance but found it as carefully unrevealing as a mask.

"Where am . . . ?" The words were cottony in her mouth. Had she been drugged? Her unease spiked and she struggled to conceal the first frisson of real panic.

He held a glass to her lips. "Drink," he said.

She hesitated. If she had been drugged, it would explain her weakness, the haze of memory. Thirst overcame caution. She took a sip. Water. Tasteless. She drank deeply.

"How do you feel?" His tone was soothing, confident.

Stalling for time, she drank until the glass was empty.

"Katherine?" He placed a hand on her shoulder.

At the touch, as if a sun had appeared, dispelling mist, full memory returned. She cringed from his hand, still cupping her shoulder, and closed her eyes, as if such a simple act could turn the clock back five months, could change the choices she had made.

She had made her first trip to the spa in December. Curiosity had brought her here and had led her to return every month since then. Eventually it had caused her to nose around the one building Verner had said was off-limits to guests. The same building, she realized, where she was now being housed. *Held.*

He reached for her hand, felt for her pulse. She steeled herself to keep from shrinking back from his fingers and the touch she had once naively believed would save her. She forced herself to meet his gaze.

"Are you hungry? Can I have something sent in for you? Perhaps some soup?"

She thought of the spa's elegant dinner room where she had last eaten, entrées that, though simple, would have been the envy of any chef back home, platters of melons and pineapple, fruit so fresh they still held the warmth of the sun. "Why is the door locked?" She hoped her voice would reveal nothing but mild inquisitiveness.

He did not answer immediately, and then, just as Kat decided he wasn't going to, he said, "For your protection. Only for your protection."

She compelled herself to continue looking steadily at him. "I want to leave," she said.

He stared at her with eyes so blue they appeared transparent. "Oh, what am I to do with you?"

The question chilled her. Her meek act was not fooling him. She had been an idiot to confront him with what she had learned. "I want to leave," she repeated. She started to rise, but he laid a hand on her shoulder and held her back.

"For now, you need to rest. Try to sleep. I'll be back to check on you again."

He switched off the light as he left. The darkness pressed through the pane of the skylight. She lay still, listening, heard the click of the door being locked. She lifted a hand to her face, felt the crepiness of her skin as if for the first time.

How had she allowed this to happen? How had she been seduced into believing his promise that age could be forestalled? When had curiosity and her excitement about finding the story of a reporter's lifetime glided into vanity? A quote teased at her memory. Something about vanity. Not from Shakespeare or the Bible, those two fonts of quotations. She was quite positive of that. No, something she read long ago. In college? Perhaps in Professor Durham's philosophy class. She recalled the separate notebook for quotes she'd kept then. Suddenly the full quote surfaced, as these things did when one stopped trying to remember. *Provided a man is not mad, he can be cured of every folly but vanity.* Well, it was vanity that had brought about her present condition. That in itself had proved a kind of madness. She stroked her cheeks, her jaw and chin and neck.

Not her.

Rousseau. That was the author of the quote. She still had her mind, at least. Verner and his "revolutionary procedures" hadn't taken that from her.

She had meant no harm, intended no offense. *Jesus, what had gone wrong?* Worse than wrong. A moan of animal anguish slipped from her throat because she understood that Verner wasn't keeping her confined here because her treatments had inexplicably gone wrong.

It was because she had discovered the truth behind the treatments— secrets that, like her, he couldn't afford to let leave.

MADISON

Maddie came awake slowly, arched her back in a deep stretch, and reached over toward the solid warmth of Jack, but instead of his shoulders, her hand slipped over bare sheets, cool beneath her fingers. Coming fully conscious, she skimmed the room with a quick glance, found his blue shirt on the bench at the foot of the bed, his trumpet on the chair by the window, its velvet-lined case propped open on the floor.

"Jack?"

The silence of the house answered her. She remembered that the previous night, before they had fallen asleep, he'd mentioned he was scheduled for an early charter. She rose, pulled on a pair of jeans, and, on impulse, reached for his shirt and slipped it on. The brushed fabric slid over her breasts, her shoulders and ribs, and her stomach contracted, warmed.

It wouldn't take much convincing to take the day off. Blow off work. Paint her toenails. Condition her hair. Eat chocolate chip ice cream straight out of the carton and moon about waiting for his return. In short, do all the things women in love were supposed to do. Or she guessed this was what women in love did. Her experience in the area until now was almost nonexistent. Instead, the habit of discipline took over.

She scooped kibble into Winks's bowl, and as if the sound were his own personal alarm, the Russian blue appeared. "Breakfast for you, coffee for me," Maddie said to the cat, who was already munching on the dry food. She poured a cup of coffee—thank God for K-cups— grabbed a tin of cookies, and headed to the studio. She saw the paper swan as soon as she walked through the door. Ornate with many folds in the wings, it sat in the middle of the smaller of her two worktables. She hadn't noticed it last night, so Jack must have made it earlier that morning while she slept. She pictured him sitting in her studio, mug of coffee at his elbow, bent over and concentrating as he created the bird, and she smiled at the image. She carried the swan to the shelf and set it with the growing collection of origami. The first and least complicated of all was a crane he had created during dinner on their first date. Over the following weeks she would come across others around the house. A star on the sill over the kitchen sink. A rose on the coffee table next to the TV remote. A turtle on the bench in the hall. A sword atop the novel she had been reading. The last had puzzled her. Such an odd object. "Think Amazon," he'd explained. "Think warrior woman. That's what I see in you." *If he only knew,* she had thought. She was full of fears. Kat was the warrior in the family.

She opened the window to the green May air. Sirens sounded somewhere in the distance, surging then fading away, off toward the east end of town, past the strip mall and Town Line Condos. Absorbed in thoughts of Jack, she paid no real attention to them, although later she would have a hazy half memory of them and wonder how she could not have paid attention. After the accident that had claimed her parents, every time she'd heard sirens, memories of the crash were triggered.

As she moved, she was aware of the scent of him rising from the fabric of his shirt, an erotic blend of early spring, Dial soap, and cigarettes, although he said he was trying to quit. And risk, too. For it smelled of that, as well. Of the vulnerability of love. She knew how dangerous it was to give your heart; the plane crash had taught her well the inevitability of loss.

She had met Jack in the spring on one of those false late-March days, a morning that pulled frost from the earth and held the promise of summer. Overnight, purple and yellow crocuses had flowered, and in sheltered spots of south-facing houses swollen forsythia buds threatened to bloom. One week later there would be a surprise dusting of snow— Cape Cod in the spring—but on that day, schoolchildren ran outside without jackets, and people considered the wisdom of taking down storm windows. On this perfect day, she met Jack.

When the doorbell rang, she had been in the studio working on the preliminary sketches for a commissioned series on women and myth. She'd been expecting a shipment from her supplier and so opened the door without hesitation. A stranger stood there, tall, just the right side of bony, and holding a black helmet tucked beneath one arm. A motorcycle stood in the drive.

"Hi." Deep voice. Hazel eyes, clean-shaven chin. Good bones. A grin her sister Kat would rate "drop dead." *Cowboy,* she thought. That lanky archetype of American masculinity. A young Sam Shepard. Her defenses rose, shutting him off as if a stage curtain had been drawn. Unconsciously, she tilted her head so that a wing of hair fell forward, shielding the damaged side of her face.

"Yes?" she said.

"Madison DiMarco?"

"Yes."

"The sculptor?"

"Yes." She scowled in puzzlement. How did he know her name?

"I was at the gallery and Lonnie gave me this address." He wore jeans and a knit shirt. No jacket. "Jack Moroni," he said, extending an arm. His sleeves were pushed up to his elbows, revealing blond hair curling on his forearms, broad capable wrists. And just like that, looking at his wrists and forearms of all things, she felt the first surprising spark of desire. No. Not surprising. Shocking. She had thought that possibility, if not dead, then close to it. She drew a breath and allowed him to take her hand, felt the strength of his.

He'd come, he said, to look at her work, hoping to purchase a piece. She drew another breath and steeled herself against that potent and unexpected hit of desire. In the fifteen years since the accident, there had only been one man, Gil, the salesman from whom she had bought a car. The very brief affair had not ended well. She accepted that that part of her life was over. She cut Jack Moroni off with a curtness that bordered on rude. "You need to talk to the gallery that handles my sales. It's the Gallery on Main. The owner is Lonnie Pearson."

"I just—" he began, but she closed the door before he could say more.

She returned to the studio, but the brief exchange—no more than a minute or two—had disturbed her. She was distracted, too, by the memory of how it had felt to have her hand enclosed by his. *Get a grip,* she told herself. Eventually, she became absorbed in her work, so deep into it that the phone startled her. She glanced at the caller ID, saw it was Lonnie.

"I heard you turned Jack away," Lonnie said without preamble.

"Who?" she said, although she knew instantly.

"Good golly, Maddie." *Good golly?* She remembered what Kat had said the first time she'd met Lonnie: *Look at her and you think: Goth. Listen to her and you think: someone's great-aunt.* Maddie had laughed. *Someone's bossy great-aunt,* she'd replied. "The guy I sent over this morning," Lonnie said.

"Oh, right." She allowed a note of irritation to creep in. "I told him you handled sales."

"I explained that to him, but when he described what he was looking for and why, I knew he needed to see everything you've done."

"Well, I don't run a gallery here. I leave that to you."

She heard Lonnie draw a long, patient inhale. "The thing is, he wants to find something special for his sister. Olivia used to be a yoga teacher at the Earth Center."

She knew the center. It occupied a space next to a shoe store on Sea Street.

"Jack's devoted to her," Lonnie said.

Maddie recalled the sight of the rangy guy at her door, the jolt of desire that had taken her, and felt a strong need to protect herself. "I don't care if he's Gandhi and the Dalai Lama packaged in one. I still don't see why you can't take care of this."

"Cut him some slack, Maddie. He's a nice guy. He wants something special for Olivia. He wants to pick out one of your masks."

"As I said, you're my dealer. You handle sales."

"You took some of your best pieces back to the studio for the piece they did on you for the *Chronicle* taping last month. As it happens, Olivia saw that segment when it aired, and she's become fascinated with your work."

Maddie had had mixed feelings about agreeing to the *Chronicle* filming, but after the program had aired on the Boston ABC affiliate, there had been a sharp spike in sales. As well as constant reminders from Lonnie to bring some of the work back to the gallery. She just hadn't gotten around to it. "So send her a catalog from the last show," she said.

"But the thing is, Maddie, Olivia's sick. Stage-four lung cancer. She's nineteen."

Nineteen. The age she had been when the life she had imagined had disappeared in flames.

"I've known the family for years and watched Olivia and Jack grow up. After college, Jack moved away, but he came back this spring to help out with Olivia's care. As I said, he's devoted to her. He wants her to have anything that might bring her some pleasure, and he thinks one of your masks would do that."

Maddie thought of Kat and her years of devotion, her unwavering attention during the months at the burn unit and the additional months of rehab after. "Okay," she said.

"Thanks, Maddie. You won't regret it."

"Right," Maddie said. She was already regretting it. Once she gave in to Lonnie, it opened the door to a stream of potential clients, each one eating into the time she had to work. She promised herself she would finally return the masks she'd taken for the taping back to the gallery.

Jack returned the next morning. Walking around the studio in silent absorption, he took his time. Often people, on looking at her work, felt compelled to remark immediately, but he studied each sculpture, in no rush to comment. The first models of various studies were displayed in a glass-fronted case. Clay, plaster of paris, wax-coated papier-mâché. Wood, bronze, and steel. Finished masks were hung throughout the room. On the far wall were her ritual masks inspired by the works of Alaskan natives and the artisans of Oceania. Her carnival masks were among the very first she had made, when she was only seventeen and just beginning to seriously study the history of masks throughout the centuries. Opulent with velvet ruffles, feathers, and colored glass, they were suspended over the archway. Above her welding bench hung a collection of highly stylized masks of porcelain: vapid faces of perfectly featured women fashioned in the manner of those crafted by Benda in the forties. Her fascination with the artist's work had begun when she was a freshman in college and had run across a fashion spread in a vintage issue of *Vogue* and had seen that what had at first glance appeared to be the flawless faces of models were really his masks.

Next to these were her fantasy pieces. "Tell me about these," Jack had said. She had become adept at reading faces to discern whether people were sincerely interested, and Jack passed the test. She'd explained how for a stretch of several years, after she had finally returned to work following the accident, she had begun creating mythical beasts, grotesque animal-like monsters. He was a good listener, and she was surprised to find herself telling him how several critics had pronounced this innovation amusing, but really it had simply been a reaction to the sterile perfection of the Benda-inspired masks.

He was skillful at conversation, at drawing her out. She found herself telling him that she had gone to art school in Providence. He told her he'd gone to Ohio State and majored in aeronautics. Unconscious that she was doing so, she took a step back from him. He told her that as a boy, he used to hang around the local airport on the weekends and how after school, when other boys were playing sports, he was doing chores in exchange for free rides. He said he'd had his private ticket by the time he was sixteen and his instrument rating at eighteen. All he'd ever wanted to do was fly. Now he was building up hours taking charters and sightseeing trips out of the local airport and hoped to sign on with a commuter airline within the year. She kept her face carefully blank when he told her this and did not tell him her father had been a pilot. Or that her parents had died in a plane crash.

When he saw her stack of CDs on a side table, he had picked up the top two, Chris Botti and Wynton Marsalis. He held them in his palm, as if reading tea leaves. He told her his most prized possession was a battered trumpet that had once belonged to Cootie Williams.

"Who?" she'd asked.

"That guy was there," he said, his voice reverent. "He knew early jazz, knew the black tradition. Hell, he *was* the black tradition. I mean the man played with Armstrong, with Ellington. He had this jungle ferocity with real sophistication behind it. He practically invented the plunger mute. He could make a horn sound like it was talking. Man, he was the ace." He laughed. "Sorry. I get carried away." He put the CDs back on the pile. "So tell me, why masks?"

She shrugged, hesitated, discomforted by a sense of intimacy that was building, a glance held a half second too long. Beneath the conversation, something that had been there throughout the morning was growing. An awkward tension, a slow dance, a dance she feared she could get lost in.

He waited in the silence. Finally, both to break the silence and because she sensed his authentic interest, she returned to the earlier subject and shared more about her research, about death masks and theatrical masks and how some cultures believed that a mask held the soul of whoever had worn it.

How could she really explain? How could she tell him how it felt to see faces, to take them into her hands, feel their imagined flesh beneath her fingers, explore and absorb the structure of their bones until, in some mysterious way, the faces became a part of her? Or how she could feel ancient stories and cultures coming alive in her own hands, of the old mask makers who would transform stories and souls into art? "I dream about faces," she finally said. "I see them as masks. I have since I was a child."

His eyes held hers. "What do you see in my face?"

He was closer now. She could smell the scent of his aftershave, a mix of spice and something close to medicinal but not unpleasantly so. He was younger than she had first thought. Midtwenties, she guessed. *Heat,* she thought. *I see heat.* The air between them shifted. She took a step back, ignored his question, and let her glance sweep along the far wall of masks. "Well, what do you think?"

He hadn't turned to the masks, just continued to look at her. "I know this is crazy, but if you really want to know . . ." He paused as if considering whether to continue and plunged on. "What I was thinking was that I'd like to kiss you."

She gasped at the audacity of his remark, then saw by his face that he, too, was surprised at his own words.

"Jesus," he said. "I'm sorry. I shouldn't have said that." He gave a sheepish grin. "Talk about no filter."

I was thinking I would really like to kiss you. The spark of that word—*kiss*—lingered in the air.

"You must think I'm some kind of asshole," he continued. "Or creep."

"It's okay," she said.

"Truly," he said. "I'm sorry."

"Forget it." As if it were possible to retrieve his charged sentence and the desire that incited it. She was relieved when he turned his attention back to the masks and she could again breathe almost normally. She guessed he would choose one of the ritual masks, but he surprised her by pointing to one of the fantasy beasts. "That one," he said. "I'd like that one."

"Are you sure?" It was dark, composed of wood and shells and shards of brass.

"Yes. That's the one."

"Why?"

"It's powerful and full of mystery. And unexpected. Olivia has always been drawn to the unexpected."

"She sounds special."

"She is." There was no missing the pride in his voice. And the sorrow. "Do you take checks?" He didn't ask the price. When she quoted it, he said, "It's worth more."

As she went to the storage closet to get packing material, the memory of the kiss that had never happened dimmed, as if she had dreamed it. When she returned, she saw Winks circling his ankles, a surprise, since the cat was shy with strangers.

"Who's this?" he said.

"Winks."

"As in tiddlywinks?"

"No, Winks as in blinking."

He raised a questioning eyebrow.

"When I first got him, he was so shy he used to hide under the bed for hours, and when he came out, he would be blinking in the brightness of the light. So I called him Winks."

He observed the cat. "I think it fits him. Unique. Like his owner."

Oh, please, she thought. *Can't you come up with a more original line?* Maybe he was right in his own assessment when he'd said she would think he was some sort of an asshole, the kind who delivered a smooth line and expected women to fall over at his attention. She wrapped the mask in bubble wrap, hesitated, then tucked her card in with it, and saw him off. *Well, that's that,* she thought and exhaled, although she had been unaware she'd been holding her breath.

"I sold a mask today," she'd told Kat when her sister phoned that night.

"That's great," Kat said. "Which one? Who bought it? Give me details."

Maddie smiled. Kat was her most passionate supporter, eager for specifics of every sale.

"One of the fantasy ones. For a girl named Olivia. She's nineteen. She has lung cancer."

"Oh, how horrid."

"Terrible. I didn't meet her. The mask was a gift." She hesitated. "From her brother."

Kat, who knew her so well, picked up on something in her voice.

"A brother, huh? Tell me more."

"There's nothing to tell." She did not mention Jack's good looks or his genuine interest in her work and certainly didn't say a word about the spark he had ignited. Nothing that would encourage Kat. Her sister and Lonnie were both always pushing her to date, to give Match.com a try. *And what would I write in my profile?* Maddie had cried in one of the few instances she gave vent to bitterness. *If you're looking for a sideshow freak, I'm your gal?*

"He was cute, right?" Kat said.

"He drives a motorcycle," Maddie said, as if that explained everything. "He won't be back. He bought the mask. It was a one and done."

But it wasn't. Jack returned the next morning. When she opened the door, he held out a small box and automatically she received it. "What's this?"

"Open it," he said. Inside was a small stone heart. "From Olivia. My sister. She wanted you to have it."

Maddie lifted the stone from its cotton nest, felt the smoothness of it beneath her fingers.

"It's quartz. Olivia said to tell you it's a power stone and purifies spiritual, mental, and physical energies. It also protects."

"She needn't have." The heart took on the warmth of her palm.

"She said to tell you she loves the mask. She had me hang it on the wall by her bed."

Maddie slid the stone into the pocket of her jeans. "Please tell her I said thanks." She moved to shut the door. "I'd better get back to work. Thanks again. I appreciate your dropping it off." Three expressions of gratitude seemed more than adequate.

A day went by and he turned up again, this time in the late afternoon. She had left the studio for the day and was about to empty Winks's litter box when the bell rang.

"Yes?" she said at the door. She wanted to be annoyed at the intrusion but instead found herself wishing she had shampooed her hair that morning. The flash of warm weather had passed, and a sea breeze was coming in from the southwest. He wore a leather jacket.

"I want to buy another mask."

She allowed herself a sigh. "Your sister?"

"This one's for my mother."

"I'm not your personal gallery, you know," she said.

"I wish," he said. Again with the killer grin.

She tried to stare him down, but he wouldn't look away. "Fine." She led him back to the studio. "Tell me a little about her. What's she like?"

He thought a minute. The grin faded. "Before or after?"

Before or after? Did everyone have a before and after in their lives? "Whichever you want."

"She used to be so steady and laughed a lot. Now, mostly, she's sad. And scared. She keeps up a pretty good face in front of Olivia, but she's not good at hiding how she feels. Never has been."

"What's her name?"

"Natalie."

Maddie considered her full collection and pointed to the last one in the row of the carnival masks. It was opulent with velvet and colored stones and feathers. It had always made her smile. "How about that one?"

He studied it. "Yes," he said. "It's perfect."

When Kat phoned that night, the first thing she said was, "How's Motorcycle Man?"

"Who?" Maddie said, stalling for time. She should be used to her sister's weird prescience, but it always took her by surprise.

"The guy who bought the mask for his sister. Has he been back?"

Maddie forced a laugh. "You've been watching too many soap operas," she said. Uncharacteristically, she was reluctant to share her every thought with Kat. She wasn't ready for her sister's questions, queries she couldn't even answer for herself. "How are things in DC? Are the cherry trees in bloom?"

"Gloriously," Kat said.

They chatted for a few more minutes, the subjects nothing special on either end. Just their touch-base call.

"Talk soon. Love you," Kat said. Her usual sign-off.

"Love you, too."

The next day, Maddie found herself listening for the roar of a Harley in the drive while she fingered the quartz heart she had taken to carrying in her pocket. But Jack didn't come, and she knew her disappointment was not a good sign. When he showed up the following day, she was determined to be aloof. "What is it this time? A cousin?"

He laughed and handed her a bottle of prosecco. "From my mother."

"Really, this is not necessary."

"She sent one instruction. She said to tell you that you have to share it with me."

"Did she really?" Skepticism coated her voice.

"She did."

What do you want from me? Instead she said, "How old are you, anyway? I'd guess probably midtwenties. Right?"

"Does it make a difference?"

Yes, she wanted to say. A big difference. She wasn't one of those women looking for a younger guy. What were they called? Panthers? Some kind of wildcat. Cougar. That was it. She wasn't looking for a man at all. She had a life. She had Kat. She had Lonnie, her all-in-one rep, movie buddy, and friend. She had her work.

She took the wine. She got two glasses.

When Kat called that Sunday, Maddie told her Jack had come back.

"Motorcycle Man? Did he buy another mask?" Kat asked.

"Well, yes. In fact, he did. For his mother."

"You're kidding."

"No. And the next time he brought a bottle of prosecco. He said it was from his mother."

"You mean he's been back twice? And you didn't call me with details? So, give it up now. What's he like?"

"He's really nice."

Kat laughed. "Nice? Hardly a glowing recommendation, but I guess it's a start."

"Well, no, I mean, he's more than nice."

"Okay. More with the dish. Good-looking? Funny? Because believe me, funny is more important than you can imagine."

"Yes. He is. He makes me laugh."

In the days that followed, Jack wooed her with persistence and patience. He found out that she liked high-end dark chocolate sprinkled with sea salt and brought her a pound from the local chocolatier. He located an out-of-print book on the history of masks and bought it for her. (She suspected he had an ally in Lonnie, who must have been feeding him info like a spy, although she'd denied it.) One day, after he'd picked her up for lunch, he stopped by his family home and introduced her to Olivia and Natalie. His mother embraced her as if they had known each other for years. Warmth and openness apparently were Moroni family traits. They were easy to be with. They broke through her usual reticence.

Just as gradually, Jack broke through her fragile resistance, one built on their age difference (eight years, she learned) and her belief that nothing good could come of this except possibly a brief fling, and that she did not need. He was proper and gentlemanly. No more talk of kissing. She was confused.

"What do you want from me?" she asked one day, giving voice to the question she had had from the beginning. It was that slip of time between evening and night, the sky a promising red in the western horizon. They had gone to a clam shack for dinner, then bought ridiculously overpriced frozen yogurt and walked to the windmill park to sit on a bench in the growing dark and finish their cones.

"This."

"What is this?"

He looked up at the billowing sails of the mill. "Friendship." The creaking of the mill's blades whispered their ancient song.

"Friendship," Maddie said.

"For a start."

"Okay," she said, even while wondering why she agreed when she didn't at all know how she felt about that. She tossed the last of the cone, now sodden, into a trash barrel by the bench. A boy and his father walked past. The boy held a leash tethered to a black lab.

"And . . . ," Jack said.

"And what?"

He stared straight ahead, as if afraid to look at her. "And I still would, you know."

"Would what?"

"Like to kiss you."

His lips were cold from the frozen yogurt. He tasted just as she had imagined he would. When she opened her eyes, she saw the boy with the lab watching them. "Let's go," she said.

"Where?"

"Home," she said.

Another two weeks passed before she called Kat, first trying her DC number and finally reaching her on her cell.

"Hey, where are you?"

"On assignment," Kat said. "What's up?"

"Well," she said. "It's about Jack . . ."

There was a silence from the other end of the wire, then: "Oh?" Kat, always vigilant on her behalf and even more protective since the accident, had kept her voice neutral.

"The thing is—the thing is, he's a pilot."

She heard Kat's sharp intake of breath. "A—a pilot?"

Maddie pictured her sister, hand at her throat, fingering the gold charm she always wore. A *K*. Not for Katherine, but for Katrina. Their mother's. Like Maddie, it had survived the crash. "Yes."

"Tell me one thing," Kat finally said. "One thing that makes you trust him. One thing that will make me trust him."

Maddie had closed her eyes and reviewed the whirl of the previous weeks, trying to choose a single thing that would convey to Kat what Jack was like. How he cared for his sister. His kindness. His patience with her. The thoughtful gifts he had found for her. Then she remembered the perfect instance. She went back to the night of the fried clams and frozen yogurt, the night she had led him to her bed. She remembered the maelstrom of emotions that had stirred in her chest. Desire, anxiety, a pulsing undercurrent of terror. It was the last that had caused her to turn from him and reach out to switch off the lamp before undressing. Only the doctors and nurses and Kat had seen the full extent of her damaged body. And, of course, the car salesman. She still could feel the shame when she recalled that one disastrous experience with Gil. His look of revulsion when he had seen her nude body. She couldn't bear to see the same expression on Jack's face. But he had stayed her hand and turned her toward him. When she dared to look, she only saw an expression she barely dared name. Not pity. Not revulsion. Only tenderness. And heat. She recalled the gentleness of his touch as he undressed her and revealed her shriveled skin, the livid scars. His words when he spoke. That is what she would tell Kat. The softness of his voice and the way that for the first time since the accident, his words had made her feel whole, undamaged. "You're beautiful," he'd said.

"The scars," she'd said.

"Everyone has scars, Maddie," he'd said. "They just hide them in different ways."

Maddie forced her mind away from the recent past—she could have played the sweet and tender memories for hours—but the day's work waited on the bench before her. She cast a glance at the origami on the window ledge, as if seeking proof that Jack really existed in more than her imagination, and then took a cookie from the tin and sat at her bench, ready to begin. Outside, the sirens sounded again, their keening cutting through the spring air.

KATHERINE

The room was too cold. They had left the air conditioner on high. Even at home in the sweltering weight of the capital's summers, Kat had welcomed the heat and rarely bothered turning on the AC. She considered the distance from the bed to the unit and wasn't at all sure that she would be able to manage it. She felt the shallow palpitations of her heart, the slippery, quick liquid of her pulse.

Two days ago, Dr. Verner had come for her in the middle of the night. She had not resisted. After the first time she had tried to run from him, he had threatened to have her restrained if she tried it again. She believed him. From now on, she had silently sworn, she would watch for her chance and not be foolish. In the examining room, her body had been poked, prodded, and scanned, vials of blood withdrawn. No longer concerned that Kat could hear, Verner dictated the results to his assistant, Helen Mercer, his voice as cold as the air that now chilled her room. Her liver and heart were still enlarged, but apparently the pace of her inexplicable aging had begun to slow. Behind the facade of his professionalism, the cool smile, she could sense his anger, as if somehow she were at fault and the flaw was not with his protocol—the diet, the weekly shots—but with a failing in her own body. There was no longer any mention of the promises he had made during her earlier trips to the clinic over the past months, assurances spoken with the passion and conviction of a man out to save the world, ones she had first come to investigate and then gradually come to accept. Until she had broken his rule and checked out the building that was off-limits.

Now she was no longer an investigative reporter following leads and nosing around. Now she was no more than a specimen on which he could experiment. Until she was no longer of use. She would not allow herself to think of what would happen then. She pushed away fear, knowing it would serve no purpose and would only sap the strength she'd need for this battle.

She had only herself to rely on. She had told no one where she was going. Not Maddie. Not even Jessica. At the thought of her colleague, a food reporter for the *Post*, she recalled the day they had met for drinks at the Mayflower's bar and how struck she had been by Jessica's appearance. At first she had suspected serious surgery but saw none of the revealing signs. Jessica not only looked younger; she looked healthy. She glowed. It hadn't taken more than a quick comment on how fabulous she looked for Jessica to launch into her story of this amazing doctor in Mexico who worked miracles. The more questions Kat asked, the more intrigued she became. According to Jessica, the doctor didn't advertise, didn't have a website, relied solely on word of mouth. Looking at her friend's face, Kat had to admit it was a better advertisement than a full-page ad in any fashion magazine.

"He calls himself an immortalist," Jessica had said.

"A what?"

"Immortalist. He truly believes we can extend life indefinitely."

"Guess he hasn't read *The Picture of Dorian Gray*," Kat had said. But she hadn't been able to stop thinking about what Jessica had said—and how fabulous she had looked—and eventually decided to fly to Mexico and check it out for herself with the intent of writing an article about the doctor and his spa. The immortalist. Such a timely subject—any editor would leap at the chance to publish her story. It was only after her second trip, a follow-up to the initial one, that Kat decided to pony up for the exorbitant cost and take part in the doctor's regimen, convincing herself it was all part of the research. If she hadn't had drinks with Jessica that day in December, she would be home now, forestalling the inroads of aging by working on her abs at her gym and sleeping with her trainer.

She turned in the bed and moaned at the ache even this slight movement caused. She curled into herself, as much for comfort as to conserve her body's heat, and after a bit, despite the chill and the pain and her fear, she drifted off.

A noise beyond the room woke her. She heard a female voice. At first, woozy, she thought it was Maddie, crying out as the dressings on her burns were changed. When she woke fully, she remembered where she was. She steeled herself against the weakness in her body. She suspected they were drugging her meals and tried to eat only the fruit and bread and items it would be difficult to conceal a sedative in. She sat up, waited a beat for her head to clear, and swung her feet to the floor. She heard the cry again. She pulled the blanket free from the mattress and, as if this thin mantle could protect her from the frigid air spewed out by the AC, shrouded it over her shoulders. Slowly she made her way across the floor, pulling the blanket tighter, and pressed her ear against the wall.

The voice was young, far too young to be Verner's assistant or one of the two elderly Mayan women who came to clean her room and tend to her. The girl called out again. A single phrase repeated over and over and muffled by the thickness of the plaster, words that seemed to be a call of both prayer and pain. Kat strained to understand. It sounded like "a way of."

She turned her mouth to the wall. "Hello? *Hola?*" Her voice was weak and to her ears sounded too frail to penetrate the cinder block walls. "*Hola?* Can you hear me?"

The rhythmic crooning from the other side did not cease. *A way of. A way of.*

Kat managed to turn off the AC and staggered back to the bed. Once she had easily run a half marathon, whipped off sit-ups as easily as she turned the pages of a book. Now traversing a few feet left her drained. Even Verner didn't know what had gone wrong or what had caused her to react so dramatically and horribly to the weekly shots he'd prescribed. As she collapsed on the mattress, she heard the echo of the girl's voice. *A way of.* Well, at the moment she couldn't see a "way of" or a way out. Not for her. Even Verner must now believe what was so clear in her body and, no doubt, on her face.

At first, horrified at the changes that had occurred in her body, she had been relieved there was no mirror, but after a while she had sought reflecting surfaces in the sparse room. The brass of the doorknob. The metallic cap of the bottle of lotion one of the Mayan women had left in the cabinet. Convex surfaces in which she might be able to study her reflection and see if there had been any change. But to no avail. Of course, she did not require any mirror to look at her hands, to see the raised and knotted veins, the papery skin that belonged on an old woman. A wave of nausea washed over her, then receded. She thought about the transfusions. Verner had sworn that they were completely safe, had explained the procedure and testing that were in place to ensure their purity. Was it possible that she had received plasma that hadn't been checked?

Verner had said that she was the only one whose body had deteriorated after receiving the infusions, and she wondered if that was true. Earlier, when it had become evident something had gone wrong, she had called Jessica and carefully questioned her about how she was doing. Her friend had nothing but praise for Verner. If there were others, wouldn't there have been publicity about it? They were hardly results one could keep hidden, even in another country.

The girl continued to cry and call out. Who was she? How had Verner found her and brought her here? Kat assumed she was young, and she felt ill. Verner had explained how the plasma they received in their transfusions had been extracted from the blood of teenagers. Now she knew better.

Surely the girl in the next room had to be missed, had to have a family who would be looking for her. Kat thought about what she now knew Verner did here, where he really sourced the cells for his therapy, and she felt horribly impotent. In spite of her exhaustion, her old fighting spirit surfaced. The sound of the girl's sobs triggered a memory so real that, for a moment, Kat could almost smell the saltiness of Maddie's sweat, feel her sister's slender hand clinging to hers in the dark.

"Just leave her alone," Carl had said when Madison's cries woke them one night during one of his rare visits to Maddie's home during her long convalescence. "Christ, she's a grown woman, not a child who needs to be coddled."

But Kat had said, "I'll be right back," chancing his anger and casting the words over her shoulder even as she padded on bare feet down the hall to the room where her sister slept. "It's all right," she would soothe as she stroked Maddie's hair, damp with sweat from her nightmare. "I'm here, honey. I'm here." She had always been there for Maddie. In all the foolishness and havoc Kat had created in her own life, the trail of failed romances and lost opportunities, Maddie was the single, shining right thing she had done, the purely unselfish act she had performed. For the past fifteen years since their parents' deaths, she had let nothing interfere with that charge, and during that time she had watched her sister grow from a traumatized nineteen-year-old into a wonderfully gifted woman whose sculptures hung in museums.

Until now. If her sister needed her now, Kat would not know. She wondered whether Maddie was trying to reach her. She remembered their recent conversations before she had flown back to Mexico and how happy Maddie had sounded. Even here, in this cold and alien room, the memory brought her comfort. She hoped that Motorcycle Man was good for her, was caring for her, was able to make her laugh. She hoped that with him, Maddie would at last learn to open her heart. To trust.

And that her trust would not be betrayed, as Kat's had been when she had innocently given it to Verner.

MADISON

Maddie slid a CD of Appalachian folk songs into the player, grabbed two more oatmeal raisin cookies from the tin—breakfast—and settled herself at the worktable. In the distance, sirens screamed their alarm, swirling and fading, contrapuntal to the wild notes of a bluegrass harp, but Maddie was so quickly absorbed in her work they barely registered. Masks stared down at her from the studio walls. For an instant she imagined the tribal eyes were watching, witnessing her reluctance to count on happiness. Except, of course, there were no eyes, only empty sockets. *A paradox,* she thought. Eyes were the most important factor in revealing character, and yet her masks had none. They could see neither her happiness nor her fear at the idea of losing it.

Only here, in this studio, could she recapture some of the person she had been before the accident. Once she had been a girl up for adventures, not foolhardy but certainly open to calculated risks and eager to discover the world beyond her immediate geography. Now the spirit of that girl was given rein only in the studio. Only here did the cautious, tentative woman she had become feel safe taking risks.

She considered the work waiting on the bench: Lady Macbeth in steel, the third in a series commissioned by an international corporation to represent women in fact and fiction. Thus far she had completed Salome and Anne Boleyn.

The Lady Macbeth mask was rough-edged and so flat it was nearly one-dimensional. It was strong, but Maddie was dissatisfied. She felt she had missed the mark on this one. Whenever she was invited to museums and universities to lecture about masks and mask making, she spoke about history and mythology, about methods and materials and about how when creating a mask, she searched for a story, a place that would serve as a point of entry for the work. But there was much she did not reveal. She did not tell her audiences how, in the best of her work, the mask itself revealed its truths.

For a week she had been listening to the strong and complicated spirit of Lady Macbeth. She had reflected on ambition and regret and had thought about disintegration and the deliberate denial of Macbeth's essential self. Still, the truth of the mask eluded her.

The CD ended. Time passed. She stared at the mask and waited. Gradually, the steel edges blurred, softened. *Tell me your secrets,* she thought. The metal seemed to shimmer and move.

"Tell me your secrets," she whispered.

They say it was regret. The thought rose up from the steel. *But it was memory that drove me mad.*

A thrill ran through Maddie. Now she could see the completed mask; a rift sliced through the center, dividing it into spheres of shadow and light. She pulled her goggles down over her face, switched on the acetylene torch, adjusted the flame, and began.

At noon she took a break. She set the torch on the bench and switched off the tank valves. Lady Macbeth, riven and enigmatic, stared up at her, and she felt a rush of satisfaction at its force.

In the kitchen, she ladled leftover tomato and lentil soup into a bowl and set it in the microwave. While it heated, she loaded the dishwasher with the dishes from the previous night's meal. As she worked, thoughts of Jack settled in. After dinner last night, when he'd been playing his trumpet, he'd closed his eyes, giving himself over to the music, and his face had become transfixed in a way that gave her a glimpse of what he would look like when he grew older, and the vision had comforted her. She recalled the touch of him, the taste of him. She pictured his grin, the crinkle of fine lines that despite his age already fanned out from his eyes. Pilot lines, he called them. From squinting into the sun. He loved flying as much as he loved jazz. He had wanted to share that passion with her, too. Again and again he'd asked her to let him take her flying. Coaxing, urging, confronting her fears with facts and statistics. Aviation, he said, was safer than driving a car.

As he'd been from the first, he was patient. Gentle. When she had been unable to fight back her fears, the terror always there since her parents' deaths, and hadn't allowed him to coax her into going up, he had told her all the things he wanted her to see, the things he wanted to share with her. He told her how different everything was from the air. The cranberry bogs and golf courses, shoals along the outer beaches, and sharply eroding sand cliffs on the Atlantic shore where cottages teetered on the brink. "I've seen all that," she had said. "When I used to go up with my father."

Still, he'd persisted. "But I want to share it with you, to show you what I love about it all—the land, its colors and contours, and how they look so different from a thousand feet. All mounds and curves. So maternal in its swells," he'd said. "I think that's why we call her Mother Earth."

She'd thought it was one of the most erotic things he'd said to her. But she did not concede. "I just can't," she'd said.

He had kept pushing. "It's not the flying that's important, Maddie. It's about the fear. Fear is like cancer: it feeds on itself, grows and spreads. I know you're afraid. I understand that. But you can't let fear keep you from experiencing beautiful things."

"Stop," she had said. "Just stop. I'm not who you think I am. So let it go."

"No, Maddie, you're not who *you* think you are."

The rest of the evening had been strained, each of them carefully polite to the other. She knew she had disappointed him and she knew she would keep doing it, because she couldn't be who he wanted her to be.

She finished the soup and rinsed the bowl. She checked the clock on the microwave and wondered when he would be back. In the early days she had not allowed herself to believe the relationship was anything more than a fling, telling herself they both understood that it was temporary. Short-lived by definition. And then he would move on. Find a woman who kept a clean house and would give him a family. Someone his own age. Someone who wasn't covered in scar tissue. She had worked to keep a part of herself sealed off. She still hadn't been open to having him move in, although he stayed over several days each week.

"Relax," Lonnie had encouraged her one night over wine. "Enjoy yourself. Jack's a wonderful guy. Don't get ahead of yourself with where it's going. Take the plunge and enjoy. Life's a risk."

Like Maddie didn't know that. She was tired of people telling her about risk and daring.

She was aware of the whack-whack of a helicopter overhead, sounds she heard as she was airlifted to the hospital, sounds she would always associate with her parents' deaths. She rarely allowed herself to think about them: a pointless exercise that only brought sorrow and loss. Moving on. That was Kat's motto, for sure. *Moving on.* She wanted to phone Kat. Now she wanted sister talk, Kat's reassurance. She picked up the phone and punched in her number. After five rings, she heard Kat's recording telling her to leave a message.

"Kat," she said, "It's me. Pick up if you're there." She waited but heard only echoing silence. "Call me," she said and hung up. She felt inexplicably edgy. She flicked on the small TV. The local network anchorwoman gazed out, her face solemn. The screen changed and a reporter, mike in hand, eyes earnestly fixed on the viewing audience, filled the screen. A LIVE graphic flashed in a box at the bottom. The camera cut to a background shot of firemen dragging hoses, working the scene. The cameraman panned the area, the length of runway, a row of private planes tied down, then zoomed in on the wreckage. Maddie could discern a fragment of tail section.

Acting independently of thought—an impulse of denial—she clicked off the set. Her hands were frigid, as if grasping ice cubes, a chill that traveled through her until she was shaking. The screen went blank. She closed her eyes, but she couldn't erase the image of the crash scene. She felt the pressure of Winks against her ankle and bent to lift him, cradled him against her chest, stroked the gray fur, tried to absorb the warmth of him. "Don't worry," she whispered into the back of his neck. "It's not him. He's fine." But she had to know. She turned the set back on.

On the screen, the reporter was talking about two fatalities, and then the newscast cut back to the anchor desk. A meteorologist nattered on about warm fronts and weather patterns. Maddie flipped to another local station. A segment with something about baby ducks was being aired.

She was hugging the cat so tightly, Winks wriggled to get free. *It wasn't Jack. Not Jack.* She picked up the phone and hit his number. He didn't answer. She scrolled down to the number for the airport office. It was busy. She pressed redial and stayed with it until she got through.

Rick, the airport manager, answered. They had met twice. "Rick? It's Madison DiMarco."

"Who?"

"Maddie. Jack Moroni's—" She struggled to find the right word to identify herself. "Girlfriend" sounded like a teenager. "Lover" sounded too intimate. "Jack's friend," she finally decided on. There was a brief silence she strained to interpret.

"Maddie." There was a definite shift in his voice. "Listen, there's been an incident here. I can't tie up the line."

"I know. I just saw the news." Her stomach was cramping now. "Is Jack there? Can I speak to him? Is he okay? I tried his cell but—"

"Maddie. I'm sorry. The FAA won't let us release any information right now."

She closed her eyes, saw again the twisted fragments of a plane made nearly unrecognizable by impact and fire. She sank to the floor, drew her knees in as if to ease the pain in her stomach. "Rick," she whispered. "Jack's all right, isn't he? He wasn't in the plane, right?" There were voices yelling in the background, a rising din that she strained to hear above. She wasn't even sure that Rick could hear her above the pandemonium.

"Listen, Maddie, I gotta go. Sorry. I'll call you back as soon as I can. Promise."

GRACIELA

"Tell me the story," Graciela used to beg her *madre*. And Inez, eyes focused on the distant sky, would recount how, just before giving birth, she'd gone to Tia Clara, who had cast the black and white corn and foreseen that the child would be a girl, a beautiful child, strong and healthy. "My name," Graciela would urge. "Tell me how I was named."

And Inez would tell her how on the night she had been born, as was their tradition, her *padre* had chosen what she would be called. "He believed you were a gift from God," she would say. "Your name," Inez would tell her, although Graciela knew this part by heart, "your name means 'Thank you for her.'"

In the dark, Graciela wondered if Inez was weeping for her now and whether she had knelt before the Virgin and prayed. She wondered, too, about Ángel. *Ángel el fisgón.* Ángel the busybody who was always running everywhere, seeing everything. He had watched her walk away from the village the day she left, and it occurred to her that perhaps he had gone to her *padre* at the taxi stand and told him this. She prayed that this was so. Even if it meant that Ángel had told him everything.

The afternoon she left home, she had waited until *siesta* time when her *madre* and the little ones were asleep, Inez snoring so loudly that at another time Graciela would have giggled at the noise. At the sight of her sisters curled in the hammock, their small bodies sweaty and deep in sleep, she had almost weakened, but she had steeled herself against this moment. Whether she stayed or left, she would bring shame to her family and break her *padre*'s heart. Better to go. Better to be thought a runaway than known as a whore. Carefully, holding her breath lest even that betray her, she'd tiptoed from the room. At the last moment, on impulse, believing that they would make her look older, she'd crammed her feet into her *madre*'s red shoes. But soon, walking along the highway that led away from town, she'd realized that wearing them had been a mistake. The walk was long, and although she was only fourteen, her feet had already grown larger than her *madre*'s. Before she had gone one mile, blisters had formed on her heels.

Now the blisters were dry and calloused: a sign that many days had passed, although she could not say how many. From the start they had kept her drugged. Sometimes she believed she had been here for weeks and at other times only days, as if time flowed as liquid as the sea and was as difficult to reckon. But perhaps, as her *abuela* believed, all time was like that, keeping its own measure and season, stretching, bending, condensing until some moments seemed to expand and last forever while other days passed in an instant. So, too, did the years pass. It seemed to Graciela that only yesterday she had been a child, and she remembered how on Sunday evenings, before the others were born, she would sit with her *madre* and *padre* on the seawall near the pier where the boat from Cozumel came in. Her parents liked to look out at the sea and watch the tourists stream down the gangplank from the ferry, but Graciela liked to look down at their feet, at the three pairs of shoes. Her *padre*'s, worn but thoroughly shined because it was Sunday; her *madre*'s red ones with impossibly high heels; and, in the middle, her own small white shoes and white socks, the tops edged with lace and carefully folded down. The rightness, the symmetry of their feet, the six shoes, filled her with joy.

More memories came. The warmth of her *padre*'s hand in hers, the roughness of her *madre*'s. The sound of the sea lapping at the shore; the ever-present smell of fish and garbage; the music of guitars; the soft swishing of her *madre*'s skirt and the clicking of her red high heels on the walkway.

Graciela stirred and shifted the new weight she carried, but her body was heavy and the bed unyielding against a spine accustomed to the curve of a hammock. She had come here for the money the woman had promised, the many pesos she needed to make her aspirations come true and rid her of the obstacles that prevented this. Graciela the dreamer, her family called her. She hadn't minded. She knew it was important to have dreams. In hers, she was rich and lived in Mérida, the white city she had seen on the postcards in the stand outside the tourist shop. She'd come to this place because it was a path to the life she wanted to live. It had seemed an easy solution. The woman had said it would be easy. But lies were as easy to believe as truths if a clever person told them.

At first she had intended to be brave, but the difficulty was that there was much to be afraid of. The cool air machine that was always on and made evil wind. The *norteamericano* with cold eyes and quick hands. The room with the hard table and lights as harsh as the summer sun, and, at night, the sound of a woman weeping in a nearby room. The reality of what would happen. So different from what she had imagined, what she had been promised.

KATHERINE

Kat was still caught in the dream that had woken her only moments before, one so convincing that she had called out her sister's name. Maddie had been alone and hurt. Needing her.

Only a dream. But so realistic that Kat couldn't shake off her apprehension. Over the years there had been times when she'd known Maddie needed her, a knowing beyond rational explanation. Like the time Maddie, then twelve, had fallen at the school playground, breaking her arm. Their parents had been off on a trip, leaving Maddie in Kat's care. Kat had been shopping—a sale at Macy's—and even before her cell phone had rung and the nurse had explained what had happened, she had known, had *known* she had to go to Maddie. She'd dropped her purchases on the counter and fled the store, driving like a maniac, so carelessly it was a wonder she hadn't caused an accident. She was in the school parking lot before her cell rang with the news. She would never forget the look of relief in Maddie's eyes when she rushed into the nurse's office, the way Maddie had run to her, her one good arm hugging Kat so tight she could hardly draw a full breath. And there had been other occasions. When Maddie was at the design school in Rhode Island and had been struggling with some difficulty. A tough final exam, a fight with a roommate. Or a boyfriend. Even Carl had commented on the prescience they shared.

The doorknob turned and Helen Mercer entered the room carrying a tray. Verner was not with her. The first time Mercer had appeared without him, Kat had pursued the possibility of creating an ally, or enlisting her sympathy, but it had quickly become apparent Mercer's alliance was unquestionably with Verner.

"Here's breakfast," Mercer said.

Kat looked at the tray without interest. Sweet bread, orange juice, sliced melon, the fluted white paper cup that held her morning's medication, the pill Verner had said might reverse the dramatic aging. And coffee, a tiny triumph for her. Caffeine was on his list of taboo foods. A toxin, he proclaimed, that poisoned the system. He forbade clients to consume any form of it, but Kat had asked for it yesterday, and now here it was on the tray. Did that mean he had softened toward her? Perhaps it would be possible to convince him to let her leave, to make him believe that she would never tell anyone what he did here. She was ready to promise him anything. "I need to see Dr. Verner." In the cat-and-mouse game she found herself in, she allowed a pleading tone to creep into her voice, the better to continue to appear docile, unthreatening.

Mercer gave her a sharp, searching look. "His schedule is quite full today."

Kat propped herself up in the bed. "I have to see him."

"I'll relay the message, but I can't promise anything." Mercer picked up the paper cup and waited for Kat to hold out her hand and take the small white pill.

Kat stared at it. For days she had taken it, hoping that it was the magic remedy that would return her to her younger self, even while a suspicion had been growing that its sole purpose was to keep her sedated. She waved it away.

Mercer's mouth tightened. "Doctor's orders."

Kat felt her resolve stiffen. Mercer's insistence only strengthened her suspicion. She permitted herself this small act of rebellion. "I don't want it."

"Orders are orders."

"I need to leave."

"You'll have to discuss that with the doctor."

"When?" She succeeded in keeping her voice level, but the effort was exhausting her.

"When he makes his rounds."

"It's important."

"Why?" Mercer's eyes narrowed at this show of resistance.

The lingering impression of the early-morning dream would not be denied. "My sister needs me."

"Your sister? You've been in touch with your sister?" Mercer cast a searching glance around the room, as if in the night a phone had been smuggled in.

"Not exactly."

Mercer grasped Kat's wrist, tightened her fingers, the grip nearly cruel.

Kat had no doubt the woman was quite capable of cruelty.

"What, then?" Mercer said.

"A dream," Kat said. "I dreamed she was in trouble and needed me."

Mercer released her wrist and turned her hand palm up, an abrupt movement that said she had no more time for fantasy or foolishness. She shook the white pill, similar in appearance to the medicine Maddie had been given in the burn unit, into Kat's hand. "Take it," she said. She passed Kat the glass of juice.

"You'll tell Dr. Verner I want to see him?"

Mercer ignored the question. "Rosa will be in later to bathe you and change your linens." She stood by the bed, watching.

The last time, Kat silently vowed as she washed the pill down with the juice. This was the last time she would swallow one of Mercer's pills. From the corridor outside, there was the sound of raised voices, a man yelling something. Mercer hurried off without a second glance at her. For one instant, when the door was open, Kat thought of shouting out for help, but before she could make a sound, the door closed behind Mercer.

It took Kat a moment to realize that she had forgotten to lock the door when she left.

If the white pill was, as she now suspected, a drug to sedate her, she figured she had ten minutes tops before the medication kicked in. She got up. She couldn't wander around in pajamas, so her first step was to get dressed. She crossed to the dresser, and a wave of panic swept her. She always worried that they would take her clothes away, and each time she checked and saw them, she allowed herself the illusion that she would go home. She opened the top drawer. No, there they were. She was being paranoid, but they had given her every reason to feel that way. She understood the danger she was to Verner.

Shakily, she pulled off the clinic's pajamas and tugged on her panties, bikini bottoms the color of flax that belonged to a different life. Her head began to swim. She closed her eyes, but that only made the dizziness increase. *I'm coming, Maddie.* She slipped first one arm and then the other into the sleeves of her blouse. *I'm coming.* She pulled on her skirt. It hung from her waist, although it had fit perfectly when she had arrived. She took one step, then two and fought off a surge of fear as a hollow ringing filled her ears. She blinked her eyes against the threatening darkness. The door was heavy and her body grew slick with sweat from the effort of opening it. Precious seconds passed as she waited a moment, listened for the voices she had heard earlier, but an eerie stillness filled the air. She stepped into the empty corridor, fought another wave of vertigo. She hadn't thought about where she could go, how far she could get. Only that she had to try.

Hang on, Maddie. I'm coming.

MADISON

Maddie paced as she waited for Rick to call back from the airport, bracing herself against the news that was to come and torturing herself with conjecture. Surely, if Jack was all right, Rick would have told her. Wouldn't he? She clung to the fragile fiber of hope that Jack had not been the pilot lost in the wreckage, but she knew what the odds were. The airport was small and was busy only in the summer when part-time residents and vacationers flew in and out, and dozens of small single- and twin-engine planes were tied down on the strips composed of asphalt and grass along the taxiway. No more than ten residents kept planes there year-round, and only Jack flew there on a regular basis. She kept moving, as if that would allow her to outrun reality, and outpace, too, the memory and flashbacks that had begun to surface. The fierce intensity of flames. The discordance of sounds, of metal tearing and the roar of fire. The haunting acrid smells, a combination of fuel and metal and a sickly odor close to floral, like that of rotting narcissus.

She forced herself to breathe. The counselor at rehab had taught her this. How to inhale, counting to four or eight, focusing only on that single inhale, and then to let it go in one long slow exhale. Again and again, in and out, until the terror abated, until the flashbacks ceased. She concentrated on that now. She continued walking, circling from room to room in the house. Doing the breathing thing. She considered driving to the airport, but the fear of what she would find there was greater than the agony of not knowing. She continued to prowl, walking from one room to another.

She found the note in the bedroom on the floor by the nightstand. It had been written on a page torn from the notebook she kept by the bed. *Maddie—I left something for you in the studio.*

The origami swan, she thought. She remembered the impossible intricacy of the folded wings. *Enjoy your day. Miss me. As I will miss you. Love, Jack.* Beneath the words, he'd sketched a cartoon of a pilot with goggles and a goofy grin waving from the cockpit of a biplane. On the side of the fuselage, he'd drawn a tiny row of hearts. She clutched the note in her fist, sank on the chair, and held his trumpet in her lap. His trumpet, the first thing she had seen on waking that morning. That morning. An eon ago. When he had left to fly a charter.

A haunting image from the noon news—the crushed tail ripped from the fuselage—wavered in her vision. After the first frozen moments, she began to cry. The noisy, nose-running, swollen-eyes kind of crying she and Kat used to call the ugly cry. Winks leaped into her lap, regarding her with his green stare.

She imagined she heard a door open downstairs, steps in the hall outside her room, but knew this could not be true. Only magical thinking of a mind that could not bear the truth.

"Maddie?"

Winks circled in her lap, kneaded her thigh with his paws.

"Maddie? Honey? It's okay."

She looked up, disbelief and confusion clouding her face. "Jack?"

He crossed and knelt at the foot of the chair. Winks hopped off her lap.

"Jack?" She ran her fingers over his cheek, his chin, his chest, as if testing reality. He used his sleeve to wipe her face, her tears and snot, then wrapped her in his arms. She allowed herself this, the presence of him, the comfort of him, the reality of him, several long moments of him. And then she pushed him away. "No." She began crying again and struck her fists against his chest.

"Stop. Maddie, stop." He grasped her wrists and held them until he felt the fight go out of her. "Tell me. What's wrong? I'm here. Just tell me."

"You didn't call! Why didn't you call? Why didn't you let me know you were all right? You should have called."

He tried to pull her close, but she held herself rigid and apart. "I thought you were dead."

He let go of her and sank down on the edge of the bed. "I'm sorry I didn't call, Maddie. Really. I am. I had a lot on my plate, diverting to Hyannis, taking care of the passengers, arranging for a ride home for them and for me to get back to the airport. Filing a report. Then when I got back, things were chaos at the field."

"You should have called," she repeated, her voice hollow.

He started to speak and then stopped, suddenly understanding. "Oh God, Maddie. I'm sorry. You're right. And I'm sorry."

She looked away.

"But you have to know I came as soon as I could get free," he said. "And I did. I came right here. You know that, right?"

What she knew was that whatever this was, whatever they had, she couldn't do it anymore. She couldn't go through this again. Couldn't live with the constant threat that he would die, too.

KATHERINE

A high buzzing echo that presaged a drugged sleep filled Kat's head. She swallowed and forced herself to go on. It had only been a minute or two since she had taken the pill. She must still have seven or eight more before she passed out. Too late, she realized she should have made herself sick, vomited up the pill. She tried to remember how far the compound gate was from the building where she was being held. Overhead the fluorescent tubes in the corridor flickered. She looked left then right but was disoriented. At one end of the hallway there were two doors. At the other end there were three. She turned left, toward the three, praying she had chosen correctly. With a hand against the wall, she steadied herself and made her way to the first door, tried the knob, half expecting it to be locked. It swung open soundlessly on oiled hinges, revealing a small space with a single overhead window, a room identical to the one she was being held in. It was empty. No need to lock a vacant room.

Kat backed away and slipped into the corridor again. She reached for the second of the three doors. Her limbs felt thicker, as if she were moving underwater. She fought the encroaching darkness. She could tell she wouldn't have much time before the medicine kicked in. Her strength was ebbing rapidly. The second door was heavier than the first. She pushed against its weight with the entire force of her body, moaning with the effort. One final push and it gave way, and she stumbled into the semidarkness of a room lit only by the ambient light from the corridor and was enveloped by a veil of steamy, tropical air. She turned to leave but the door swung shut, cutting off all light. She reached out and felt the concrete wall, swept her hand along the rough surface, feeling for a switch, fighting a growing sense of panic and disorientation. There: she had it. Instantly the room was flooded with light. Overhead spotlights glared down intensely, and she raised a hand to shield her eyes while her pupils adjusted. The first thing she saw was the steel table with metal stirrups that stood in the center of the room. Lining the far wall was a bank of closed cabinets, several of which she could see were secured with padlocks. This was not the room where Verner had examined her.

Every instinct screamed to get out, but she remained rooted in place. Another wave of dizziness, stronger than the earlier one, overtook her. It was an effort to move. She lurched forward, stumbled toward the table, recoiled at the cold touch of the steel. Broad canvas tie-down straps were attached to the side. Identical strips hung from the stirrups. A supply cart stood to the left. She saw bottles and jars, sterile dressings, surgical gloves and instruments: a speculum with gleaming, curved blades, stretched forceps, a hypodermic that looked nearly a foot long, scissors, scalpels, curettes with honed edges. A stool was at one end of the table, and at the other were canisters of gas, tubes.

A noise echoed from beyond the door. A sound escaped her lips, a single gasp of fear. Exposed and vulnerable, she edged toward the wall. Even as she crept toward the switch, her eyes took in more details. An IV pole. A stethoscope and blood-pressure cuff hanging from the frame. And—this her eyes found last—by the foot of the metal table, a suction cannula, the vacuum no larger than a bucket, to which was attached a hose. The transparent tubing was darkened from repetitive use.

She had stumbled into the room where Verner harvested the fetal tissue.

Backing away in horror, Kat felt the blackness closing in.

MADISON

Maddie had fallen asleep on the couch and woke thick-tongued and dry-mouthed, as if she had been drinking. Remembering the Ambien, she groaned. She had taken the tablet after midnight. A week had passed since she had broken things off with Jack, and she was desperate to escape the emptiness of loss. She stared sightlessly up at the ceiling. A bleak inertia gripped her. The phone rang, but she did not move. The machine would pick up. Sooner or later she would have to get on with routine. Work. Something.

The phone rang again. It had been several days since he had called, leaving messages that she'd instantly deleted. Cold turkey was best. Move on. A swift, sharp break was better than a lingering one. There was no sense in delaying it when an ending was inevitable, as she had seen from the beginning it was fated to be. She counted the rings, waiting for voice mail to pick up. After a moment she heard a female voice. Not Jack, then. She closed her eyes against the disappointment that took her. Time would heal that, make her stronger. The caller continued to leave a message. *Probably Lonnie,* she thought. And then: *Kat.*

About time, she thought. Usually they talked at least once a week, but when she'd called Kat after she broke off with Jack, there had been no answer, and, oddly, her sister had not responded to the messages she'd left on her voice mail. Maddie wondered where her sister was off to now and why she hadn't mentioned a trip.

She stumbled from the couch, her legs unsteady. She tried to remember whether she had taken one or two of the white tablets. She felt a pulsing in her temples. Bending forward, protectively, like an aged person afraid of falling, she went into the kitchen and played back the message.

"Hi, Maddie."

Not Kat. Her disappointment was sharp. She had wanted it to be her sister. Needed it to be. Wherever Kat was—probably on assignment—Maddie hoped she would be back soon. And again, she tried to remember if during their last conversation Kat had said anything about going away.

"Maddie, it's Meredith. Where are you?"

Not now, not Meredith of all people. The woman was one of the group of artists whom the Gallery on Main represented. She painted oversize canvases with expansive scenes of meadows and rustic fences with a single focus in the center of each. Maddie remembered one of a partridge. Meredith had explained that she had come upon the bird frozen stiff in a snowdrift and had taken it home to paint, propping its neck straight with toothpicks as it thawed so she could complete the painting. Maddie reached out to erase the message.

"I was hoping to get you before you left the house," Meredith continued before Maddie could punch delete. "I was wondering if you would like to have lunch after the lecture? Someplace close. The East Coast Grill?"

What lecture? Maddie tried to concentrate. The pulsing in her temples swelled, slid behind her eyes. What the hell was Meredith talking about? Then she remembered. She had promised to give a slide presentation to Meredith's art history class. She glanced at the clock. Nine thirty. She crossed to the kitchen desk, shuffled through a stack of old mail, located her appointment book, checked the date. There it was, written in her own careful script: *M's class. 10:30. Slides and talk.* She looked back at the clock. That gave her a half hour to shower, dress, and gather materials and a half hour to get to the college. Or cancel. Plead illness. The thought was enormously tempting. But she'd made the commitment, and it was too late to back out. Plus, Meredith was the sort of person who banked away things like that. Maddie could hear her voice ten years on. "Remember that time you promised to lecture to my art history class and you blew me off at the last minute?"

She needed coffee. She dropped in a pod, got out a mug. If she skipped the shower she could buy herself a few minutes. She carried the coffee into the studio and found the cartridges for the slide projector. She had been promising herself to switch everything to the computer—PowerPoint presentations were what people expected these days—but she had yet to get around to it. She stared at the cartridges, trying to remember what she had promised to speak about. A lecture on the Sacred Power of Masks? Or the Use of Masks in Ritual? Maybe it was the Meaning and Function of Masks. There wasn't time to sort through them or to call Meredith. She grabbed the closest one. She would just wing it. As she turned to leave, she caught sight of the row of origami objects on the shelf and felt the swift thrust of unexpected pain. Swan. Rose. Crane. Turtle. Sword. She knew she should get rid of them but so far had been unable to bring herself to destroy them. So beautifully and carefully crafted. So intricate. She would throw them away eventually. Just not yet.

Upstairs, she couldn't avoid seeing the empty chair at the foot of the bed. Nothing of Jack's remained there. Even his absence was a presence. She turned and sorted through her clothes, clumsy from a combination of the Ambien hangover and haste. Although her rib cage constricted with just the thought of it, she supposed she should wear a bra, much as she hated the idea. One of the perks of working at home was the freedom to dress completely for comfort. She rummaged through a drawer, pulled one out. She reached into the closet to retrieve her favorite blouse, a long-sleeved top in a soft shade of lavender that Kat had given her. When she saw the shirt Jack had left behind, she felt a jolt.

But that was how it would be for a while, she guessed. When she saw a Harley on the road, caught sight of the back of a tall slim guy, heard the name Jack. Eventually, she knew, she would grow numb to these things, but right now she wanted to crawl back into bed and stay there for weeks. Months.

Life goes on. Another thing she'd learned.

She pulled out the lavender blouse and a pair of dark gray slacks and shut the closet door. She brushed her hair and applied concealer foundation to the scarred side of her face. *False advertising,* she thought wryly. The makeup did not live up to its name.

She arrived at the college eight minutes late.

"We were so worried." Meredith's words were thick with fake concern and suggested that the only acceptable excuse would be if Maddie had shown up in a full-body cast. *Passive-aggressive.* Lonnie once had said that if Meredith were a dog, she would piss on your foot while licking your hand. "How can someone who looks like a Botticelli painting be such a bitch?" Lonnie had asked.

Maddie wished she had canceled after all.

It took them several minutes to set up the projector. Maddie still moved with awkward gestures. She could have used another cup of coffee to snap fully awake. Once Meredith leaned in and whispered, "Are you all right? You look hungover." Several students seated nearby overheard. A girl with copper earrings smirked.

Meredith introduced her to the class. Faces stared up. Maddie looked out at expressions ranging from interested to slightly bored to curious: whether about the subject of her talk or Maddie herself she couldn't tell. She wondered how much Meredith had told the class about her. She bent her head so the curtain of hair fell forward, partially concealing the map of scars. "To a large extent," she began, "the original significance of the mask has been forgotten in the civilized world." Her voice sounded hollow, as if it belonged to someone else. She signaled for Meredith to pull down the shade and lower the lights, then pressed the remote. The carousel clicked forward; the first slide slipped into place. An Etruscan mask of hammered bronze flashed onto the screen. She swallowed back a sound. The cartridge she had grabbed held the slides of death masks. She heard herself identify the one on the screen by material, date, and origin. "This is a death mask," she said. "These masks hold the mystery between two phases of existence." She pressed the remote, forwarding the carousel. "Some of the finest of the genre can be found in the Aleutians." Click. The carousel turned again. "The African masks were of particular importance in their funeral rites." Her tone grew stronger as she settled into the familiar material. She advanced the slides and identified death masks from Egypt and Cambodia and Siam. This was a talk she could give in her sleep.

Another slide slipped from its slot in the carousel and dropped into the projector. Chips of turquoise rimmed in gold illuminated the mask. A half dozen teeth remained affixed to the gaping mouth. "This is an unusual example," she said, "in that the turquoise mosaic is laid over the actual skull of a human."

"What country is it from?" a boy asked.

"Mexico," she answered. Immediately she remembered the trip she had taken with Kat. Mexico, the enchanted land. Then, suddenly, inexplicably chilled, she trembled.

GRACIELA

The woman in the next room had finally stopped crying. Earlier, Graciela had heard a commotion outside in the corridor. There had been voices—the stern one of the doctor and then the woman who was always with him, the woman who had come up to her one day in the village and promised her money, seeing what even Graciela's own *madre* had not seen. With relief, Graciela had listened to the woman's solution for her problem. Beneath the voices in the corridor, running like an underground river, flowed the eerie moaning that made her skin prickle. Since then, she had heard a woman crying and calling out. This made her think of her *madre*. She wondered again if Inez was weeping for her.

She tried to move, but her body was disobedient from the shot that had been given to her. From the start she had intended to be brave. But there was much to be afraid of in this place. When fear fingered its way in, she reminded herself of her *abuela*'s name for her: *Mi pequeña valiente.* My little brave one. She heard the sea echo inside her ears and swallowed against the thickness of her throat. Overhead, the light hanging from the ceiling blurred and sharpened, blurred and sharpened. She shut her eyes and allowed the dark to swallow her.

Soon the hour of dawn will come. In the night, the high priests have prepared her, painting her skin with blue dye, perfuming her hair, forcing the ceremonial gourd of balché to her lips, holding it there until all the bitter wine is swallowed. She is naked. In the heap of jade beads and pottery, in the offerings of zapotes and tapel piled at her head, she sees the string tied to the red shell. Since she was five, her mother had laced it around her waist, replacing it with a bigger one each year on her birthday. It was to come off forever when she turned twelve, but the Nacom in the crocodile mask had removed it weeks ago, the first day the Ah Kin began fasting.

Since birth she has been prepared for this. When she was a toddler, just walking, her madre had dangled a tiny pitch bead from a string tied to her hair until her eyes, focused on the bead, had become permanently crossed. And when she was younger still, her forehead had been flattened between two blocks so that the top of her scalp was squeezed into a pointy hump. Later a tooth was drilled to hold a jade pellet, and pendants were hung from her ears. All that work and pain. All to make her most desirable to the gods.

Somewhere from a distance, she hears the screech of a macaw, then, closer, the cough of a jaguar. In spite of the intoxicating balché, fear envelops her.

Graciela was awakened by the sound of her own voice crying out. Her heart pulsed in her chest like that of a captured animal. She fought to lift her head, to look down at her body. A moment passed before she trusted the truth of her own eyes. There was no blue paint on her skin. She was not naked but wore the shift they had given her when they took away her clothes, a worn cotton garment that did not tie shut.

She had been dreaming. That was all. She was not a child painted blue. That girl had been only a dream. A dream spirit from long ago. Again she heard her *abuela*'s voice, speaking old wisdom. *Such spirits will not harm us. But if we allow them, they will warn us.* Tia Clara had echoed this during the times they had talked together about the gift that Graciela shared with the old seer.

Was the girl-child spirit trying to warn her? Or had it been a vision brought on by the medicine? She dropped her head back on the pillow, fought the darkness, but soon slipped off again.

Dawn is near. She who has been chosen hears the Ah kin *begin to chant, praying to the* Chacs. *At one side of the altar, a priest waves a broom through the air, spreading the sweet clouds of the burning copal. Another claps wooden sticks together, and the noise of this thunder rises above the sounds of shell trumpets and bone flutes. The beat of the turtle drum swells; her own heart climbs to meet it.*

The hands of the high priests stroke her body, lift her up. Fear flickers and her head swims from the wine, given to her so she will not fight as she is carried to the cenote. *Soon she will fly. Not up, but down. Down into the darkness of the* cenote. *Soon she will join those who have gone before her, deep in the earth where the silent waters flow.*

Again, Graciela woke crying out. Her *abuela* was right. The child spirit was trying to warn her. She wanted to leave this place. She would tell this to the *norteamericano* when he came. She had changed her mind. She wanted to go home, back to her family. She would keep the infant that grew inside her belly. She didn't want the money the woman had promised. She called out to her *madre*, to her *abuela. Take me home.*

But when the *norteamericano* finally appeared, his face floated in the air, and she could not lift her voice to reach him. For a moment she fought the growing shadows. Far away, a woman cried. Was it a dream? And then she surrendered, encircled by the mist.

MADISON

Pleading another appointment, Maddie turned down Meredith's invitation for lunch. Once she was outside the college and in the fresh air, the lingering effects of the Ambien dissipated. By the time she got home, she felt stronger, steadier, the weird episode or panic attack or whatever it had been pushed from her memory.

She unloaded the projector and slide cartridge and then went upstairs to strip off her bra and change into jeans and an old cotton smock she used for working in the studio. She was reaching for the smock when she again saw Jack's shirt in the closet. Instantly she flashed to the day she had ended things with him. The final fight. "I thought you were dead. I thought you were in the crash," she'd screamed, still caught in the grief and pain of losing him. He had crossed the room to her, and she'd been swept by the immense relief of seeing him, being in his arms.

"I had to divert to an alternate airport," he'd explained again.

"You should have called." How could he not have called to tell her he was safe? He knew her history. Knew what she must have been thinking. It was unforgivable that he hadn't phoned, had put her through hell. Relief was replaced by anger. *How could he have not called?*

The phone rang, pulling her from the memory.

"You're a hard one to get hold of," Lonnie said.

"I was at the college."

"You need to get a cell. Join the modern world."

"So you say." Both Lonnie and Kat were always pushing her to get a cell phone. She saw no need.

"What were you doing at the college?"

"A good question. In a weak moment, I promised Meredith I'd do a slideshow for her class." She plopped down on the bed.

"Oh, you have weak moments, do you?"

"What's that supposed to mean?"

"I thought you were steel, unbending. That's what I hear."

"Jack? That's what this is about? That's why you called?"

"What happened, Maddie? You seemed so happy and then—bam—it's over. Closed book."

"What are you, his mother?"

"You know he's in love with you."

"What? He told you that?" She was unprepared to hear this and wished Lonnie hadn't told her.

"As a matter of fact, he did."

"So you're his confessor, too?"

"Maddie, sweetheart. I've known Jack since he was a boy. I'm like a second mother. He had to talk to someone, and I'm glad it was me. Look, he only told me his side of the story, and since you won't talk about it, that's all I've heard. God knows how traumatic it was for you when you thought he'd crashed, but he didn't. That's the thing, Maddie. He didn't crash. He's alive and he wants to be with you. And I saw how you were with him. How he made you laugh. He's one of the good guys. I can't believe you'd throw away that chance at life."

"In case you didn't notice," Maddie said, her voice stiff, "I already have a life."

"I didn't say *a life*, Maddie. I said life."

She waited a beat. "I don't want to argue, Lonnie."

"Oh, Maddie. Just think about it. What is life but a marriage of change and chance? Change is inevitable. Chance is frivolous, a series of what-ifs, a throw of the dice we don't even know have been cast. You're not the only one with pain, Maddie. I've watched Jack grow up, seen him work for everything he has, watched the way he stepped in after his father left, and seen the way he's been there for his mother and his sister. One thing I know for sure about Jack is that he is worth the gamble."

Jack. A man who was devoted to his dying sister. A Renaissance man who played jazz and the blues and created exquisite paper sculptures. A man who had seen her as a warrior woman, who thought she was beautiful in spite of her scarred face and body.

Jack. The handsome twenty-six-year-old who no doubt had women lining up to be with him, who was a pilot and put his life in peril with every flight, no matter how safe he believed flying was. Jack who hadn't thought to call her to let her know he was alive and safe.

Maddie felt a wave of exhaustion.

"He misses you, Maddie. He's hurt."

Maddie let the silence on her end swell.

"He really loves you."

"He just thinks he does." She stood up, as if a movement would settle her heart, quench the flash of desire. She couldn't afford to get weak-willed. "He'll get over it."

KATHERINE

Kat no longer held out any hope that Verner would help her. If she was ever going to return to her life in DC, she would have to find a way to do it herself. She was working on that. She devised a Plan A, a Plan B, and, although this was least likely, a plan she called Omega. One way or another, she would get out of there.

On the days when she felt strong and clever enough to avoid the drugs dissolved in her food, her old fierceness would surface as if it had only been asleep and gathering strength. She would pass the long hours mentally documenting everything she knew about Verner and what he did here. The pregnant girls he brought here. His procedures. Not just unethical. Insane. She had no paper, pens, or pencils, but she imagined a notebook in her mind, and there she wrote, remembering details, forming sentences, laying out the framework of the story she would tell once she got out of there. She would lead with her experience in December during her first visit to Retirada de la Playa, which she'd imagined would lead to a story and would also be a chance for some rest and rejuvenation after a difficult year in which she had gone through another breakup and two of her pieces, done on spec, had been rejected. She would candidly document how she had been seduced by the elegance of the spa and by Verner's promise that aging could be delayed. Now, after the fact, she wondered how she could have bought what he was selling. Had she left her brains at the door? During her stint as a consumer reporter she knew well the validity of the axiom that if something was too good to be true, it probably was. And yet, perhaps still feeling the sting of the previous year's rejections, she had succumbed to his promises.

She would write about her return in January, when she'd had the first in the monthly series of shots that were central to his treatment, injections he had maintained were a combination of vitamins and vital minerals that declined as one aged, as well as an infusion of plasma culled from young blood and a cocktail injection of human growth hormone. He had supplied the guests with papers declaring the efficacy of the last. And another shot when she returned in March. The readers, drawn in just as she had been, would learn how in April, she began to notice changes, but not those Verner had promised. Her hairdresser remarked on it, too. "You need to hydrate, honey," she'd told her. "And sugar is death for the complexion. Hydrate and avoid sugar if you want to keep your skin in good shape. And consider Rogaine for the hair loss."

When he entered the room, she turned her face away and waited while he conducted his evaluation. They rarely spoke to each other now. She closed her eyes and floated off while he examined her, heard him speak to Mercer, their voices devoid of emotion, cool, without remorse. They were a pair, the two of them. He ordered more blood. What good could that possibly do? She opened her eyes and looked down at her arm, the thin skin bruised purple from the needles. *More blood.* Verner the Vampire. But even as she shrank from his touch, even now some part of her held out hope that he would be able to find a solution. *Like a doomed man, hoping the noose would break before his neck snapped,* she thought wryly. Stubborn, she had been called in the past, but her hope was based, she knew, on a fierce desire to live.

Once he was done with her, he patted her shoulder in a fake gesture of concern and left the room. Before Mercer followed him, she handed Kat the usual white pill. Dutifully she took it and pretended to swallow. Feign resignation. Lure them into complacency. When she looked up, she found Mercer's eyes on her. She knew she must be careful because Mercer was more difficult to fool than the local Mayan women, more suspicious. She had asked Kat to open her mouth and checked to see that the pill was swallowed, but Kat had learned the trick of tucking the pill up by the gum line by her back tooth. Once, uncharacteristically, Mercer had changed the sheets on the bed, had even flipped the mattress over, although menial tasks were far beneath her. Kat had been grateful she had hidden the stash of pills so cleverly. She fell back on the pillow and closed her eyes, feigning sleep while she waited for Mercer to leave. When she was sure she was alone, she retrieved the white pill and wiped it dry on her gown. Holding it in the palm of her hand, she allowed herself a nod of satisfaction.

The bed had a simple metal frame. Two square posts at the head, side slats, two more posts at the foot. The posts were capped at the top, and she had discovered she could pry off one with the spoon she had slipped from a dinner tray. The post on the left held her stash, wrapped in a length of toilet paper. Now she wedged off the top and experienced a flush of relief when she saw the square of white. She always feared the wadded paper would become dislodged and slip down into the hollow post. She unfolded the paper. She now had five pills. She did not know how many would be enough. Twenty? She settled on thirty to be sure. The pills were her Plan Omega. She would fight to escape. That was Plan A. But if that failed, she would at least be in control of how she died.

But even when reviewing this desperate plan, she would think of the story she needed to tell, that the world outside needed to know, and her determination to escape returned. And when she thought of Maddie, a fierce *no* to the pills would vibrate inside her chest, breaking through the shroud of despair, a mandate forcing her to fight, to hold on. When this happened, she would think out the exposé she would write and would review the ways she might get out of there.

She didn't know which of the two would prove her eventual release: her escape or the pills.

MADISON

She hadn't expected Lonnie to understand why she couldn't continue with Jack. Certainly Jack hadn't been able to. As she had throughout her life and especially after their parents had died, she knew the only one she could turn to and trust was Kat. Kat would understand everything. Maddie felt a longing for her sister that was physical. The house echoed, as empty and claustrophobic as a tomb.

She checked the time. Eleven fifteen. Too late? But Kat was a night owl. Always had been. She called the cell first and then, when there was no answer, Maddie tried to quell her rising anxiety. Kat was probably on assignment. Hadn't she said that during their last conversation? She was always flying away, off to distant locations in search of a story readers would love. Maddie searched her memory. She tried to recall whether Kat had mentioned specifics about her plans. The fault was Maddie's. She had been so wrapped up with Jack that she had ignored almost everything else outside the studio. Jack and her work. The past days and weeks had gone by in a rainbow spectrum of passion and play. But that was no excuse. How had she let the time elapse without questioning the silence from Kat's end?

The last conversation she could remember was when she had told Kat about Jack being a pilot. She remembered how Kat had let a silence stretch on a bit after Maddie had told her about him. She had waited for the inevitable warnings and cautions, all based on her sister's desire to protect her. Instead, after a long moment, Kat had said, "Well, don't do anything I wouldn't do," and then laughed. They both knew that left a pretty wide swath for Maddie to frolic in. After the call ended, Maddie had wondered if at last her sister was seeing her as a grown woman, able to take care of herself.

But that was nearly three weeks ago. Now Maddie's unrest was edging toward . . . not panic—Kat was a grown woman and often traveled—but something close. Three weeks without a call wasn't alarming, but it was unusual. She thought of her sister, alone in DC. What if she had fallen in her apartment? The bathroom, site of unforgiving surfaces, cast-iron tubs, glass doors, and fatal accidents. Unbidden, a picture came to mind: Kat, facedown in the bath, her hair matted with blood. Or lying on her bed, eyes open, mouth distorted in the rictus of death. Kat was only forty-four, but women younger than that died. Strokes. Heart attacks. It wasn't outside the realm of possibility.

Other scenarios crowded in, brutal images born of a thousand headlines. Muggings and murders were common events in Washington. Kat had told her this herself, had, in fact, written a feature cautioning about the dangers of being a woman alone in the city. The piece had been filled with advice on how to stay safe: advice Maddie knew that Kat, being Kat, didn't always follow.

She imagined her sister's body lying on a street or on a shadowed, grassy strip at the Mall where Kat sometimes ran. Or dead, hidden by the brush along the running path by the canal in Georgetown. Maddie wiped her hand over her eyes as if this simple gesture could erase fear. Momentarily, she considered calling the DC police or one of the hospitals in the area, but at the thought of making such a call, she convinced herself she was overreacting, not being realistic. Surely if something had really happened to Kat, someone would have been in touch with Maddie by now. No, Kat was away on a freelance assignment and, being Kat, had become consumed with work. The answer was as simple as that. Maddie was overreacting out of her own neediness. She took a Ambien and went to bed. Things were always better in the morning. Daylight had the power to wash away worries that the night gave birth to.

Except in the morning, Maddie again felt the anxiety, which now lay separated by only a whisper from more full-blown alarm. Was Kat all right? Who would know? Who could she call? She realized with a start that the list was short. Kat's work was freelance so there were no colleagues she could check in with. As for friends, at one point she would have known of a dozen people to phone, but now she knew fewer of Kat's friends. Somehow, without her being conscious of it, their worlds had drifted apart. Perhaps Izzy would know something. Why hadn't she thought of her before?

The DC row house had been divided in half. The other flat belonged to an older woman whom Kat had befriended, an overweight widow on a federal pension who had the improbable name of Isadora Duncan, although she looked no more like her namesake than a straw resembled a beer keg. Izzy's hygiene was questionable, and the one or two times Maddie had accompanied Kat there she had noticed the trash contained a suspiciously high number of empty wine bottles, but for reasons incomprehensible to Maddie, Kat adored her. "Old Izzy likes her sherry," Kat had once said, "but she's all right. She's a survivor. I've learned a lot about life from her."

She dug out Izzy's number. She let it ring and ring but there was no answer, not even voice mail. She considered calling Carl, but hesitated. There had to be someone else. She had never grown close to either of Kat's husbands. The first had lasted only two months. You can barely count that as a marriage, Kat used to say. More like a blind date carried too far. Carl, her second husband, lasted longer. Maddie had a deeper dislike of Carl, a senate lawyer who carried himself with a cocky self-importance she associated with that profession. His family had owned the parking franchise at a Maryland racetrack, a business that, according to Kat, brought in a truly astonishing amount of money. Maddie had pegged him as a bully early on and was surprised when Kat married him. For a smart woman her sister was clueless in her choice of a husband and in the prenup she'd agreed to.

She didn't want to call him and tried to convince herself Kat was fine, but eventually, around noon, her concern for her sister outweighed her reluctance. She still had the number for Carl's home in Maryland in her old address book. It occurred to her he might have moved, but she remembered his virulence during the divorce and how he had pronounced that he had designed the place himself—his dream house— and that Kat would get it over his dead body. He had been beyond acrimonious. He had been vicious, a part of his personality he had kept hidden. Maddie had tried to talk about it to Kat—had he been abusive?—but Kat shook off that question. "Here's the thing about Carl," she finally said when Maddie kept pushing. "He can't stand a woman who disagrees with him. About anything. He doesn't want anyone to outshine him. He doesn't want any demands. The surest way to incur his wrath is to stand up to him." Maddie, remembering how Carl could turn on the charm when he chose to, said, "Sounds like Jekyll and Hyde." Kat had laughed. "It's not like I didn't see the red flags waving from the start. I just chose to ignore them. Oh, well. Free now and moving forward."

The phone rang twice before a woman answered. Her voice was thin and slightly nasal. Young. Kat's replacement. Maddie wondered if she was malleable, agreeable, undemanding.

"Is Carl there?"

"Who's calling?"

"Maddie DiMarco."

"Hold on." The clicking of high heels faded off—*who wore high heels at home?*—replaced in a minute by heavy footsteps and then Carl's voice, as big and beefy as he was. "Hello."

"Hi, Carl." She could imagine his mouth already tightened in impatience.

"What can I do for you?" His voice was smooth. His professional voice.

"I'm sorry to bother you. It's Kat. I'm worried about her. I've been trying to reach her, but there's never an answer. Have you talked to her lately?"

He barked a curt laugh. "Not likely. Your sister and I are no longer in communication."

"I tried her neighbor but didn't get an answer. I didn't know who else to call. I'm really concerned about her. It isn't like her to not be in touch."

His smooth veneer dropped like a stage curtain. "Well, as I said, I don't know anything about her, and take it from me, kid, worrying about your sister is a royal waste of time. If there's one thing Kat knows how to do, it's how to take care of herself."

Maddie heard the sharp clicking of heels in the background and a woman's voice but could not distinguish what his wife—or whoever she was—was saying. "But she hasn't been answering her phone or returning the messages I've left. Don't you think that's odd?"

"I think just about everything that sister of yours does is odd."

Maddie bit back a retort. Jesus, did he think she'd be calling him if she had anyone else to call? "I'm really worried, Carl. I was wondering . . ."

"Wondering what?"

"Well, if you would drive into the city and check. Just check and see that she's okay, that she hasn't had an accident or something." She doubted he would agree to this, but she had to try, had to convey her worries. The image of Kat unconscious in the bathtub flitted across her vision.

Again, the barking laugh. "I'll tell you something, kid. I wouldn't cross the fucking street for your precious sister. You want someone to check on her, you'd better call the cops."

"She could be hurt. Or worse."

"Hey, if my luck was that good, I'd be playing the lottery," he said, his voice thick with indifference.

He hung up before Maddie could reply. She felt adrift. Maybe phoning the Georgetown police made sense. Or she could go check herself. Do what she had just asked Carl to do. She glanced at the clock, saw it was quarter to one. If she left now, she could be in Washington by eight. Nine, if she hit traffic going through New York. It would be better than waiting, pacing, worrying, imagining.

Waging hope against a sense of futility, she again tried Kat's numbers, tried not to hear an ominous tone in every unanswered ring. No better luck with a call to Izzy. She finished the coffee and rinsed out the mug. She knew she would continue to worry and would be unable to work until she did something. She opened the file drawer in her desk. As the executors of each other's estates, she and Kat had traded envelopes holding details of their lives. Kat's had been thicker. It held a computer printout listing the names of Kat's insurance company and the bank where she held accounts, a copy of her will, a list of her internet passwords, and a key to her house. Maddie took the key. She did the breathing thing she'd learned to do to avert an attack, but her skin felt too tight, her pulse raced. It took no more than fifteen minutes to pack a few things and fill two bowls of kibble for Winks. She was in the car when she remembered she hadn't changed his litter box and went back in to do that. She thought about calling Lonnie, but, still miffed from their last conversation, she didn't.

There was a multicar accident on I-95 in Connecticut. Staring at the flashing lights ahead on the highway, it hit her that if she hadn't gone back to tend to the litter box, she very well might have been in the accident, and she thought about Lonnie's comments about chance. Capricious chance. More flashing lights swooped by. Tow trucks and an ambulance. An hour later she was again on her way. A pit stop for gas and a bathroom break added more time to the trip. By the time she turned onto P Street, it was close to midnight. The pavement was wet from an earlier shower. It took her another ten minutes before she found a parking spot two blocks from Kat's house. She'd worn Reeboks and her feet were quiet on the deserted sidewalk, but, spooked, she couldn't resist looking over her shoulder. By the last half block, she was close to jogging.

The Georgian row house had been Carl's base when he worked in the capital for any stretch of time, and after the divorce it was the only thing Kat walked away with. At the time, Kat had told Maddie that she'd heard rumors that Carl had used the place to entertain women—DC hangers-on, reporters, secretaries—and she hadn't wanted it. Even if the rumors were unfounded, the house held sour memories. But Kat had said that to fight Carl on the prenup would have cost far more than she would have gained. So he got the house in Maryland and she kept the Georgetown property. Not a bad trade-off, Kat had said. Five years in a marriage wrong from the get-go in exchange for her freedom and the row house. She spent almost a year renovating it and redecorating it, erasing every trace of Carl.

Maddie rang the bell, heard its faint chime through the door, and waited, hoping against reason that her sister would answer. Her hand shook as she reached for the rail to steady herself, and she tried to prepare herself for what she might find inside. Finally, she took the key from her bag and unlocked the door. The air inside was stale, the silence total.

"Kat?" Her voice echoed, and she shivered against the sudden chill that touched her spine in spite of the May heat. She flicked on the wall switch, and light flooded the entry hall and living room. The furniture—upholstered in a cream and forest-green print fabric—had been rearranged since her last visit. It was as perfect as a stage set. "Kat?"

The dining alcove angled off to the left. She switched on the chandelier, an antique of crystal that Kat had discovered in the back room of a shop in Alexandria. Soft lighting lit the long glass-topped table, the wrought-iron wine stand, and the Duncan Phyfe sideboard that had belonged to their parents. It held a collection of jewel-toned goblets. A bay window looked out over P Street. Three orchids filled the wide windowsill, cutting off the view from the bottom half of the mullioned panes. Their outer leaves were yellow and curled; petals as dry as tissue paper littered the sill and floor. Another tongue of ice ran the length of her back. Kat pampered these plants, coddled them, even named them, as if they were the children or pets she never had. She headed into the kitchen.

Clutter greeted her, so uncommon for Kat, who demanded order. Fast-food containers were on the café table. Dirty dishes—a mug, small china bowl, two tumblers—sat in the sink. The trash container was partially filled. Maddie smelled the rankness of something organic gone bad. Her breath quickened, and the raspiness of it echoed in the empty house.

She stiffened her shoulders and headed for the bedroom. The room was vacant and she exhaled in relief. If something had happened to Kat, it hadn't happened there. Still, she couldn't shake off a mounting apprehension. The bed had been carelessly made. She forced herself to look at the sheets and pillow slips. No stains. No blood. Still, her hands trembled, her heart raced.

She continued to the bathroom, bracing herself for what lay beyond the closed door. She twisted the knob, half expecting resistance from Kat's body crumpled on the floor, but the door swung open. A towel was draped over the side of the tub. The vanity was covered with cosmetic jars and a wicker basket that held an assortment of lipstick tubes and mascara wands. There was a hair dryer, still plugged into the outlet, and four brushes and various bottles containing vitamins. Maddie held each item, as if examining for clues. She picked the bottles up, read the labels. A, E, C, D, and B complex capsules in addition to a multivitamin pill and an iron tablet. This struck Maddie as extreme overkill, but then she didn't even take C to ward off colds. She picked up one of the brushes. The rounded bristle end struck her as impossibly fat. She drew a long ash-colored hair from it. What could she possibly learn from that?

A pair of Kat's panties lay on the floor by the shower. They were a pale green, bikini-style, with the crotch exposed, as if Kat had just moments before stepped out of them. A white terry-cloth garment hung from the hook on the back of the door, the kind of lush robe that high-class hotels provided for guests. Three words were embroidered in blue floss on the breast pocket: RETIRADA DE LA PLAYA. Although Kat spoke the language fluently, Maddie's high school Spanish, never great to begin with, was beyond rusty. She considered possible translations. Refuge by the shore? Retirement by the shore? Something like that, anyway. A souvenir from some trip, she supposed. Mexico? Spain? She checked the deep side pockets and the smaller one with the blue stitching but found nothing. Not even a tissue. She left the bathroom and returned to Kat's bedroom.

The answering machine was on the bedside table. She punched the button and listened to her own voice relay the messages she had left over the past few days. A woman named Lucille had called four times, a man with a liquid voice and southern accent had left two brief "call me" messages but no name, a half dozen robo calls. There were a number of hang-ups.

A pair of thin cotton gloves lay next to the machine. Maddie picked them up, laid them against her cheek. The familiar sweetness of Kat's almond-oil cream filled her nostrils. As long as she could remember, her sister had slept wearing gloves like these to pamper her hands and nails. She held them for several minutes, breathing in the scent, and then returned them to the table.

Back in the kitchen, she opened the refrigerator and surveyed the few staples. A pint of half-and-half gone sour, a jar of capers, another of tiny cocktail onions, a tin of coffee, a container of moldy lo mein, a baggie with four bagels inside. In the freezer compartment she found a pint of sour cherry low-fat ice cream, two ice trays, and an unopened bottle of Absolut. The door that led to the rear courtyard was bolted shut.

The small room Kat used as her combo office, gym, and—for Maddie's occasional visits—spare bedroom was neater than Kat's room or the kitchen. Circling the rowing machine and two sets of dumbbells, Maddie crossed to the two-drawer file. The top one held folders, and she took out the first one. Notes and research for articles her sister had written. The other files held more of the same. The bottom drawer was empty.

A combination printer/fax/copier sat on top of the cabinet. The internet modem was on the floor by the desk. Kat's laptop was gone, its absence briefly reassuring. If Kat was off on an assignment, she would have taken it with her. Maddie could find nothing unusual. There was the normal paraphernalia of a home office. Reams of paper, a mug containing an array of pencils and pens, a coaster for the mug of coffee Kat always drank when she was working on a story. A three-shelf bookcase held several atlases, *The Chicago Manual of Style*, a variety of books, both fiction and biographies. The bottom shelf held stacks of magazines that Kat had written for, most of them from the periodical where she had been on staff until it went defunct. On top of the bookcase were framed photos of Kat with various people, some of whom Maddie recognized as the subjects of profiles she had written. In the back, partially obscured by a photo of Kat with the artistic director of Lincoln Center, was a small snapshot of Maddie. It had been taken when she was a sophomore in college and had spent spring break with Kat. She was sitting on a bench by the pool in front of the Jefferson Memorial. The cherry trees were in bloom. That was the last photo Maddie remembered Kat taking of her. Before the accident.

She went back to the kitchen and shot the deadbolt open, stepped into the brick courtyard edged with boxwood. A circular wrought-iron table and four chairs occupied the center. These had been painted with a dark green enamel, and spots of rust were visible on the arms of two of the chairs. A small border of thirsty-looking herbs lined the back side of the kitchen wall. Even in the moonlight, Maddie recognized sage, tarragon, and rosemary. *Rosemary for remembrance.* In the kitchen, she filled the tumbler that she'd seen in the sink and carried it out to the courtyard. It took ten trips before she was satisfied that the herbs were resuscitated.

She should call the police. But say what? She was exhausted, beyond exhausted, and unable to deal with even the thought of dealing with the inevitable questions. She would need to be alert. Another few hours wouldn't matter now. And what could they really do in the middle of the night? She went through the house, turning off the lights she had switched on. Then she stripped to her underwear and crawled into Kat's bed. The sheets were silky. Kat loved luxury. A single sheet probably cost more than Maddie spent in years for one set. Before she turned off the lamp next to the bed, she got back up and rechecked the bolts on the front door and the one in the kitchen. On the way back to bed, she turned on a small lamp in the hall, a circle of light to dispel the dark.

She watched the clock tick off the minutes. It was well after two. When she was a girl and couldn't sleep because she was afraid of nightmares, she would get up and go into Kat's room and get into the bed. Her sister wouldn't say anything, just move over to make room for her. She would stroke Maddie's hair back from her face. The memory was so vivid, so strong. Longing for the comfort only Kat could bring her, she reached for the cotton gloves, held them to her cheek, again inhaling the almond scent. At last she drifted off. Despite her anxiety and worry, she fell into a sound sleep, the first time she'd slept so deeply since Jack had left.

MADISON

The dream was an old one. Maddie moaned in her sleep while it played on, unfolding to its own ordained conclusion. Her father is at the controls, her mother in the copilot's seat. She is in the back. The sun is bouncing off the nose of the Piper, so bright it hurts her eyes. Her father glances back over his shoulder at her, but his face is distorted: not her father but someone else at the wheel, a stranger who means to do her harm.

Maddie woke trembling from the dream's insistent realism. She closed her eyes, forced her mind to the present. She was in Kat's bedroom in Georgetown. Safe in Kat's bed. But the return of the dream—it had been years since it had troubled her—disturbed her. Her body felt bloated with memory, each treacherous cell bent on recalling what she had been determined to shut out. A therapist she had seen briefly in the hospital had told her that coming to terms with memory was a way of making sense of the present, a concept she thought inane.

"I don't remember," she told the therapist. This was not entirely true. She did remember some of the crash. And her father's voice above the crackle of flames. *Get out, pumpkin. Get out and run.* But perhaps that wasn't even a real memory. Perhaps she had made it up. She had been told that her parents had died on impact.

She felt edgy, her heart rate irregular, signs of an impending anxiety attack. She knew she would get no more sleep. She forced herself to take deep breaths. It had been weeks since she'd had an attack, and she had left her meds at home. The bedside clock read five fifteen. She found Kat's glove twisted in the sheets and brought it to her face. Now the scent of almonds was no longer comforting. It seemed too sweet. She got up, shook off a momentary nausea, headed for the kitchen. Being active, moving, often helped derail an attack before it switched into high gear.

She brewed coffee. The bagels were stale—more wood than dough—but she managed to get half of one down, which helped the nausea while she worked on a plan. She rehearsed what she would tell the police, trying to strike the right note: concern but not hysteria. She forced herself to wait until it was after eight before she placed the call, filling the hours between with searching her sister's rooms again, but she uncovered nothing new.

The dispatcher took her information and told her a patrolman would be there within an hour. While she was waiting, she found a watering can, a graceful copper vessel with a long, curved spout. At home, Maddie used a plastic milk jug to water her houseplants, but Kat wouldn't think of using something like that. The copper can held less water than it would appear, and it took several trips to again water the herbs on the back patio and the orchids in the dining room. She swept up the desiccated blossoms on the floor.

They would want a photo of Kat, she supposed. Wasn't that what the police asked for in missing persons cases? The implication of this chilled her. She took a framed shot from the top of the office bookcase, a photo of her sister with a famous violinist whose name she could not recall. And clothes: they would want to know what she might be wearing. She froze, paralyzed by the unreality of the situation, then went to the closet. She couldn't conceive of owning so many clothes. Shoeboxes covered the entirety of the floor. She fingered through several hangers before she gave up. There wasn't a chance in a trillion she would know what was missing.

She was in the bathroom when the doorbell rang. Before she answered it, she picked up Kat's panties off the floor and dropped them in the hamper.

"Ms. DiMarco?"

The patrolman was in his fifties with a deeply lined face and gray hair that spoke of long experience. She felt hopeful.

"Ms. DiMarco?" he repeated.

She nodded.

"I'm Officer Segerman. The station sent me over." His eyes widened as he took in her scars, a look she'd grown used to, and then an expression of professional detachment slid into place. "You reported a missing person?"

"Yes." She identified herself as Kat's sister and told him about Kat's disappearance. He took down Kat's specifics. Her full name, age, physical appearance, marital status, the last time Maddie had had contact with her. Then he snapped his notebook shut.

"Do you mind if I take a look around?"

"No. Of course not." She followed him as he checked each room, went to the back patio.

"And you arrived this morning?"

"Last night. I drove down from Massachusetts."

"And this is how you found the place?"

"Yes. I slept in the bed last night and made coffee this morning." She didn't think it important to mention the bagel.

He made a note in his book. "And that's all."

"Oh, I played the messages on her machine when I first got here."

"What time was that?"

"Around midnight."

"Where's the phone?"

"There are two. One in the bedroom and an extension in the office. I played the messages on the one in the bedroom." She waited while he listened to the messages. He had dandruff on the shoulders of his uniform.

"Do you know who Lucille is?"

"No."

"What about the male? Did you recognize his voice?"

"No."

"Does your sister live alone here?"

"Yes."

"And you said she was divorced?"

"Yes. About fourteen years ago." She heard her voice, surprised at how calm and steady it was as she answered his questions, revealing no sign of her inner fears. "I called Carl yesterday, before I drove down, but he hadn't heard from her. I don't think they stay in touch. He's remarried."

"Any boyfriends?"

"No. Not for a while now." Was that even true?

"Any history of alcohol or drug abuse?"

"No. None." Of that she was confident.

"Has she ever done anything like this before? Just gone off without telling you?"

"No. We're very close. She'd tell me if she was going to be away for a long time."

"But you don't recognize the people who left messages."

"No."

"So maybe not that close, after all."

Maddie didn't bother to respond. What did he know about her and Kat?

"Does she have a job?"

"She's a journalist."

"Have you tried her employer?"

"She's freelance. She writes articles. Travel pieces. Celebrity profiles. Other assignments."

"I take it that her job involves some travel."

"Yes."

"Is it possible that she's just off on an assignment? Out of the country?"

"I suppose it's possible. But it isn't like her to be out of touch for such a length of time."

"Listen, Ms. DiMarco. There's nothing here to suggest foul play. No signs of struggle. Your sister is an adult. As you said yourself, she travels for her work. Chances are that's where she is now. Or perhaps a new boyfriend."

"So that's it?"

"I don't know what else we can do."

The hope she had allowed herself earlier faded.

"I can put in a routine report, and after twenty-four hours they might assign a detective to check in with you. Put out an ATL."

"ATL?" She hated acronyms.

"Attempt to locate."

Maddie fought to keep the panic out of her voice. "Listen, I really think something's wrong. I know there aren't any signs of a struggle, but there *are* signs. The dishes in the sink. And her orchids needed watering."

Officer Segerman smiled. "Ms. DiMarco, if we had to check on dried-out plants, we'd be too busy to catch the bad guys."

She clenched her jaw to contain her anger, to keep from yelling at him.

MADISON

It was intolerable to think of waiting twenty-four hours. There had to be something she could do, someone she could call who might have some knowledge.

Izzy.

From the front stoop, Maddie saw that the shades of the two street-level windows were drawn closed. She pressed the buzzer. Waited. Pressed again. Although it was nearing ten o'clock, she supposed Izzy could still be in bed. She knocked on the door, then gave one last try with the bell, heard the five-note chime ringing on the other side of the door. Finally, she gave up and returned to Kat's.

Maybe Izzy wouldn't answer the door, but perhaps she would respond to a phone call. She searched for a phone directory in Kat's office desk. The contents were in neat order, the tidiness a sharp contrast to the perpetual clutter of Maddie's own desk. She opened the top drawer and found several pens and pencils, some paper clips in a small rosewood box, a book of stamps, a folder of paid invoices—mostly utilities and Bank of America credit card statements—a short stack of stationery in an elegant cream stock with Kat's address embossed on the envelopes in a sable brown. Even in an age where communication was predominately by email and text, Kat still liked to correspond by letter. The drawer contained the usual paraphernalia but no directory for Georgetown. Nothing private beyond the file of invoices. No letters or personal papers. No checkbook.

Disappointed, Maddie shoved the drawer in, encountered resistance. She pushed harder, but again the drawer stopped short of closing completely. She slid it free of the desk, bent to look in the opening, and saw a dark object in the shadowy recess. She felt a catch of excitement that faded quickly when she retrieved only an address book. She leafed through and found nothing but a handful of listings entered, as if Kat had begun putting in names but had lost the book before she could finish or had given up on the book and entered contact info in her iPhone instead. She flipped through the pages, found her own name, numbers for a nail salon, a gym, and one other listing: Picasso's. There was a number and street address for the last but no further notation. It could be an art gallery or restaurant or one of those trendy cafés that were always popping up in Georgetown. Not much to go on, but it was a start, and better than sitting around imagining the worst while waiting for the twenty-four hours to pass before she could follow up with the police. The address for Picasso's was on Thirty-Fifth Street, not more than a ten-minute walk. She'd start there.

She headed west on P. It felt good to be outside and walking. She had forgotten how much she liked this part of the city. She had stayed with Kat for one entire summer, and they had explored the rest of the capital, done all the tourist things—all the Smithsonian buildings, the national monuments, the art galleries, crossing the river to Arlington and the cemetery—but her favorite times had been spent in Georgetown. She had filled nearly an entire sketchbook with drawings of the picturesque row houses along the towpath of the Chesapeake and Ohio Canal. Unbidden, catching her completely off guard, she thought of Jack, imagined sharing with him the city Kat loved.

She nearly missed Picasso's. The entrance was stark, offering no clue to what lay inside. A curved black awning sheltered the door. The front windows were tinted. On one was written Picasso's in elegant script in the same funereal shade as the awning. She pushed open the etched-glass door and entered. Immediately, Maddie recognized it as the kind of beauty salon where the cost of a haircut started north of three hundred. The place smelled of hair spray and the scent of vanilla that wafted from a mister near the front desk. Maddie preferred the smell of paint, epoxy, and turpentine any day of the week. The decor was chrome and black with pale gray carpeting. Adele was blasting from ceiling speakers. No one sat at the receptionist's counter. A thin black woman clad in leopard-print tights and a pale, smoke-gray smock brushed by. She carried a silver tray holding bottled water and porcelain coffee cups. "Be right with you," she chirped. Kat sneezed in response. The fake vanilla mist was making her eyes water.

There was a small bank of shampoo stations on the far wall, and four women lay back with heads arched into the basins. Another wall held four styling chairs. Three stylists dressed in the signature gray smocks cut locks or wielded dryers or applied thick, paste-like product to clients' hair with brushes.

"May I help you?" A tall man, dark hair streaked at the temples with egg-yolk yellow, approached. He held a pair of scissors in his left hand and absently opened and closed them as he neared.

"Are you the owner?"

"Lordy, no, darling." He laughed. "I'm just one of the lowly laborers. Malcolm," he added by way of introduction. He scrutinized her face, scars, hair. She recognized the look. Kat's voice echoed. *You've got to do something with that hair of yours.*

"If you are here to see Phillipe, you're out of luck, honey," he said. "It's his day off. Besides, he only takes referrals. The rest of us are booked for the day." His gaze again took in her scars. The shears flicked open and shut. "But if you are not in a hurry, one of us might be able to fit you in."

"I'm not here for an appointment." She took a deep breath. "My name is Maddie DiMarco. My sister is Katherine Clayton. I think she's a client here."

"Clayton?" He thought. "I'm coming up dry, honey. Blonde or brunette?"

The girl in the leopard tights, still carrying the tray, sashayed over. "You want to know who does Ms. Clayton?"

"Yes."

"You know her," she said to Malcolm. "The tall ash blonde with green eyes. She's one of Lucille's standing appointments. Every Thursday."

Lucille. The name left on Kat's machine.

Malcolm turned toward the rear of the shop and pointed to a bony woman with hair the red of mahogany. "That's Lucille."

"Thanks."

"No problem, love." He withdrew a card from a small saucer on the counter. "Here's my card. If you reconsider the cut, call." He tilted his head and narrowed his eyes. "I see you with something whimsical. Layered. Something feathered around your face. A cut that would define your features."

She took the card and shoved it in her bag, knowing she would toss it as soon as she left. Malcolm would have to live with the disappointment. Lucille looked like she should be in high school, but as Maddie drew closer she saw she was older. Her forehead was broad, her chin pointed, her ears triple pierced. Maddie felt the first real surge of optimism. Weren't hairdressers supposed to be the recipient of confidences, privy to their clients' innermost lives? What had Kat shared with Lucille?

"Lucille? My name is Maddie DiMarco, Katherine Clayton's sister. Do you have a minute?"

"Sure. Give me five."

"Okay."

She was painting strands of hair with a brush, then wrapping the strands with foil. Just watching, Maddie felt her scalp itch. "But we've got to make it quick. My next cut is waiting."

"Thanks." Maddie tried to curtain her impatience. Finally, she was going to speak to someone Kat had seen recently, a link to her sister's current life.

"Do you want water or coffee or something while I finish up?"

"No. I'm fine. Thanks." It was closer to ten minutes before Lucille finished with the foiling, and each minute felt like an hour.

"Be right back," the stylist said. "Just going to tell my next cut that I'll be right with her."

"Sure," Maddie said.

"So what's up?" Lucille said when she returned. "Is Katherine okay? I mean, is she sick or something?"

"What makes you ask?"

"Well, I haven't seen her since her last appointment in April. To tell you the truth, she didn't look too great the last time I saw her. Real tired. I told her it was all right to burn the candle at both ends when you're twenty, but you can't get away with doing it once you're on the north side of forty. When she didn't return my calls, I thought maybe she had switched to another salon."

"Why?" Maddie was still processing the disturbing idea that Kat had looked ill.

Lucille shrugged. "It happens. I was kind of surprised, though."

"Why?"

"She seemed happy here. Recommended me to some people. Tipped well. Usually when a client is unhappy, the first thing you notice is that the tips fall off." She tilted her head, leaned in closer. "So what happened? Is she sick?"

Maddie lowered her voice. "I don't know." It occurred to her that she really didn't know. Was it possible that Kat was ill? But why wouldn't she have told her? Why would she keep something like that secret? The shapeless possibilities that had shadowed Maddie for the past days took a more concrete form. *Cancer.*

"You don't know?"

"I can't find her. She—she's disappeared." As soon as the words were spoken, she wanted to recall them. So dramatic. So frightening.

"Disappeared?" Lucille's yelp attracted the attention of the stylists at the shampoo sinks.

"I'm sure it's nothing. A vacation, or off on assignment or something." Now she sounded like the cop. Segerman. In truth, she wasn't certain of anything. "Do you remember the last time she came in?"

"You want the exact date?"

"That might help."

"Sure. No problem." Lucille crossed to the appointment book and paged through the register. "Kat has disappeared," she confided to the receptionist. "This is her sister."

"Disappeared? You're kidding."

"I'm not sure," Maddie interrupted. "I think she could be on assignment. I've been away, and we've not been in touch for a while. I'm trying to track her down." Kat would be horrified to learn she had been telling people she had disappeared.

"April fifteenth," Lucille said. "Color and cut." She flipped ahead several more pages. "Yeah. That was her last time. On Thursday. Her standing appointment."

"She had her hair cut every week?"

"Shampoo and blow-dry every week. Color and cut every month."

"The last time she was here, did she say anything about a trip, or that she would be away?"

"No. She just blew off her appointments. No call. No cancellation or explanation. Nothing. Just didn't show. That's why I thought she must have changed salons. Look, I'm sorry, but I've got someone waiting."

Maddie considered asking the girl at the desk if Kat had said anything to her about a trip, but that seemed improbable. If she hadn't said anything to Lucille, she wouldn't have confided to the receptionist.

Another fit of sneezing hit her. She had to get out of there before she developed hives.

Outside, she paused a moment to let what she had learned in the salon sink in. Kat had missed appointments without explanation. She had appeared unwell. What had happened to her? If Kat was really ill, why had she kept this information from her? Her sense of urgency increased. She was determined to pursue every lead, no matter what it led to. Naomi's Nails was next on the list. Maddie rechecked the address. Two blocks south. The sky was darkening. She hadn't brought an umbrella and stepped up her pace. Students from the university, Georgetown matrons, and tourists in T-shirts and shorts crowded around her. Out of habit she noticed faces, the shapes and bones and lines. A couple walked by arm in arm, laughing. The man had narrow shoulders. Jack. The burden of sorrow—the knife of loss—washed over her. How physical a pain heartache was. She stopped in midstride, gave it a moment, and then pressed on. One lesson life had taught her was that pain was tolerable, and eventually the worst would pass. Eventually, thoughts of Jack wouldn't overwhelm her. Eventually, she would be numb.

At the nail salon, the story was the same. Kat had missed her biweekly appointment in April. No cancellation. No notice. She just hadn't shown up and hadn't been in since. There was nothing more the staff could tell her. When Maddie went outside, the rain had already begun. Other pedestrians, as unprepared as she, hurried along, folding into the rain and wind. Maddie checked the last address from Kat's book. The gym was five blocks away. Her leg began to ache, as it did whenever she overexerted or when it rained. She flagged down a cab. The driver, an Algerian, judging from his cabdriver ID, wanted to talk. She stifled a groan. The entire morning of racing around from one stop to the next in search of answers was beginning to feel like an idiot's pursuit. Whatever had been going on with Kat, she clearly hadn't wanted to confide in anyone.

The gym was a surprise. She had envisioned a fashionable place with free weights in bright colors and high-tech machines, one of those clubs heavy on special features like saunas, steam rooms, and women's dressing areas stocked with thick towels, hair dryers, and shower gels, where Lycra-clad housewives and professionals struggled to keep their butts high and their thighs firm.

This place was a throwback to the days before Pilates and step classes. Grimy brick walls were exposed, and bare pipes hung from the ceiling. The synthetic commercial carpet was years overdue for replacing, and the smell of sweat was not camouflaged by any floral deodorizer or misting machines. There were several apparatuses, but the majority of equipment consisted of free weights, bars, and incline benches. The coverings on one or two of the benches had been mended with silver duct tape. Black-and-white photos of bodybuilders, several of them autographed, hung on the wall behind the counter. Judging by the style, Maddie guessed they dated from the '40s and '50s. She could not imagine Kat working out here. How had her sister even discovered the place?

A half dozen men were lifting, but they did not break their concentration when she entered. There was no pause in the rhythm of the weights clanging. In one corner she saw a well-built older man jabbing a punching bag. Even from a distance of several yards, she could see the jolt pass up his arms each time a fist hit the bag. He looked faintly familiar, and it took her a moment or two to make the connection. He was the national political correspondent for one of the networks. Much shorter than he appeared on TV.

"Help you?" The man behind the desk was young, blond, and tan. He wore a T-shirt with the logo of a sports drink on the front. Even through the fabric, Maddie could make out the planes of sharply defined muscles.

"Hi. I'm hoping you can give me some information." She couldn't shake the sense that she knew him. His voice, if not his face, was vaguely familiar. Another reporter moonlighting here?

"Tom." He held out a hand and she offered hers, praying he'd curb any macho need to crush it. He was assessing her: not in a sexual way, she realized, but clinically. Checking out muscle tone, body fat. Again, as she had in the salon, she knew she fell short of the place's standard. "I'm looking for someone."

"Name?"

What was it with this guy? Didn't he know how to form complete sentences?

"Katherine. Katherine Clayton."

A flicker of recognition crossed his face, followed immediately by one of caution. "Yeah, sure. I know her." The caution was still there, as well as something else that she couldn't identify.

"You do?"

"Sure. Tightest abs I've ever seen on a woman over thirty." He smiled. "Let me tell you, she puts women half her age to shame. Can toss off fifty sit-ups like she's dealing cards." His voice shifted, less cautious, more caring. "Is she okay?"

Maddie was more prepared now that she'd told the story at Picasso's and Naomi's Nails, but it still was awkward. How did you tell people that your sister was missing? "I don't know."

"You don't know?"

"I was hoping you might know something."

He hesitated. "Then you haven't talked to her. Kat didn't say anything to you about me?"

"No." She caught his eyes. He reddened and looked away and she got it. He had slept with her sister. "When was the last time you saw her?"

He didn't need to check any appointment book. "April."

That matched what she had learned earlier at two salons.

"You're Kat's sister?"

She nodded, waited for the inevitable reaction. *You don't look alike. I would never have guessed you were related.* But he surprised her by saying, "I can see that. There's *something* about you that reminds me of her. You see her, tell her if she wants to keep those killer abs, she'd better get back here."

"Okay. I'll pass the message on."

She was at the door when he called out. "Tell her I miss her. Tell her to come back."

There was a break in the rain, and she decided to walk back to the house. She took her time, realizing she was avoiding the empty rooms that awaited her. As she approached the building, she noticed the shades were still drawn on Izzy's windows. She checked her watch. It was nearly noon. She hesitated and then rang the bell, holding it in place for several long moments before turning away. Maybe they were both in there, lying inside the apartment. Dead. A flicker of hysteria caught in her chest, and she willed it away. She heard the echo of Kat's voice, remembered how her sister always had the ability to allay her fears and soothe away her worries. *Stay calm. Stay reasonable.* She stepped back on the sidewalk. A growing pressure behind her eyes signaled the beginning of a headache. She had eaten little since grabbing a coffee and cellophane-wrapped pastry when she'd stopped for gas on the trip down the day before. And the stale half bagel earlier that morning. The idea of food wasn't appealing, but fasting was giving her a headache. She'd passed a café a few blocks back. She reversed course and headed there.

They were in the middle of the late-morning rush, and there was a fifteen-minute wait before she could be seated. While she waited, she surveyed the menu board. All the breakfast sandwiches were made with croissants filled with a number of choices. Scrambled eggs with ham or prosciutto, or salmon. Or sautéed veggies. Even the French toast was made with croissants. The idea that appealed to Maddie most was coffee. She ordered a cup and a simple scrambled egg. But once she was served, she was so jumpy she could barely manage a mouthful. She tried to formulate a plan for the rest of the day, but could think of nothing. She had informed the police and followed up on the only leads she had. The idea of Kat's empty rooms came close to triggering panic. She had nowhere to go. Knew no one else in the city. She considered finding a cinema in the area. A film would occupy at least a couple of hours. Anything, even staring sightlessly at a screen, was better than the echoing silence of Kat's place. The waitress gave her directions to a two-screen theater not too far away. The walk took her back by Picasso's. She paused beneath the black awning and, on impulse—perhaps there was one thing Kat had said that Lucille had remembered after she'd left—she opened the door. It was even possible that Malcolm or one of the others might have overheard her talking to another client.

He smiled when he saw her. "Changed your mind about that haircut, I see," he said.

MADISON

Almost to the minute that the twenty-four-hour window elapsed, Maddie called the precinct. She was handed off from person to person and put on hold three times before reaching the detective.

"Are you at the address you gave Officer Segerman?" John Miller asked after he'd identified himself. "Yes? Give me twenty minutes and I'll be there."

Miller was a black man with powerful features, a face that in another time and place she would have wanted to sketch. He wore a well-tailored sports coat and carried himself with a confidence that was more reassuring than off-putting. He began by taking the same information she had covered with Segerman. Her sister's full name. Employment. Friends.

"I've been through this with the other officer," she said, struggling to conceal her impatience.

"Bear with me." He continued with the routine questions, but listened with an intensity and attention that suggested he was hearing more than simple answers and that nothing would escape his intelligence. Her hopes rose.

He motioned for her to take a chair and then sat opposite her, leaning forward, his voice calm, low.

"Do you remember the date that you last spoke with your sister?"

"Not exactly," she said. "It was in the middle of April."

"Did she sound upset? Depressed?"

"No. Not at all."

"What did you talk about?"

"Mostly we talked about what was going on in my life." She hesitated and tugged at a wispy strand of hair that circled her chin. *Elfin.* That's how Malcolm said the new style made her look. It had been a mistake. She missed her long hair. Missed the concealment it had afforded her, felt naked in her exposure. And all for naught. Malcolm had been unable to offer anything more about Kat. "She was asking about a new relationship I was in."

"Can you remember if she mentioned anything about going away? A trip or vacation she was thinking about?"

"No." Then she reconsidered. "She might have said something about an assignment. I'm not sure."

"And that's the last time you spoke? Roughly a month ago."

"Yes."

"Since that time have you tried to contact her? Email? Text?"

"I've tried calling. We don't text. I don't have a cell phone."

He smiled. "Well, that's a sentence you don't hear much these days."

"That's what people tell me." When she told people she didn't have a cell, they always made her feel like the last holdout from the ice age.

"To get back to your sister, you did try to call her."

"Yes."

"Okay," he said. "Tell me everything. Anything. Even if you don't think it's relevant."

She explained how she had tried to get hold of Kat in recent weeks but that her calls had gone unanswered. She told him of her brief conversation with Carl and his unwillingness to check on Kat.

"What's their history?"

"They're divorced."

"Was he abusive? Did your sister have any reason to fear him?"

"They've both moved on. He's remarried. She's—" Maddie paused. *She's what?* she wondered. *As content as she professes?* She recalled the way Kat now described herself, and she parroted her words to Miller. "She's happily divorced." But was she? Really?

He asked for Carl's name and telephone number, made a note of it. "Go on," he said.

Maddie told him how her worry had grown, her sense that something was wrong, that Kat would never just fall off the face of the planet without checking in with her. She led him through the previous day, her futile attempt to learn anything from the neighbor, her visits to the hair and nail salons and the gym where Kat had worked out.

He scribbled notes while she talked. When she was finished, he walked through the rooms, taking longer than Segerman had. Again, she sensed that he was missing nothing. In the bathroom, he opened the bottles of supplements, checked the capsules and tablets in each. "Is your sister a health nut?"

"No. Not really." She hated feeling that she had to defend Kat against unspoken assumptions.

"What about drugs? Or alcohol? Any problems or history there?"

"No. No. Never."

He took in the bedroom from the doorway and then crossed to the closet and opened the door, pulled out a few garments. She saw him check the labels. "Do you know if any of her clothes are missing?"

"I did look, but I wouldn't really know if anything was gone."

He stared at the clothes, crowded hanger to hanger. "I can see why." In the hall, he stopped and studied the mask that Kat had hung there. It was one of the Benda copies, a depiction of perfect, porcelain beauty, expressionless, the mystery of the unknown. Or the hidden. Over the years Maddie had given several of her sculptures to Kat, but this was the only one that her sister had chosen to display.

"Interesting," he said.

She did not tell him that she had created it.

They returned to the living room. "Can I get you something? Coffee?"

"You read my mind."

"There isn't any cream."

"Black is fine."

He followed her to the kitchen and watched while she got out mugs, pulled out two K-cups. She was aware of his gaze, searching the room, studying her, assessing. His silence was unnerving. She wished he would tell her what he was thinking. She wondered if he was taking Kat's absence seriously. While he was thorough, he certainly wasn't acting with any urgency. "What are you going to do now?" she asked. "Yesterday the other officer mentioned putting out an"—she struggled to remember the acronym—"an ATL."

"Yes. We'll do that. And tomorrow, if you still haven't heard from her, we'll put out a missing persons, but to be honest with you, at this point, with the information we have, there's not cause for a fuller investigation."

"Why?"

"For starters, there's no sign of a struggle here. Nothing out of place. Earlier, before I left the station, I checked the log, and there's no record of any calls from your sister reporting prowlers or stalkers. And you yourself said she might have said she was going off on an assignment."

"Something is wrong." Her voice was shrill with frustration. "I'm telling you, something is really wrong." She handed him the coffee.

He set his notebook down and took the cup. "Thanks." He maintained his measured, soothing tone. "Ms. DiMarco, here's what we can do. I'll have someone run a check on the DC hospitals. We'll speak to your sister's friends if you'll give us names and contacts, although I suspect you've already done this. Have you been in touch with her physician?"

"Her physician?"

"To see if she's had a recent physical, received a test result that would upset her. Something that might have made her want to be alone."

"Yes. I checked," she lied. "Kat is perfectly healthy." She didn't want Miller to delay his investigation while he waited for her to chase after Kat's doctor. If anything was wrong, Kat would have told her. She was certain of that. Well, almost certain. She recalled Lucille saying Kat had looked tired. Drawn.

"We can check her car registration and driver's license," Miller continued, "see if either of them were due to expire and have been renewed in the past months."

"Kat doesn't own a car." Her sister's laughter slipped into the room. *Forget cars. That's why God invented taxis.* The memory was cut abruptly by the sound of Miller slapping his palm on the table.

"I knew there was something I was missing."

"What?"

"Her mail. Where is your sister's mail?"

Maddie was a step behind. "I don't understand."

"There's a mail slot in the front door. Does she have it delivered here, or does she pick it up at the post office?"

"Here."

"Did you see it when you came in yesterday? Pick it up and put it somewhere?"

"No."

"Well, where is it? If she's like most people, the catalogs and junk mail alone should be piled ankle deep. Unless she had it held for her at the post office. Which would mean she made plans to be away for a while."

"But she didn't," Maddie said. "She didn't make plans to be away."

"Why do you say that?"

"Well, when I arrived yesterday, there was a pint of cream in the refrigerator, and it had turned sour. If Kat had planned to be away, she would have dumped it before she left. And then there's her orchids."

"Her orchids?"

"Yes." She pointed to the alcove in the dining room, the three plants in the bay window. "When I got here, they were completely dry. There were dead blossoms on the floor. If Kat was going to be away for more than a week or ten days, she would have asked Izzy—Mrs. Duncan—to water them. She was quite precise about their care. A quarter cup of cold water every week. She was exact about that. Too little and they dried out, too much and the roots rotted."

"This Mrs. Duncan?" Miller checked his notes. "That would be the neighbor?"

"Yes."

He rose, crossed to the dining alcove, returning a moment later. "They're not dry now."

"I watered them. Yesterday. When I arrived."

He fixed her with a steady gaze, then flipped back several pages in his notebooks and scanned the scribbles. "In your initial report, you told Officer Segerman you didn't touch anything but the bed where you said you slept that night, the phone, the answering machine, and—" He checked the notes again. "And some things in the kitchen when you made coffee. You didn't mention the orchids."

"I guess I just forgot. What does it matter?"

"Was there anything else you forgot to mention?" His voice was even, no unpleasant emphasis, but she felt accused.

"No." Then she remembered the panties. "Well, there is one other thing."

He raised an eyebrow, waited.

"Only one thing. There was a pair of panties on the bathroom floor. I put them in the hamper."

"Why?"

"Why?" She parroted the word dumbly.

"Why did you do that?"

Why had she? Because Kat would have wanted her to? Because looking at the bikini bottoms—such an intimate thing—had made her want to protect Kat, especially from the eyes of strangers? "It seemed like a violation to think of anyone else seeing them."

"Anything else you can remember?" His tone had cooled.

"No."

He let his gaze survey the room. "Is your sister wealthy? I mean, this is a good address, a nice place, a closet filled with good clothes."

"The house was part of her divorce settlement. Kat's not rich, but I don't think she has a lot of financial worries, if that's what you're asking. She's comfortable. We were both left money when our parents died."

"Does she have a will?"

"Yes." Where was this heading? Surely he couldn't possibly think she had anything to do with Kat's absence. The idea was beyond insane.

"Do you know who her beneficiaries might be?"

Beneficiaries? Jesus, did he think Kat was dead? "No. I mean, I guess I would be. There's no other family."

Abruptly, he changed topics. "Has she ever, even just once, gone off without telling you?"

"No." Then she remembered.

He read her face. "What?"

"Well, once, right after Kat got divorced from Carl, she went away for a couple of weeks."

"Where?"

"I don't remember. A country inn somewhere. Or maybe a spa. I think it was somewhere in Virginia." Instinctively she decided not to tell him about the other time Kat had disappeared for a week shortly after her divorce from Carl. *To have work done,* she'd said. *You got a facelift?* Maddie had said. *God, no,* Kat had replied. *Don't make it sound so dramatic. Just a couple of nips and tucks, that's all. No big deal.* Maddie didn't tell this to Miller. She wanted him to care about Kat, not see her as a woman who could afford to fight the ravages of growing older.

"Here's what I think," he was saying. "I think your sister has gone on a vacation. A trip. Maybe alone. Maybe with someone else. Or maybe she's working. I think you should go home. In a day or two, maybe a week, you'll probably hear from her. A call. A postcard from Vermont. Or Paris. Or I don't know the hell where."

For a minute, Maddie allowed herself to believe what he was saying. An assignment. Or a man. After all, hadn't she been swept away with Jack? It hurt to remember how swept away she had been during those weeks. But wasn't it possible something like that could have happened with Kat?

Miller rose, slipped his notebook into the inside pocket of his sports jacket. "In the meantime, like I said, I'll make a few inquiries. I'll inquire at the post office and ask about her mail. I'll check out her bank, see if any large deposits have been withdrawn. I'll try to reach her neighbor. You go home. We'll keep you informed." He took a billfold from his hip pocket, opened it and handed her a card. "If you think of anything, let us know."

"Right." She tried to find his promise reassuring, but she was frustrated. She wanted action. Not words.

"If I'm not in, they'll take a message at the precinct, or you can leave it in my box."

"Okay."

"One last thing. It would help if you'd give us a recent photo of your sister."

Maddie had been right that he would want a photo. She went to Kat's office and got the picture of Kat with the violinist. She looked into her sister's smiling face. *Where are you? What's happened to you?* "Will this do?" she asked as she handed it to Miller.

He looked at the photo. "Yes. We can crop the guy out and enlarge it. I'll get the original back to you."

She saw him out. When she picked up his cup, the coffee was cold. He hadn't taken a swallow. *Go home,* he'd advised. *Back to Massachusetts.* She supposed she should. There was little more she could do here. And she hadn't arranged for cat care when she left, and Winks would be needing food and fresh water. Still, leaving felt like giving up. She didn't know what to do. In another weak moment, she considered calling Jack and asking for his advice. She hated to admit to herself how seductive the idea was, and that made it easier to push it away. She was on her own here. She switched on automatic pilot.

She straightened up the bedroom, found fresh linens and remade the bed, gathered the few things she had brought with her. Before she left, she did the one last chore she could do for Kat. She carried each of the three orchids into the kitchen and set them in the sink. Adjusting the faucet so the water flow was gentle, she sprayed the leaves, rinsing off dust. That would keep them for another week or two. She was picking up one of the pots to return to the windowsill when she caught her finger on the rim. Her fingernail bent back, tore. All the frustration, anger, and fear she had managed to hold back during Miller's visit erupted and tears spilled. "Shit," she whispered. Then: "Damn you, Kat. Where are you?"

She left the pots in the sink. In the bathroom, she combed through Kat's cosmetics, checked the medicine cabinet. This was Kat's place. There had to be at least one emery board somewhere. She opened the top drawer of the vanity, pawed through the collection of brushes, combs, and hair clips. In the second drawer she found a bag of cotton squares Kat used to remove makeup and two green washcloths. She was pushing the cloths aside when something jabbed her finger. She cried out and pulled her hand back. A drop of blood welled up on the pad of her index finger, and she watched it fall on the slab of marble vanity. As she stared, a shiver ran through her. She reached carefully back into the drawer and removed the green cloths, placed them on the counter, unfolded them. She stared at the object, dumbstruck.

What about drugs? the detective had asked. *Any problems or history there?*

No, she'd answered, completely confident of this.

Nestled between the folds of soft terry lay a syringe.

KATHERINE

Damn you, Kat.

The voice was so clear, as distinct as if Maddie were there in the room with her. The echo rang on and on. *Damn you, Kat.* Impossible, of course. She had been dreaming or hallucinating. Again. It was becoming more and more difficult to separate reality from the dreams and drug-induced imaginings caused from the pills she had twice given in to and allowed herself for release from her situation. Nor could she trust her perceptions of time. When had Verner last been in to examine her?

The night sky shone down through the skylight. The moon was nearly full, its phases her only method of tracing the passage of days. Soon Helen Mercer would arrive to give her the evening medication. She was brisk and struck Kat as being void of emotion, but she had observed the woman touch Verner's shoulder in a way that suggested an intimacy between them. Since the day Kat had been found unconscious on the hall floor, Mercer had been checking on her more frequently and taking more care to ensure the door was locked when she left. The Mayan women, too, seemed more wary. She had been foolish to try to escape after taking the pill. She would be more careful in the future and not squander an opportunity when it arose. The way they were watching her, she doubted she would have more than one chance to escape. She had to be patient. Watch for it. Take it.

She had tried to speak to the two Mayan women who brought her meals and explain that she was being held here and wanted to get out. She didn't know if they understood what she was saying, or if they only pretended not to. One of them—the one whose name she did not know yet—even avoided eye contact, but several times Kat had looked up to see the other one staring at her with an expression she couldn't read. Her name was Rosa, and she was the kinder of the two, always taking an extra moment to rub Kat's back after she had bathed her. Kat was unsure how much the woman understood of what happened in this place. Her face was impassive, and when Kat had tried to speak to her, hoping to enlist her as an ally—trying both Spanish and English—the woman had not responded. Once, relying on her compassion and the times she had brushed her hair even though this was something Kat could do herself, she had asked her for help, but a look of panic had crossed her face and she had fled.

Mostly Kat pretended to be passive and did what she was asked, giving them no trouble, playing possum while figuring out a way to get out of there.

She continued to mentally compose the piece she would write exposing Verner and the many questions that remained unanswered, questions an editor would want her to pursue. Where did Verner find the pregnant girls? Had they come willingly to the clinic? How did he get away with it? Did people in the village know? She remembered the time she had spent in Playa del Pedro on her first two trips to the clinic. At the memory, unbidden, a smile softened her face.

In this whole nightmarish experience, there had been that one lovely promise. Where might it have led? She wondered what the handsome diver was doing, if he thought about her, if he wondered why, despite her promise, she hadn't returned. Occasionally she allowed herself the fantasy that he would come looking for her, would rescue her like the hero from a fairy tale. She had hated those stories, even as a child, believing that the princess locked in the tower or cooking for the dwarfs while they toiled in the mine, the girl sleeping in the glass coffin, all of them should have rescued themselves. Yet here she was, fantasizing that a tall, handsome diver would arrive in the night to save her. *Hell,* she would scold herself, *he doesn't even know where I am.* But in the night she continued to think of him. His eyes, which seemed to suggest he understood all the things she had long ago learned not to speak of. If she believed in such things, if age and experience had not disabused her of the romantic notion, she would have called him a soul mate.

She passed time, too, lost in memory. When her grandmother was dying, Kat had visited her in the nursing home. "What do you do all day, just lying there?" she had asked.

Her nana was legally blind at that point and could neither read nor watch television. "Oh, I have my memories," Nana had replied. "In the end, that's all we have. Our memories." So Kat would go over the past. She would think back to when she was young and had the arrogance of youth, a time when—what was it an older man she'd dated when she was in her twenties had said?—when the world was her oyster. She traveled through the geography and geology of her life, thinking about the places and countries she had visited. The people she had interviewed. The wonders of the world, of life, so easy to take for granted. She recalled every man who ever loved her. Every man who had left her. Every man she had loved and left. Again, she thought about the diver and felt the loss of something that had only just begun. Only begun but filled with such promise.

Occasionally she would travel back to her childhood. Even now, after all these years, she could recall the sound of her mother's laughter, the manly scent of her father. After the plane crash she had had little time to explore or express her grief because her time and energy were focused on Maddie. Now, long-suppressed sorrow would take her in the morning hours, and she would find herself fingering the gold *K* on the chain at her throat and missing them with a pain that burned. Sometimes, half-asleep, she could almost hear them. *You always were the practical one,* she could hear her father say. *And smart,* her mother would chime in. *So smart.*

Not so smart or practical now. She remembered all of her sins, her acts of foolishness and transgressions. Pride and lust. Always, she remembered Maddie. The recollections of Maddie in the burn unit were particularly vivid. She was amazed at the power of memory.

"You have a killer memory," Carl had said when they were first married, like it was a good thing, and then later, right before the divorce, he said it more like it was a curse. But she knew memory didn't kill. It made her whole.

A key turned in the lock and her attention snapped back to the present. Would it be Verner? It was too early for an excursion to the pool. Was he coming to draw more blood to see how her profile was changing?

"Hola." The Mayan woman came with the tray, avoiding Kat's gaze. A moment or two later, the door opened and Mercer entered. The Mayan left, and Verner's assistant sat on the end of the bed and watched while Kat ate a few mouthfuls of rice, of black beans and sliced banana. There was no coffee today, only a cup of a liquid that tasted of cinnamon and honey. She took a cautious sip, trying to discern any bitterness that might reveal a drug, and finding none, drank it all. When she was finished, Mercer handed her the little paper cup holding the white pill, watching while Kat took it. She lay back and closed her eyes, conscious even behind closed lids of Mercer watching her. Finally she heard her walk away, the door close, the lock turn.

She waited a moment or two and then poked her finger in her mouth and dislodged the pill from where it was tucked in her cheek. She stared at it, then wiped the pill clean of her saliva and concealed it with the others.

Her last thoughts before sleep were of Maddie. It had been a mistake not to tell her sister her plans. She had kept them hidden out of shame, of appearing foolish and vain. And the very last thing she would ever do was make Maddie feel bad about her own scars while Kat focused on preserving her own looks. But Maddie wouldn't have judged her. Too late to rectify that mistake now. Maddie would be worried as the weeks passed with no word from her. More than worried. Probably frantic. The thought of causing her distress made Kat's heart race. Would Maddie call the police? The idea brought a slender ray of hope, a light almost immediately extinguished. No one would ever find her here. She had left no track to follow. No one knew she was here, with the slight possibility of Víctor, the diver, but when she returned to Playa she hadn't even gone to see him, unwilling to reveal to him what was happening to her. And even if by some miracle he or Maddie managed to find her and rescue her, what then? She raised a hand to her face. What then?

"Maddie," she whispered aloud. "Forgive me."

MADISON

The overnight bag where she had stashed the syringe occupied the front passenger's seat, its presence so huge it might as well have been a person. Might as well have been glowing with radioactive material. She should have stored it in the trunk. Out of sight. Out of mind. As if that were even possible. The questions it posed circled through her mind. Insulin? Some other medication? Or a more dangerous drug. She pushed the last thought away.

The trip back up the coast seemed endless. As the miles rolled by she surfed from station to station on the radio, eventually giving up. Music stations grated, even the classical ones, and her mind was so active, thoughts and fears circling endlessly, that talk shows were impossible to follow. When she wasn't thinking about Kat, or Jack, she kept returning to the worries and regrets of the past and ruminating over fears about the future, both of which were as futile to effect as a fly's ability to stop a tornado.

The hours of sitting in the car had aggravated her lame leg. The ache progressed from dull to throbbing. She alternately tensed and relaxed her calf muscles and shifted her weight in her seat. If she wasn't able to stand and stretch pretty soon, her thigh muscles would start to spasm.

She stopped to get gas just after she crossed over the state line into Rhode Island. She stood outside the restroom and did some standing yoga poses, which helped a bit. She consoled herself that she was on the last stage of the trip and soon would be home, where a hot bath and her own bed awaited.

Winks met her at the door, winding in and around her ankles, mewing in reproach at being abandoned. His food bowls were empty. Maddie was glad to have something to do, glad for the companionship. She dropped her stuff on the kitchen bench, but avoided looking at the radioactive overnight bag. She filled Winks's bowl, gave him fresh water, and changed his litter box. "There you go. Am I forgiven?" Her voice echoed in the emptiness of the house. She turned on the CD player to fill the echoing stillness. She passed over the Chris Botti disc. It would be a long time before she could listen to a trumpet without thinking of Jack. She selected another, and the first notes of a blues guitar wove through the air. Muddy Waters wailing about the seamy side of life. Perfect.

She made herself a peanut butter and orange marmalade sandwich— comfort food from her childhood—and ate it standing at the kitchen sink, trying not to think about Kat. She kept her eyes averted from the overnight bag while she finished the sandwich. She would deal with it in the morning.

Overcome with exhaustion from the long drive and the events of the past days, she opted for two Advil in place of a hot bath, switched off the CD, and headed up to bed. The ghost echo of a wild-voiced blues man crying that he couldn't be satisfied lingered in the air.

After an hour of tossing, she gave up on sleep and descended to the kitchen. The luggage was on the bench where she had dropped it. Waiting. Unable to ignore it any longer, she opened the bag. The green washcloth was where she had packed it. She unfolded it and stared at the syringe. There was a reasonable explanation. Detective Miller had asked about Kat's health. The staff at the salon had said she looked tired, worn. She reconsidered the possibility that her sister was ill with something that required self-administered injections. But surely Kat would have shared this.

Drugs? Miller had asked about that, too. It seemed inconceivable that Kat would use drugs. She had once broken off a friendship with a woman when she discovered she did coke on the weekends. "I don't need that shit in my life, and I don't need friends who do," Kat had said. Even so, Maddie couldn't deny the reality of the syringe: physical evidence of a Kat she didn't know; it mocked her. What version of herself had Kat kept secret? What secrets had she concealed?

Her throat closed with fear. And anger, too. She folded the washcloth over the syringe and put it in a drawer, as if once it were hidden the secrets it suggested would also disappear.

TIA CLARA

Tia Clara watched as the white van with blue lettering on the driver's door passed on its way from the airport in Cancún through the village to its final destination. There was no dust on the sides of the van or dead bugs smeared on the windshield. Everyone knew it belonged to the *norteamericano* doctor who owned the sprawling compound on the outskirts of the village. Tia Clara knew evil could be concealed behind many masks and, despite the man's occupation and money and the steady flow of foreigners who arrived to stay at his spa, the doctor was a wicked man. She kept her fingers crossed inside her apron pocket on those few occasions when he passed by, enclosed in his second shell of putrid green, a vibration so vivid she was always amazed that even those without the gift couldn't see it. Although she would have admitted this to no one, she was afraid that in a contest, his power—that of wealth and bad medicine—would be stronger than hers.

The name of his place was Retirada de la Playa, but whenever they spoke of it, the villagers, openly blessing themselves, called it El Lugar del Diablo. Once, more than twenty years ago, a chapel stood on the same site. It had been a thick-walled adobe hut that smelled of greasy wax and mice. Women brought offerings there to set before the statue of the Virgin. Stubby candles and *tortillas*, *calabaza*, and plaits of their children's hair. Their husbands, conch fishermen and poor farmers, left *cigarrillos* and, on occasion, *cervezas*. In this way, the people asked for her blessings. Once, long ago, Tia Clara had done this, too.

Like much of Quintana Roo, the village occupied land composed of limestone and coral, no more than a living rock, a stone sponge really. From this they wrested gardens, rough patches of earth where they grew squash and peppers, beans and thin rows of corn. From the gulf, the men pulled conch and *huachinango*. All this they received as a benediction from their Virgin.

Tia Clara cast a glance to the heavens, calculating the date the chapel had fallen. She remembered that the job had taken less than half a day and had been carried out by a crew of *gringo* workers who had been brought in to construct the new clinic. From a stand of nearby brush, she had watched the demolition with others from the village, listening as the crew laughed among themselves at the offerings, the fading photographs and limp paper flowers, moldy oranges and squash, cigarettes and beer. But their laughter was hollow, and when the first wall collapsed, the operator of the bulldozer had crossed himself with a furtive movement.

In place of the adobe chapel, an immense wooden building had been erected, an H-shaped structure with a courtyard in the north cup of the H and an azure-tiled pool in the south, near an opening to a deep underground river. Two additional buildings—a residence for the doctor and a low structure constructed of concrete blocks—completed the complex. The entire compound was enclosed by a fence of concrete.

The doctor was a man of shrewd eyes, and although he offered generous wages, because he had leveled their chapel, no one from Playa would cook or clean for him, so he was forced to hire Mayan labor from Ramul, farther down the coast.

Some believed it was called El Lugar del Diablo because of the whispers that a girl in trouble could go there to make her baby disappear, although these were only whispers and were never proved. The old ones, like Tia Clara, knew it was because who but a devil would destroy a chapel?

Tia Clara watched the white van disappear around the corner as it headed down the highway toward the complex. She wondered who rode within. She turned away. The foolish souls who went there were deserving of their fate. It was not her concern.

MADISON

The DC area code appeared on her caller ID. It wasn't Kat's number.

"Ms. DiMarco?"

"Yes."

"Detective Miller."

She remembered him as he sat in Kat's kitchen, ignoring the cup of coffee he had accepted. She sank onto a chair and tried to prepare herself for what he had to say.

"I'm glad I reached you," he said. "We've made a bit of progress here."

Progress. Progress was good. Hopeful. No one called bad news "progress," did they?

"First of all, we managed to get hold of Mrs. Duncan, your sister's neighbor."

"Is she all right?"

"She's fine. She was away overnight visiting her daughter and grandson in Richmond."

Maddie had no idea Izzy had a grandchild. "Does she know where Kat is?"

"She doesn't."

Disappointment stabbed her chest. "And this is what you think of as progress?"

"No. There's more. Before your sister left, she asked Mrs. Duncan to pick up her mail. One mystery solved."

"So Kat planned to go away?" But if this were so, wouldn't Kat have arranged to have Izzy water the orchids?

"Yes."

"Did she tell Izzy—Mrs. Duncan—where she was going?" Or maybe she hadn't planned to be gone long. A few days—enough to ask to have the mail picked up—but not long enough to worry about cream in the fridge or watering the plants.

"No."

She waited for him to go on, to tell her what the next step would be, heard the rustle of paper on his end. The little he had told her was a tease. She wanted to know more. Wanted action. Miller's silence stretched on. Finally she broke it. "Detective? Where do we go from here?"

"There isn't much more we can do, Ms. DiMarco. We've entered her in the system. There's no evidence of foul play. She made arrangements for her neighbor to pick up her mail, which suggests she planned to be away for a while. But, like I said, she's in the system. If something comes up, we'll let you know."

"Right," Maddie said. After she hung up, she turned to gaze out the window, dull with exhaustion and disappointment. She couldn't escape the sense that Miller had not pursued Kat's disappearance vigorously enough. It occurred to her that maybe Kat had said more to Izzy but, confident that Kat was safe, Izzy had chosen not to confide this to the detective. It wasn't totally beyond possibility that Kat was involved in a romantic affair. She retrieved the envelope Kat had given her, shuffled through the papers until she came to a list of names and numbers. Lawyer. Accountant.

A boy answered the phone. "Hello?"

"This is Madison DiMarco. Is Izzy there?"

"Gram, hey, Gram. It's for you. Some woman named Madison wants to talk to you."

"Maddie, dear," Izzy said. "How are you?"

How was she? Alone. Afraid. Her gaze fell on the overnight bag. Worried to distraction about Kat. That's how she was. "Okay," she said.

"I was going to call you later," Izzy said. "A detective was here asking about Katherine."

"I know. He just called. He told me Kat asked you to take in her mail."

"She did. I've got a sackful for her. The detective didn't seem interested in it. Said I should just keep it. He said Katherine would probably be showing up any day now."

"I know. That's what he told me, too. But I'm worried. It isn't like Kat to just disappear and not let me know where she was going. Did she say anything to you about her plans? Something you didn't want to tell the police. Something private."

"No. She didn't."

"Really?"

"Really. Don't touch that, dear."

It was a moment before Maddie realized Izzy was speaking to the child.

"You're worried, aren't you?" Izzy said.

"Yes. I am."

She was relieved when Izzy didn't try and tell her that she was overreacting or that Kat could take care of herself.

"What are you going to do?"

"Honestly? I don't know." A helpless weariness settled on her. "I don't know what I can do."

"Is there anything I can do?"

"No. Well, yes, actually, there is. You have a key, right?"

"Yes."

"Would you take care of her orchids?"

"Of course, dear."

"I watered them before I left, so they'll be okay for a week."

"With any luck, Katherine will be back to water them herself."

"With any luck." The words sounded false to her own ears. Something wasn't right. She lifted a hand to her mouth and bit at a thumbnail.

"And what about her mail? Shall I keep it here?"

The mail. "Izzy," she said. "I just had an idea. Would you sort through it, pull out anything from her credit card company? It's Bank of America."

"Sure. Do you want to hold on, or shall I call you back?"

"I'll wait while you look."

"Tommy," Izzy called out. "Tommy, will you get that big bag that's out in the hall and bring it to me?"

While Izzy sorted through Kat's mail, Maddie put the phone on speaker and paced the kitchen.

"Got it," Izzy finally said.

"Open it," Maddie said.

"Are you sure?"

"Absolutely. I promise that Kat won't mind." She listened to the sound of paper ripping.

"Well, there's only one charge. For American Airlines. That's it."

She took in the news, the first solid clue as to where Kat might be. "And just the one?"

"Yes. For American Airlines."

"Can you read me the transaction number?" She scribbled it down as Izzy recited it.

After she hung up, Maddie shuffled through the papers in Kat's envelope until she found the one with the usernames and passwords, grateful for Kat's obsessive organization. She went on the bank's site and logged onto Kat's account. An hour later and two calls to customer service and she had more information. It wasn't much, but she was making progress. More than Detective Miller and the Georgetown police had.

Miller wasn't at his desk, so Maddie left a message. He returned the call a half hour later.

"I think Kat's in Mexico."

"What makes you say that?"

"The last charge on her credit card was for an American Airlines flight to Mexico. And nothing since then."

"Nothing else?"

"No. That's not like Kat. She charges everything. Even groceries. She uses the points she accrues for travel."

"Okay. This is a help, Ms. DiMarco. You did good work."

His praise warmed her.

"We'll start by contacting TSA," he continued. "We'll have them do a passport check of her exit and entry records. We can see if she reentered the States after her last trip there."

"And then what?"

"Let's take this a step at a time. We'll begin with TSA. I'll get back to you as soon as we know anything."

"Thank you." After she hung up, she paced from room to room, as if by constantly moving she could expedite Miller's work. How long would it take for a TSA check? It couldn't require much. Everything was computerized. She stopped pacing long enough to make a sandwich—she hadn't eaten lunch, but, too hyped to eat, she managed no more than one bite. Finally, she turned to work, her ever-reliable method of coping.

Maddie spent the next two hours in her studio with Lady Macbeth. The riven mask seemed more haunted than ever. It was late afternoon before she heard from Miller.

"Does your sister know anyone in Mexico? Friends or family or business associates? Specifically in the Yucatán?"

"Kat. No. Why?"

"Are you certain? Or just not that you know of?"

"Why?"

"According to TSA records, Katherine Clayton has booked flights to Cancún four times since December. Do you know of any reason she might want to do that? Why she would take multiple trips to Mexico?"

"No. No, I don't."

The syringe. *What about drugs? Any problems there?*

"During the time of the first trip, there was also a charge for a hotel in a village down the coast from Cancún. The Hotel Molcas in a place called Playa del Pedro. She stayed there two nights."

"What do we do now? Have you called the hotel? Or checked with the Mexican police?" Maddie recalled news reports of crime on the other side of the border. Abductions. Rapes. Murders. Crimes even in places one would expect to be safe. All-inclusive resorts. High-end hotels.

"Well, since there is no record of her returning to the States from the last trip, it's now out of our jurisdiction. We'll transfer it to the State Department. They'll be the ones to follow up."

"Does that mean you'll stop looking? Do you even care?" The accusation was unfair, she knew.

He paused as if considering whether to say more. When he finally spoke, his voice was heavy. "Ms. DiMarco—Madison—" he began. He paused again.

"What?"

"The State Department will do everything they can. They care. We care. We care about the hundreds of women who are reported missing."

"Are you actually telling me that hundreds of women are missing?"

A long pause. "No. In reality, it's probably much more."

Her body went rigid. Why on earth would he tell her this? He had told her not to worry, that Kat would probably call or show up any day. Did he really believe that? Why even mention that hundreds of women were missing?

Kat, she thought. *Kat, where are you?*

KATHERINE

Night became day. Day became night.

Kat watched and waited. In front of Verner and Mercer, she presented a docile and beaten facade. She made no more mention about revealing his protocol. It had been a mistake to threaten him. How could she have not seen that? Her new approach was to appeal to his vanity, to pretend to admire his genius, to pretend that he could correct what had happened to her. She confessed boredom and asked him if, while she was there, there was some way she could be of assistance, anything she could do to help out. He had been suspicious. She had forced herself to hold his gaze. "Perhaps I will think of something," he had said. When he and Mercer left, he did not lock the door. Suspecting it was a test, she forced herself not to open it, determined to win at his cat-and-mouse game. She asked for books, for paper and pencil or pen, and was given the books, two romance novels, but not the writing materials. She continued to try to befriend Rosa and was aware of the small signs she was succeeding. One evening the Mayan woman brought in salve, which she rubbed into Kat's scalp and her thinning hair. When she left, she did not lock the door. Kat waited impatiently, and when she was unable to be patient any longer, she opened it and slipped out into the corridor, scouting like a spy. She found that the outer doors were locked. She prowled a bit, opening two doors and peering into empty rooms. As far as she could tell, she and the girl she had heard crying were currently the only occupants of the building at night, although during the day, she often heard activity in the halls. She tried the girl's door but it was locked, and when she knocked and called out, there had been no response.

She thought about men and women who had been imprisoned, some, like her, in solitary confinement. What had kept them sane? What kept them from sinking into despair? She thought of prisoners, famous and unknown, who had not only survived but had emerged from the experience whole.

Kat resolved to be one of the survivors. She felt stronger and dared to hope that now that she was no longer taking the injections, her body was healing itself. She would find a way to escape. In spite of what she had promised him, she knew Verner had to be stopped.

Day became night. Night became day.

Kat plotted and schemed and considered ways of escape.

On one dark night of despair, she counted the white pills. Now she had fifteen.

MADISON

Hundreds of missing women. The more she thought about Miller's callous statement, the angrier Maddie became. Of course it wasn't true. Ridiculous. Why would he toss such a statistic out? If it were remotely true, wouldn't there be a national outcry? International outrage?

She logged on at her computer and typed "missing women" in the search box on her home page. Within minutes she was caught up in the world of vanished women. Miller had been wrong. Not hundreds. Thousands of women were reported missing every year in the United States alone. Thousands more throughout the world. An epidemic, one article proclaimed.

How was it possible? Maddie's hand trembled on the mouse. How was it conceivable that such a huge number of women went missing? Disappeared. Vanished, never to be found. Like some immense act performed by an evil magician.

The stories and statistics she read as she scrolled through the internet were haunting, and she was sickened by them. The voices of the missing seemed to echo through her house. At last she clicked off the computer, grabbed her car keys, and headed out to escape them and the fear they engendered. As she drove, without destination, just following the streets around and out of town and then doubling back, she thought over what she had learned thus far. Although discredited by the police as not particularly unusual, she thought about the dying orchids. The rotting food in the trash. The souring milk in the refrigerator. The series of appointments that Kat had missed. She tried to imagine what would have caused Kat to rush off, leaving such disarray in her wake. She could think of nothing further than she had during the call with Izzy. Kat had only expected to be away for a short time.

She reviewed what the bank had relayed about the charges on Kat's credit card statements. And, lastly, she listened to her own intuition. Kat was in trouble. As she headed back to town, the car, as if of its own volition, slowed as she passed the airport. Jack's Harley wasn't in the parking lot. Nor was the jeep he used in foul weather. And if he had been there, what then? Would she have stopped? What could she have said to him? Even if she wanted to see him, she had burned that bridge when she'd made it clear to him that he was out of her life. Recalling their last conversation, her coldness and accusations, she felt ashamed. He had deserved better.

The need to talk with someone was overwhelming. She continued on and drove straight to the Gallery on Main. Lonnie was alone, sitting at her desk catching up on paperwork. "Hey," she said when she saw Maddie. "Great haircut."

Maddie fingered the short strands, wondered how long it would take to grow out. It had been a rash act, and all for nothing, as she hadn't learned one more thing at the salon. Well, that's what came of acting out of desperation instead of careful thought.

"It was a mistake."

Lonnie shot her a crooked grin. "In my experience, when a woman decides to radically change her hair, it is rarely a mistake. So what's up?"

"Kat's missing." The words, propelled by her concern for her sister, burst out.

Lonnie set her pen down. "What do you mean, missing?"

"She's gone. She's disappeared."

"Holy cow," she said. "First of all, sit down. You look like you haven't slept in a month." She paused and gave her a more searching look. "Actually, you look like you could use a drink. If it weren't ten in the morning, I'd bring out the Johnnie Black I keep in the back room." She came around the desk and sat next to Maddie. "So what's going on?"

Maddie took a ragged breath and tried to get her thoughts in order. Would Lonnie think she was being melodramatic? She could have used the scotch. Bit by bit, stumbling at first, she told her everything. Kat's disappearance. The trip she had taken to DC and the conversations she'd had with Detective Miller, what the detective had said about missing women. She told her what she had learned about Kat's credit card charges for trips to Mexico. All of it. When she was done, Lonnie got up and went into the back room, returning minutes later with a bottle and two glasses.

"So are you going to go?" she asked.

"Go where?"

"Mexico."

"Mexico? God, no." Just the thought of going there, of flying, shot adrenaline through her body. "Why would I do that?" Maddie stared at Lonnie as if she had suggested she walk across the ceiling, but her friend was calmly pouring a shot in each glass.

"Because that's the last place you know for sure that Kat was."

"What can I do there? Like I just told you, the State Department is going to follow up on this. What do you think I can do that the authorities can't? They have the resources and the connections."

Lonnie handed her one of the glasses. "Do you think Kat is really in trouble?"

She looked away. She thought of what she had read about the thousands of missing women. Lonnie waited. "Yes," she said, relieved to finally share her fears openly. "I do. And I'm scared."

"And if you were missing, what would Kat do?"

"That's unfair." She knew if she were missing, Kat would do whatever it took, move whatever mountain blocked the path, in her determination to find her. But she wasn't as gritty or as strong as Kat. Never had been. Even before the accident. Kat was indomitable, not her. Kat was like the mythical warriors. Hippolyta. Antiope. An Amazon. Even as Maddie rejected and dismissed any idea of her own strength, the thought of the origami sword Jack had given her came, unbidden, to mind.

"Is it?"

"Yes." Why did Lonnie keep pushing? She knew about her fear of flying, about her panic attacks. She took a sip of scotch, stalling. "I don't even speak Spanish."

Lonnie surprised her by laughing. "So get a dictionary."

"Why are you doing this?"

"Doing what?"

"Pushing me like this. Suggesting I fly off on some wild goose chase."

"But it isn't wild, Maddie. Didn't you just tell me that the last record of Kat going anywhere is the flight she charged to Mexico? And there's no record of her returning?"

"But Mexico?"

"Stop acting like this. It's not China, for cripe's sake."

"I'd have to fly."

"Yes. You would." Lonnie's voice was firm. And kind. "You would have to fly. So get some pills, knock yourself out for the duration of the flight. People do that all the time."

"Does this make sense? I mean, what can I even do there?"

"For starters, you said you have the name of the village where Kat stayed on one of her trips. You have the name of the hotel. You can canvass the town, show Kat's photo to everyone you see. At least try."

"And what if I can't find out anything? What if I can't find Kat?" Her desire for action had been fueling her all day, but now, with Lonnie pushing, she pulled back, full of doubt. And fear.

"At least you will have tried. And you will know you have done everything you can. What's the alternative? To sit at home waiting? And waiting? Not knowing? You'd be taking action, and believe me, that always feels better."

Lonnie's confidence surprised her. She wished she could match it. "But I'm not you. And I'm not Kat. I don't know if I can."

Lonnie placed her hand on Maddie's arm. "I do. I know you can."

"If I did go, would you come with me?" It nearly killed her to ask this favor.

"Oh jeez, honey, I wish I could. And if I could, I would. You know that, right?"

Maddie nodded.

"Look at it this way: you probably won't be gone much longer than you were when you went to Washington. Just a little further away. And you'll know you will have done what Kat would have done for you."

Maddie winced. "That's your last shot? Guilt?"

"Whatever it takes. So you'll go?"

Maddie took a deep breath, followed by a gulp of the scotch. "Maybe." That was the most she could concede.

Lonnie took it as a yes. "Okay. How can I help? What can I do?"

"Nothing."

"What about Winks? Shall I arrange for someone to take care of him? You know I'd take him if I didn't break out in hives."

Everything was moving too fast. She hadn't even committed to going. "I don't know."

"Don't worry. I'll take care of it. Just leave a sheet with his schedule. I'll pick up a sack of cat treats for the cause."

"Who would you get?" She equivocated, thinking of all the reasons it would be impossible.

"I think Jeannie will do it. You know how crazy she is about animals." Jeannie was a senior in Dexter High who helped out in the gallery on weekends and during showings. "Any idea when you'll be leaving?"

She felt swept up in a current of Lonnie's making. "Slow down, will you? Let me just think about this." She finished the scotch.

Lonnie took the empty glass from her and gave her a hug. "I have faith in you. Now, get moving. Call if you want morale reinforcement. I'll be here."

In the car, she sat for a moment before starting the engine. Why the hell had she even gone to the gallery? Why had she confided in Lonnie, who would push her into doing something she honestly didn't know if she was capable of doing?

Later she would wonder if that was precisely for that reason she had gone there. One bridge she hadn't broken.

When she got home, she googled flights. With luck there would be no seats and she could tell Lonnie she had tried, but there was a flight that departed Logan at eight the next morning, which meant arriving at the airport around five. Add the hour and a half drive to Boston and she'd have to get up around three. Just the idea of walking through the gate and onto the plane, being confined during the flight—all of it made her skin prickle. She thought about what Lonnie had said. *If you were missing, what would Kat do?*

Anything, she thought. *Kat would do anything.* Her fingers were icy as she clicked on the "Buy" button, confirming the reservation. All that was left to do was pack a bag and write out detailed instructions for Jeannie about Winks's care and feeding.

She stood in front of the closet, grabbing a few items suitable for a hot climate. As she flicked through the hangers, her fingers brushed against Jack's shirt and froze. She paused and then allowed herself this single indulgence, this single regression, this hollow, brief, and foolish comfort of the scent of him: she put on Jack's shirt. She should have been prepared but wasn't. She was swept by memories of him. The crinkly lines that fanned out from his eyes. His tenderness. And patience. She steeled herself against them, but she did not take off his shirt.

The only way to keep going was to keep the escape route open: she could still change her mind at the last minute. This knowledge reassured her as she checked off tasks as if for someone else. It didn't take long to finish packing. Her passport was in the desk. She hadn't used it in years, but Kat, ever optimistic, had insisted she keep it valid. She took some cash from her stash to convert to pesos when she landed at the airport. She put together a zip bag with travel-size toiletries, remembering to add the vial of Xanax. Just the thought of being on the flight and having a bad attack was enough to bring one on. In the kitchen, she checked the refrigerator. She imagined she would be gone for three days, four at most, but remembering the cream turned sour in Kat's refrigerator, she took out a few perishables, tossed them in the trash, and set the bag outside for pickup.

She took Winks's food from the cabinet where it was stored, set it on the counter, and began writing the instructions, detailing the morning and late-afternoon feedings, the need to change his litter box every day. "Imperative," she wrote and underscored the word. Russian blues were a breed notoriously fastidious about this. A doorbell interrupted her. She had not heard a car in the drive.

She opened the door and might as well have touched a live wire. "Jack?" she said. "What are you doing here?"

He hesitated, testing the water, then smiled. "I think people normally start with a 'Hey, how's it going.'"

"What do you want?"

The smile slipped a bit at her coolness. He tipped his head to one side and regarded her. "You cut your hair."

She brushed the wispy bangs aside, wondering if he liked it and angry that she cared. "It'll grow back."

"I like it. It suits you." His gaze dropped and an expression she couldn't read passed over his face. And then his smile returned.

It took a moment to understand, and then she was mortified. She'd forgotten she'd put on his damn shirt. He would think she was acting like a teenager mooning over a lost love. Struggling to reestablish control, to think of what to say that would erase his smile, she stepped back. "I didn't expect to see you here."

"Lonnie sent me. She said you were looking for someone to take care of Winks for a bit."

Lonnie. The traitor. It gave her great satisfaction to say, "I have someone. Jeannie, a girl who helps out in the gallery."

"I know. Lonnie asked her, but Jeannie can't do it. Looks like you're stuck with me."

She scrambled to come up with a reason to refuse. "The thing is, I don't know how long I'll be gone or anything." The urge to tell him everything was powerful. A momentary fit of madness—what else— made her long to throw herself at him. She evaded his eyes, hoped he couldn't read her face or sense her agitation, the desire he always sparked in her, the confusion of emotions, one of which, she had to admit, was guilt for the sharp way she had ended their relationship. She allowed herself to acknowledge it. "Why are you being this way?"

He frowned. "What way?"

She searched for the word. "Nice," she finally settled on.

"Would it be better if I wasn't?"

She paused. He waited. "Probably," she finally admitted.

He laughed. The exchange, her honesty, his response, all reminded her of how it had been, how easy things were, until that day and they weren't.

At that moment Winks wandered in. Ignoring Maddie, he went straight for Jack and rubbed against his ankles. Jack picked him up and the cat relaxed in his arms, with a deep throaty purr that signaled complete contentment. *Another traitor,* she thought, *but this time without an edge.*

"Actually, you'd be doing me a favor. It's for Olivia. If it's okay with you, I'd like to take Winks over there to keep her company."

His mention of Olivia altered something in the atmosphere. Maddie softened. "Oh, Jack. I'm sorry. You caught me off guard. I should have asked. How is she?"

Jack looked out at a middle distance, lost for a moment. "It depends," he said. "It varies. At first, she was optimistic. She was determined to beat it. You're alike that way. Fighters."

Maddie started to interrupt, to refute this vision he had of her, the one Lonnie had of her, but he continued before she could speak. "Now she's more resigned. Some days she's angry. Pissed, actually. Other days, she seems calm. Almost at peace with the idea of dying. Like an old monk or something. The truth is, we're losing her."

"Oh, Jack. I'm so sorry." *I'm sorry.* Such empty words. Words she had heard so often after her parents' deaths. Recalling the pain of that loss, the ache that never went away, her impulse was to reach out, embrace him. Instead, she shoved her hand in her pocket and cupped the quartz heart that she had taken to carrying with her, the smoothness of the stone oddly comforting. "Is there anything I can do?" Another thing people had said to her. And, of course, there was nothing. But still she couldn't avoid the guilt that she hadn't reached out to Olivia.

"I don't think so," he said. "Lonnie told me about Kat. She said you're going to Mexico."

She held back for a moment and then surrendered to the need to confide in him. "She pushed me into going, actually. I still question whether I should let the Mexican police and the American State Department handle it. What do you think? Do you think I'm crazy to go looking for Kat?" It was a relief to ask his advice.

He stroked Winks's back, thoughtful for a moment. "I don't know, Maddie. What I do know is that if it were me and if Olivia was missing, I would go. I would go wherever I had to and do whatever it took to find her."

It felt so natural to reach for his hand. "Thanks, Jack."

"What's your plan?"

"I made a reservation."

He didn't say anything.

"For a flight." She withdrew her hand.

"Are you scared?" Concern flooded his voice.

"To tell you the truth, I don't know if I can do it." She heard the weakness in her voice, how small it sounded, and hated how much vulnerability it revealed.

"You can. I know you can." He stroked Winks and looked at her. "But you don't have to do it alone."

"What do you mean?"

"I could go with you."

"Why? Why would you do that?"

"Because I care."

She was stunned into silence. After everything, he still would offer to do this for her. He didn't push, just waited for her to decide. It was this, his lack of insistence and of course the idea of not having to go alone, that settled it for her. Maddie capitulated, sensing it signified something more, but she was unwilling to follow that thought.

"When's your flight?"

"Tomorrow morning. Eight a.m."

"Airline?"

She told him.

He handed Winks to her and pulled out his cell. While he made his reservation, she paced the kitchen wondering what she was doing, what door she was opening, already having second thoughts, even as she tried to still the thrill of seeing him again.

He was on the phone with the airlines for some time. When he finally reached for his wallet to pull out a credit card, she gave him hers. He shook his head, but she pressed it into his hands.

"Want the good news or bad?" he asked when he hung up.

"Bad," she said immediately. Always best to get it over with.

"They didn't have an available seat next to the one you'd booked."

"Oh." She had already begun to rely on the idea of him sitting next to her, the comfort of it. She might as well go alone. "What's the good news?"

"We've been upgraded to business. Adjoining seats."

She wondered what he had told them to arrange for that.

"Okay," he said. "That takes care of the flight. Where are you staying? What hotel?"

She realized she hadn't thought that far ahead. "I haven't made a reservation."

"I can do that."

"Wait." She went to where she had scribbled notes from Kat's credit charges. "The Hotel Molcas," she said. "That's where Kat stayed at least once."

When he reached the hotel desk, he switched to Spanish. *Of course he speaks Spanish,* she thought. What didn't he do? She wondered what other mysteries she hadn't learned in their too brief time together. "Separate rooms," she said, determination returning to her voice. "Reserve separate rooms." She wanted it clear.

He eyed her with an expression impossible to interpret. "All set," he said when he hung up.

"And we have separate rooms?"

"Yes," he said with a show of exaggerated patience. "I reserved two rooms."

She nodded.

"Well, let's get the show on the road. I assume Winks has a travel case?"

"I'll get it, and a bag for the food." She handed the cat back to him. In the basement, she retrieved the case and took a few minutes before returning to the kitchen. If she was going to change her mind, now was the moment.

Usually when Winks spied the travel case, he disappeared, but now he stayed in Jack's arms. She leaned in to stroke Winks, gave him one last nuzzle, and, while her face was in the vicinity of Jack's chest, she tilted her face to his and their eyes met. She held it as if the gaze itself was an exchange of something, then broke it and gave him a quick kiss on the cheek. "Thanks. For everything."

"Sure." He settled Winks in the carrying case and took it out to his car. He returned for the bag of food. "I'll pick you up a little before three a.m. Does that sound good?"

"Yes."

"Right. Okay, then." As he turned to go, he said, "You should keep it."

"What's that?"

"The shirt. Keep it. It looks better on you than it ever did on me."

Her face flamed. He was out the door before she could think of a response.

ÁNGEL

On his way back to the ticket booth by the pier, Ángel spied María the maid watching him from a second-floor window of the Hotel Molcas. He gave no sign that he had seen her, but there was a slight shift in his step. He took a quick hop and flipped in the air, ending in a handstand. His gold chain and crucifix dangled against his chin, drawing a dart of sunlight. Balancing easily, he covered the remaining yards to the booth on his hands. A quick flip and he was upright again. Daring a swift side glance, he saw her raise a hand to her mouth to conceal a shy smile.

Still without acknowledging María, he disappeared into the booth. He dusted off his palms, tucked the crucifix into his shirt, and retrieved his comb from the shelf beneath the ticket window. It was a handsome comb, neon green, eight inches in length, with tiny sparkles embedded in the plastic. All in all, a comb worthy of the head of Ángel Morales. Bending forward, he eyed his reflection in the mirror wedged on the narrow shelf. He combed his hair back with a long sweeping motion, repeating the gesture until he was satisfied. He returned the comb to the shelf and pulled the tall stool to one side of the window into a triangle of shade and waited. A prince surveying his domain.

Even at four o'clock, heat shimmered over the square, slowing one's step, sucking the breath from one's lungs. On the veranda of the hotel the luncheon crowd had disappeared and waiters readied tables for the evening meal, covering them with linens, cloths so startlingly white that Ángel could not imagine what it must be like to eat on them.

Along Avenida Cinco, the *federales* strode back and forth, their carbines slung across their chests. The backs of their uniforms' shirts were patterned with sweat. At the edge of the water a man ran, his legs pumping with exaggerated movements, his face twisted with effort. He dragged air into his mouth, gaping like a snapper stranded on shore. It was craziness to run in such heat. No one but a *gringo* would run beneath such a sun. Automatically Ángel cataloged the man's clothes. *Calzones cortos.* "Shorts," he said to himself. *Zapatos.* "Shoes." He reached again toward the shelf and took a Spanish-English dictionary from its place next to the mirror. The paperback was water-stained and missing several pages. Víctor, the diver, had given it to him, and dreams had awakened in Ángel that day, yearnings that would have astonished his *madre* and *padre* had he ever shared them. He leafed through the pages until he located the words and smiled, pleased with the accuracy of his translations.

It had been his grasp of English, limited though it was, that had led to this job, that and his quick mind for figures. José, the old man who had sold tickets before, was always giving inexact change to the tourists. This was understandable, of course, an easy thing to do with the confusion over the old pesos and the nuevos pesos, but it often resulted in arguments and one time had involved the *policía*.

Ángel believed José's mistakes were honest ones, but it was easy to cheat the tourists who, afraid of looking ignorant, often did not count their change. Ángel always gave the correct change to every tourist. He had learned a peculiar thing about them. They would yell for the *policía* if they believed you had cheated them of a single peso, but the same *gringos* would easily hand over five pesos if you politely gave them directions or answered their questions about the ruins or where to hire boats for fishing or diving, information they could have had for free.

Nothing about the *gringos* made sense to him. They were always moving, like the man running in the hot sun. They swam, they ran, they ate and drank. They traveled to the ruins. They went horseback riding and snorkeling and they shopped for souvenirs. Still, he had observed that no matter how much they did, their eyes stayed hungry, wanting more.

A horn sounded on the far side of the square, and the bus from Cancún slowed to a halt, disgorging passengers. Everything about them suggested they were trying too hard to have fun. As he surveyed the passengers, one caught his eye. She had on loose blue pants and a cotton shirt with long sleeves, but these could not conceal her bony frame. Ángel preferred women who wore more meat on their bones, like María, the maid, who had breasts and hips that would cradle a man. Or Graciela, who, in spite of her age, had the curves of a woman.

He looked again at the tourist in blue slacks. She and her companion walked toward him. A long-billed cap shielded the woman's face. They paused, as if to get their bearings. As they drew closer, he saw the woman's scars that the long-billed cap had hidden when he had looked at her from a distance.

At that moment he saw another girl and immediately forgot about the thin *gringa*. *"María Santísima."* He exhaled the words. In front of his eyes was Graciela. It had been three weeks now, and her family had been frantic with sorrow at her disappearance. Each night her *padre* drank too much and each day he slept in the seat of his taxi. Her *madre*'s knees were swollen from the hours she spent kneeling in the village church, praying for the return of her daughter. And in Ángel's own house, his *madre* watched his sisters carefully, as if Graciela's disappearance were contagious. The villagers also remembered Marisa Gómez, who had vanished months ago. Now, in front of his eyes, here was Graciela stepping off the bus from Cancún. His instinct was to turn away, to ignore her and hope she would cause no trouble. But almost at once, he saw with relief that this girl was not Graciela after all, but someone older. The girl darted swift glances at each face she passed, as if searching for someone. She held her woven shawl tight around her shoulders as she stepped closer to the square.

Ángel went back to watching life unfold around the square and on the pier. Occasionally he sold tickets. Sometimes he flirted with a pretty girl. He forgot about the thin woman with the scars and the girl he had mistaken for Graciela.

MADISON

She survived the flights. Four words. She. Survived. The. Flights. An encyclopedia of meaning.

She endured the panic. The hyperventilating. The dizziness that made her stumble when she walked down the Jetway to the plane. The leg from Boston to Miami had been the hardest. Before they boarded, Jack had said, "Think of this as a desensitizing exercise. By the time we land in Cancún, you'll feel like an experienced flier."

"I doubt it," she had said. Did desensitizing even work? If so, would being next to Jack for hours on end work on numbing her feelings for him, the electric and persistent jolt she continued to feel at the sight of him, his touch, his smell? Could it quell those? She refused to allow herself to dwell on the what-ifs. If he were older. If she were younger. If she could be the woman he thought she was. If he were anything but a pilot. If she would ever be capable of trust. All the things that she'd known from the beginning would prevent a lasting relationship.

He had talked nonstop from the moment of liftoff on the flight from Logan to Miami. He told her about the first fight he had ever been in—kindergarten—and all the male rites of passage. He told her about the house he had grown up in and his favorite hiding places.

"Would you please be quiet," she had said at one point.

"Why? Does my talking bother you?"

"Yes," she'd said.

"Why?"

She'd thought for a minute. "It's distracting."

"That's kind of the point," he'd said.

In spite of herself, Maddie had to laugh. He joined her. The flight attendant smiled at them. "Let me guess," she said. "Honeymoon, right?"

There was an awkward pause and Jack spoke first. "Not yet," he said.

Maddie shifted in her seat, creating distance between them.

Jack continued to chatter. Once, before landing, they hit a pocket of turbulence, and she gripped the armrest and white-knuckled it through.

"Are you doing okay?" he asked.

"Fine," she managed.

"Good girl," he said.

The flight from Miami to Cancún was easier. She had a stirring of anxiety as she went aboard, but she experienced no dizziness or sweats of panic. She didn't know whether the drugs were kicking in or if it was Jack's desensitizing theory at work.

"Well, look at you," Jack said, grinning. "You're getting to be an old hand at this."

"Does that mean on this flight you won't continue to walk and talk me through every day of your life?" she teased. But she felt a quiet, green sprout of pride. She was doing it! She was actually flying. She wouldn't have believed it possible.

As they drew closer to their destination, Jack asked her what her plan was once they arrived.

"Get to the hotel," she said. "I guess take it from there. And check in with the local police. I know they've been alerted about Kat."

The bus drive down the coast from Cancún was long, and two women occupying the seats behind them talked incessantly. "Well, will you look at that," one was saying. "Look, May. Out the window."

Maddie turned to see what had captured their attention. Off to the left of the road, a half dozen militiamen encircled a car pulled off to the side. They carried weapons and even in the oppressive heat wore helmets.

"Federal troops of some kind," the woman continued. "They're probably searching for drugs. These countries are infested with drugs."

"Cartels," said the other. "I read about it in *Time*. Thank goodness we booked a safe resort."

Maddie's thoughts returned to the syringe she had found in Kat's bathroom. Not possible. Not drugs. There had to be some other explanation. But why had it been hidden between the two green washcloths? Why not just set it in the drawer? Kat lived alone; there was no need to conceal it from view. Was it to keep it out of her own sight? Just one more puzzle piece in the huge mystery. She sighed and watched the landscape unfold as the bus rolled along. They passed a decrepit ranch and a field where several swayback horses grazed. Ahead she saw a collection of hovels and one-room shacks covered with palm-thatched roofs. Chickens and tan-skinned children ran freely in the open space.

"Imagine," said the woman behind her. "In this day and age. Ringworm must be rampant."

Jack squeezed her hand at this, and their eyes met in sympathy. If Kat had been there, she would have turned to the woman and said something. Maddie could almost hear her. *People like you shouldn't be allowed out of the house,* Kat would have said. At the thought of her sister, all the unanswered questions flowed in. Why had Kat gone to Playa del Pedro? Would staff at the hotel remember her? Had she stayed there each time? Was she there now? With each mile, Maddie was closer to finding answers. The bus ride stretched on endlessly.

The Hotel Molcas was a white two-story building overlooking the water. A dining pavilion occupied the front. The desk clerk, a Mexican of indeterminate age whose name tag read Luis Castillo, smiled at them, revealing two front teeth rimmed with gold. His English was better than her Spanish, and between them registration was accomplished. Jack stood back and let her take charge. As she had with the airfares, Maddie insisted on paying. She suspected this was something they would argue about later, after they found Kat. While the clerk was running her credit card, she took a street map of the village from a stack on the counter.

She signed the slip and Jack accepted their keys. Adjoining rooms. Numbers 25 and 27. The clerk signaled for the bellboy.

"*Un momento, por favor,*" she said.

"*Qué pasa?*"

She reached into her tote and took out a picture of Kat. It had been taken two years ago at a party in DC. Kat wore a sapphire gown that showed off her coloring to good effect. Maddie handed the photo to the clerk. "I'm looking for this woman. Have you seen her?"

He gazed at the photo. "*Sí,*" he said, smiling widely.

"You've seen her?" Her voice broke. Could it be that simple? A single question and she would find Kat?

"*Sí. Muy linda,*" he said.

"Where? Here? Recently?" The words spilled out.

His gilt-toothed smile was replaced by a frown. "*Muy bonita,*" he said with a frown and handed the photo back, as if he wanted no trouble.

Jack listened to the exchange but did not interrupt. She was grateful that he continued to let her take the lead. She fumbled through her tote for her dictionary. "*Mi hermana.*"

"Ah." The smile returned in its full, golden glory.

"Have you seen her?"

"No, *señorita.* No." His eyes were sorrowful to have disappointed her.

Their rooms were on the second floor. She left Jack in the corridor, promising to meet him later. The bellboy swung her door open, revealing a bedroom decorated in bright blues and greens and facing out to the sea. Drapes in a coarse fabric framed the window. A ceiling fan turned lazily, its blades barely stirring the air. Alone, she sat on the edge of the broad, low bed. She was drained by the tropical heat and exhausted physically and emotionally from the long day of travel. The urge to fall back and sleep was nearly irresistible. And impossible. She was here not to sleep but to follow the trail that would lead her to Kat.

She rose, crossed to the dresser, uncapped the liter of bottled water provided by the hotel, and drank deeply. She peeled off her shirt and slacks and headed for the shower, hoping it would revive her. After she toweled dry, she used more of the bottled water to brush her teeth. She pulled on a loose ankle-length shift, grabbed her room key and tote, and headed out. The first imperative was coffee. She passed Jack's door but did not knock. She was determined to maintain some independence and not rely on him too much.

Out on the dining veranda, the maître d' led her to a table dressed with spotless linen. "Welcome to Playa del Pedro," he said as he seated her. Before he could turn away, she took out Kat's photo. His eyes lit in appreciation.

"She was here. In Playa. She stayed here at the hotel. Do you remember her?"

"No." Like the desk clerk, he seemed sad to disappoint her. As soon as he departed, a waiter approached with a silver pot. She nodded, watched him pour. As he turned to go, she gestured for him to wait. She placed Kat's photo on the table. *"Mi hermana,"* she said. He did not remember Kat, either.

She looked around the room for other staff members but saw only the maître d' and her waiter. She felt foolish at how naive she had been to think finding Kat would be a smooth ride. Her impulse was to get up and start immediately rushing around, showing Kat's picture to everyone she met, but she needed a better sense of the town, a chance to get her bearings before she started out, and perhaps to discover some hint of what had drawn Kat here not just once but several times. And, of course, she needed to check in with the local police.

The coffee was strong and revived her somewhat. At the airport in Miami, Jack had picked up a guidebook to the Yucatán that she had tucked into her tote, and she pulled it out and began to skim through the pages until she located the section on Playa del Pedro. A tropical climate, she read, with cooling trade winds.

She turned the pages impatiently. The land was composed of lime-stone and coral, one living rock, like a stone sponge. Innumerable rivers ran beneath the earth, streams and subterranean lakes. Maddie could almost picture them, a secret network flowing underground. A para-graph instructed the reader about how to contact companies that con-ducted excursions into these rivers. Just the thought of being enclosed in a stream underground made her feel claustrophobic. She could no more imagine signing up for such a tour than scaling a rock face. But would Kat? Perhaps. Kat was always open to adventures. But she liked new ones, not reruns. It seemed unlikely that she would return several times solely for the experience of the underground rivers.

She flipped to the next page. Playa del Pedro, she read, was a small fishing village that had once been populated by workers from the chicle and hemp and coconut plantations. Hundreds of years before that, it had been the mainland departure point for Mayan pilgrims visiting the temples on Cozumel. Its more recent history was predictable. In the late 1960s, divers had discovered the offshore reefs that had some of the best diving on the coast. Maddie's attention was caught. She could definitely see Kat diving, exploring the reefs. She made a mental note to pursue this avenue.

She set the book aside. She stared out at the street and the square beyond. Directly adjacent to the hotel was a *palapa* restaurant with tour-ists seated at the bar. Automatically, Maddie scanned the faces but did not see her sister. On the pedestrian walkway, several vendors hawked ice cream and fresh fruit while smooth-skinned boys with broad faces kicked a ball between the carts with admirable nimbleness. Although it was well past four, bathers still swam in the ocean. Close to shore, near-naked children took turns throwing stones at something in the water. She watched as two dusky-skinned girls with shy smiles emerged dripping from the sea. They were young and lovely, and Maddie imagined that if one pierced their skin, a liquid as sweet as the juice of a papaya would run.

The heat penetrated her bones, loosening something in the marrow. She felt something tremble and shift like a tectonic plate. It would be so easy, if things were different, to surrender to the magic of the land. The heat, the colors, the people. For just one extraordinary moment she could almost forget everything. Had that been the appeal for Kat? Not great adventures, not new experiences. Something as simple as that? Something so un-Kat-like?

But why had her sister never mentioned it? Why the secrecy? Had she needed to carve out a little distance between them?

She left the hotel terrace and headed for the waterfront. As she walked along the pedestrian walkway, she continued to search faces, looking for Kat. The breeze brushed her skin. She reviewed the plan of action she had formulated during the flight from Miami. She would go to the local police station. And then she would canvass the shops and little cafés. She would show everyone she met the photo of Kat. Her sister—tall and blonde and lovely—would surely stand out, even among the tourists who came to the village.

Somewhere, someone would recognize her.

TIA CLARA

A song was coming to Tia Clara. The thin whirling drone of cicadas swirled around her. She knew this melody. This was how death sang. She moved restlessly in her chair, her chest tight with knowledge that such a melody presaged a vision. If she could, she would free herself of such apparitions. She was getting too old. A vein in her foot throbbed in agreement. The swelling in her knees and feet grew worse every day.

"*Buenos días,* Tia Clara." Ángel Morales passed by her table on his way home from the ticket booth.

"*Buenos días.*" What a demon the boy was. A *fisgón.* A busybody who ran everywhere and saw everything. A troublemaker with the mind of an accountant. Well, soon the village would be rid of him. Although he had spoken of his dreams to no one, except perhaps that son-of-a-dog Víctor the diver, Tia Clara knew that Ángel would work at the ticket booth for only a few months more. Then he would depart for the border, and from there he would continue north to California, running away from responsibilities. The fortune-teller closed her eyes, suddenly weary. It was no business of hers. The song of the cicadas, dim for a moment, again grew loud in her ears. The green canary hopped nervously in its cage, scattering seed. The air around the table grew heavy. In the square, tourists wandered from shop to shop, vendor stall to vendor stall. Some sat at sidewalk cafés and sipped salt-rimmed margaritas. A stray dog slunk by. Then, not a block away, from the direction of the silver shop owned by a young couple from Mérida came the sounds of commotion. Tia Clara craned her head forward. Other heads peered from shop fronts. The cause of the disturbance was a pig.

It probably belongs to Pedro Mendes, Tia Clara thought. Not too long ago such a sight would not have caused a second glance in Playa. There was a time when pigs and chickens had wandered freely throughout the village, but much had changed in recent years. In spite of the warning song of cicadas that spiraled in her head, the significance of the animal had not yet occurred to her. The pig squealed. More heads appeared in doorways; a crowd began to gather. Not just the *gringos*, but the people of Playa. "Look," they called to one another. *"Un cochino. Un cochino."*

Tia Clara recognized Gomez the butcher in the middle of the throng. Several of the *gringos* aimed their little cameras at the animal, who was now frozen in the center of the *calle*, tiny, shrewd eyes darting about, looking for escape. There was more laughter, but it fell hollow on the fortune-teller's ears. Now, she understood. *Un cochino.* The one who roots in the underearth. The cloven-hoofed seeker of truth. Her hands made a feeble shooing motion. Beneath her blouse, her heart beat quickly. *Un cochino.* The finder of that which was hidden. The past and the sins it held could not remain forever hidden. The air began to vibrate, trembling like a living thing. Again, the sound of cicadas whirled in the air. As if summoned by Pedro Mendes's pig, a waking vision began to appear. Tia Clara relaxed and prepared herself to be revisited by memory.

The ghost woman was thin, her bones robbed of the sweetness of flesh, exactly as Tia Clara remembered. She was dressed in white, and Tia Clara narrowed her eyes against so much brightness in the midday sun. The phantom had decorated herself in gold. A thin bracelet circled her wrist, and from her throat hung a chain with an amulet in the shape of a *K*. The bright jewelry and the white clothing could not conceal the sickly second shell of this woman that was of both body and spirit. Dark brown holes throbbed in the shell. The serpent power in the base of her belly was shriveled to the size of a dried kernel of corn.

The wind stirred, and as quickly as it had appeared, the vision disappeared. Then the air stilled; the vibrations quieted. The shriek of cicadas faded away. The sounds of the village enfolded her. In front of the silver shop, the crowd still surrounded the pig. She watched with little interest as the animal saw a window of escape, darted through an opening in the circle of legs, and disappeared into an alley. The tourists drifted away. Gomez the butcher returned to his shop, his shoulders drooping with disappointment, his left hand absently wiping the red-stained apron that girded his belly.

Tia Clara sank back in her chair, wishing to brush away the memory of the apparition of the *gringa*, but it was stubborn and did not fade as willingly as that. *This has nothing to do with me,* she told herself. But even so, she thought of the *cochino*, rooting in the earth, uncovering what lay buried. She reached from beneath the table and took out her old deck from the box, unfolded the woven scarf that protected it. Eyes closed, she shuffled the cards. Still without looking, she pulled out a card and held it in her lap. Finally, she looked. *La Torre.* Destruction.

The wind began to whisper. In a voice as faint as an infant's sigh, it spoke to her of the coming of the woman of many scars. The woman of the masks. She shut her ears to the words of the wind. This was not her business. But her hands trembled as she wrapped the cards and returned them to their box. This had nothing to do with her. Nothing to do with her past and ghosts long banished. The sea that knew all—her past, her sins, the ghosts that haunted—laughed. The unexpected opportunity they held for her to atone. *Pah.* She spat on the ground. She took a pinch of chia from the little sack and flung it out to the air, appeasing hungry souls that might wait.

Old fool, she told herself.

MADISON

Maddie looked back toward the Molcas and wondered what Jack was doing. The thought brought with it a little ache, an ache that never really disappeared but was triggered by small things, in the same way that her leg was triggered. It would be fine, strong, and then a storm would hit or she would overexercise, and her hip and thigh would throb with a deep ache. Her feelings for Jack were like that. She decided to continue on her own for a while.

It was past the height of the winter tourist season, but the avenue was crowded. Families walked together as the afternoon approached its end. Little girls in dresses and leather sandals ran in circles laughing. Again, it occurred to Maddie that if she had come for another reason, it would be easy to be enchanted by this place. She studied the Mayan faces with their long, elegant noses rising without indentation to slanting foreheads. A mother and child crossed the sand to sit near her. As Maddie looked at them, she imagined she could have been peering back through the curtain of hundreds of years. The woman wore a traditional *huipil*. She was self-contained and handsome, and her face seemed to hold both the beauty and the sorrow of her native land. The history of this country. The girl had dark eyes and long, shiny plaits interwoven with red ribbon. She cast a furtive glance Maddie's way and, seeing her scars, quickly looked away.

She shook off all her musing. This was getting her nowhere. She retrieved the street map from her tote and unfolded it. The police station was located next to the post office, several blocks north of the hotel on Avenida Juarez. She would start there.

The officer on duty put aside his magazine and looked up when she entered. His ID badge identified him as Officer Ruiz.

"May I help you, *señorita*?" His English was formal and nearly flawless.

"*Sí,*" she said and found herself telling yet another official about Kat's disappearance. In the middle of her recitation, two voices raised in anger came from an adjoining room, but Ruiz, attentive to her story, ignored them, as if they were of no more importance than the buzzing of a single fly. He made a few notes, and when she was done he fingered through a stack of reports on his desk. "Ah, yes," he said, withdrawing one. "We have received an inquiry from your Department of State about this missing woman." Her pulse quickened. For the first time since arriving, someone in Playa knew of Kat, knew she was missing. He scanned the report. From across the desk, Maddie could see a faxed copy of the photo of Kat she had given to the DC police. The violinist had been cropped out. "Naturally, we wish to help," Ruiz said, "but I am afraid we have not been successful in finding any information about your sister. We have informed your authorities of this."

Tears threatened. She had come all this way pulled by the sense that she would find Kat, only to meet more roadblocks, only to encounter another official who could not help. "*Gracias,*" she said, unwilling to let him see the weakness of her tears, the enormity of her failure. "But you will continue to investigate, *sí*?"

"Of, course, *señorita*," he said. His eyes returned to his paperwork, dismissing her.

She left the station and, momentarily confused, turned left instead of right toward the route that would have led her back to the hotel. She passed a silver shop and next to that a souvenir shop, where displays of thick Mexican glass and pottery crowded the shelves, along with mass-produced clay reproductions of Mayan gods, evidence she had seen in other places of how authentic cultures had become perverted by the god of commerce. Another shelf held baskets. On the wall above hung a smattering of cheap papier-mâché and wooden masks. She scanned them with a practiced eye. Bats and snakes, mermaids and devils, one of which bore an amusing resemblance to Richard Nixon. She knew Mexico had a strong mask culture with a tradition that went back thousands of years to pre-conquest times. She was familiar with the material of the traditional masks, bone and wood, skin and leather, and knew, too, the recent and sophisticated work of José Rodríguez.

The masks in this shop were cheap copies of the traditional masks, unworthy of the rich custom. It angered and offended her to see them. Who would buy them? And what would they do with such crap once they returned home?

She pulled out Kat's photo and showed it to the clerk. The man shook his head. He had not seen her. She exited the shop, crossed the intersection, and approached a small church. A Spanish-style stucco building with red shutters, it was smaller than the surrounding build-ings, the size, really, of a single-car garage. On the north side of the building, a loudspeaker had been bolted to the roof, the source of the folk music that blared out over the square. Atop the south face were three wooden crosses. Maddie considered the building. The last place in the world she would ever expect to find Kat was in a church. Of that she was certain. Neither of them had ever found much comfort in religion.

Several fruit vendors sat in the shade of the north wall of the church. She stopped and watched as one vendor chose a piece of fruit and began peeling the rind. Her knife was broad-bladed and resembled a half-scale machete. The child at her feet reached up for a slice of the melon, and the woman handed him one without comment or smile, returning to her work before he had even taken a bite. *What is her story?* Maddie wondered. *Is she happy? Has she known sickness? Or loss?* Her impassive face revealed nothing. Maddie approached her and showed her Kat's photo. The woman shook her head and continued slicing melon. Two Mayan women, squat-bodied, no taller than an average fifth grader, passed her, walking with loose-limbed gaits. She listened to the pat, pat, pat of their sandals slapping against bare soles. She caught up with them and held out the photo. They shook their heads and continued on.

She turned in the direction of the Hotel Molcas, but as she passed the entrance of the church, her feet detoured from the path, as if on their own. Quickly, before her mind could regain control, they led her inside. The interior was plain. Plaster walls painted white, with fluorescent tubes hanging from the ceiling. Orange paper flowers decorated the altar. Crude wooden benches with narrow seats took up most of the space. At the front, flanking the altar, two niches were framed by white lace curtains made of plastic. In one, a boldly painted plaster statue of the Virgin resided. In the other, one of the Madonna and child. A dozen candles flickered on narrow tables set beneath each icon.

Two old women with heavy bodies and thin hair, so alike they must have been sisters, sat near the front, shoulders touching, despite the near-empty church. Maddie could hear the rhythmic droning as faint as that of wasps as they recited their rosaries. What were they seeking? Solace? Redemption? Blessings? Or perhaps nothing more than the mindless comfort of ritual, spewing out syllables that by their very familiarity comforted. There was one other woman in the church. She knelt before the statue of the Virgin. The woman was weeping, her figure bent in a posture Maddie recognized as the broken carriage of grief. As if such emotion were contagious, Maddie was struck with the desire to run, followed almost instantly by the urge to go to the woman and hold her, cry with her until their tears mingled and formed a river of sorrow too deep to be measured, denied, or ignored. What loss, she wondered, did the kneeling woman grieve?

Maddie had to flee the church and the weeping woman. Her head throbbed. She crossed the square, heading back to the hotel, and passed another street vendor, this one an old woman, wrinkled and fat, with two braids of white hair roping down her back. Her wares—blankets and shawls and belts—hung from a wooden frame. She sat behind a small table on which, improbably, was a wire cage with a small green bird inside, its prehensile claws curled around a roost. The old woman was staring at her with eyes so unfocused that for an instant Maddie believed her to be blind. She noticed on the table a small card. ADIVINACIÓN, a small sign read. She dug out her dictionary and looked up the word. Prophesies. She turned to continue to the hotel when, as clearly as if her sister stood beside her, she heard Kat's laughter. Of course. This was exactly the kind of thing Kat would do. She would have been unable to resist the whole scene. The old woman, the fortunes, the bird. Hope, that terrible thing with feathers, took hold. Of course Kat would have talked to the old woman. She stepped forward and once again drew out the photo of Kat. *"Mi hermana,"* she told the old woman.

The fortune-teller ignored the picture.

"Mi hermana," Maddie repeated.

The old woman looked straight at her with unsettling, unfocused eyes. Maddie would not have persisted, but at that instant the woman lifted a gnarled and swollen finger and motioned for her to come close.

Maddie's pulse rushed. Did the old woman know something?

The fortune-teller reached for a shawl and pushed it toward Maddie. "You buy?" she asked.

Oh. Just another street vendor wanting to make a sale. *"No, no, gracias."*

The old woman folded the shawl and placed it back on display. Then she pointed a bent finger at the sign.

If she had been superstitious, Maddie would have said a shadow, presaging evil, flitted through her. But she did not believe in such things. Even so, she did not move. She did not want her fortune told.

But she understood the mechanisms of the marketplace. To gain information, she needed to buy something. She indicated the shawl the woman had rehung on the frame. She fumbled in her tote and pulled out some pesos. "How much?"

She did not bargain. When the transaction was completed, she again showed Kat's photo.

The old fortune-teller shook her head.

TIA CLARA

The life of Playa played out around Tia Clara. She watched the tourists wandering the streets, listened to the music of the Tejano singers pouring out from the speaker atop the church. Today, perhaps because she was tired, or perhaps because she was plagued by the memory of many ghosts, now it seemed that the colors that hung above the village were shifting. Memories, emerging this morning like sargasso floating on the surface of the sea, tired her. Perhaps she should have stayed home. But memory waited there as well. There was no escaping. She leaned back in her chair. A woman approached. Even from a distance Tia Clara could see she held a heavy heart. She beckoned her to the table. The woman paused, and again Tia Clara motioned for her to approach.

When the stranger drew close, the fortune-teller saw her clearly, saw what had been hidden by the shadow of her hat. It was the woman of scars. The woman of many masks. The stranger was handing her a photo. In the cage, the bird began to hop about fretfully, pulling at the yarn that fastened the mirror to the wires.

The *gringa* set the photo on the table. *"Mi hermana,"* she said.

Tia Clara took a shawl from the display and pushed it forward, pretending to misunderstand, to offer a bargain. She needed more time to decide. *Tell her,* a voice urged. *Tell her what you know.* She resisted, stalling for time.

Tell her. The voice was more urgent now. *No,* whispered another voice, one filled with bitterness. *Tell her nothing. This is not any business of mine. Do not become involved in the affairs of the gringos.* That way always led to complications. To problems. "No." She pushed the picture away, a sharp gesture, and fixed her attention on the shawl, carefully folding it and placing it back on the frame that Felipe Leones, the carpenter, had built for her. She would let fate determine what to tell the woman. She pointed to the sign offering a reading, but the woman shook her head, and so it was decided.

Even after the *gringa* reconsidered and stayed to buy the shawl, Tia Clara did not waver from her decision and did not tell her what she knew about the woman with the golden *K* hanging at her throat. She would not be responsible for the troubles of others. It was not her concern. But she remembered her recent premonition on the morning of the shrouded dawn that foretold of the coming of the woman of many scars. And Tia Clara knew doubt. The makers of masks held more power than most. For the second time that day she took a pinch of chia and tossed it in the air to assuage the spirits and protect herself.

MADISON

Maddie reviewed the exchange with the old fortune-teller. In spite of her denial, Maddie was certain she had seen a flash of recognition in the old woman's eyes when she had looked at Kat's photo. But why would she have lied? Or had she been mistaken, and the crafty expression she had glimpsed had simply been the slyness of a street vendor?

As she headed back to the hotel, she paused on the pedestrian walkway and watched the bathers in the placid sea. One woman was swimming apart from the others. She swam without a cap, and her hair clung to her scalp like a helmet of gold. She cut through the water with a steady crawl, her long arms scissoring the air in strong strokes. The woman reminded her of Kat and how much she loved to swim. Tears filled her eyes.

She continued on, past the beachfront *palapa* where tourists drank while a mariachi band played. The doubt that had claimed her in the police station faded. She would not give up yet. She would talk to every employee at the Molcas, where Kat had once stayed. She would canvass the entire village if she had to, go into every shop and restaurant, show Kat's photo to every vendor.

As she crossed to the steps leading to the hotel terrace, she saw Jack—even from the back she would have recognized him. The wash of desire warmed her. The desensitization program wasn't working yet.

"Hi," she said, unable to conceal the catch in her voice.

He turned and she saw he was talking on his cell phone. "Mom," he mouthed.

"Is everything okay?" she whispered. *Olivia,* she thought. A picture of the girl—her impish humor, her adoration for Jack, her courage in the face of her illness—flashed before her, and she mentally crossed her fingers that everything was all right.

He nodded. "She's right here," he said into the phone. "Do you want to say hello?"

Before she could wave it off, he handed the phone to her.

"Hi, Maddie," Natalie said. "I am so glad I managed to reach Jack."

Her breath caught. "What's wrong? Is Olivia all right?"

"Nothing's wrong, dear. Quite the opposite, in fact. But I was calling to make sure you two arrived safely."

This was the first time they had spoken since she had broken it off with Jack, and the warmth in Natalie's voice eased the awkwardness she'd felt. She pictured her the first time she had met Jack's mother and Olivia: she had been struck by what she had seen in their faces and had wondered if kindness ran in families, like a trait for curly hair or long fingers. "Yes. Just a little tired from the trip."

"What's it like there? I've always wanted to go to Mexico but have never been."

Maddie looked out from the hotel veranda, took in the colors and sounds and people. "Unfiltered," she said. "Everything is pretty much unfiltered." She laughed. "Right now there's a mariachi band playing on the veranda of a restaurant across the street and folk songs being broadcast from the roof of the village church. Which is really more of a chapel."

"It sounds delightful."

"Yes."

"Jack told us why you are there. Have you been able to find out anything about Katherine?"

"Not yet." She heard the note of motherly concern in Natalie's voice, and a wash of grief at the loss of her own mother took her.

"Well, you must be tired. I'll let you go get some sleep. We're pulling for you. You just call if you want a shot of moral support."

Tears welled in her eyes. "Thanks, Natalie."

"Olivia sends her love."

She pictured Jack's sister, her sweet smile, the laugh that still held a touch of mischief that gave Maddie a hint of what Olivia had been like before she grew so ill. "How's Winks? I hope he isn't too much care for her."

"No. In fact, we think he's her good luck charm. We've had some very hopeful news. Olivia has been accepted into a study. Her doctors believe she's in the very small minority who are candidates for an experimental procedure. They are cautiously optimistic. We're keeping our fingers crossed."

"That's wonderful." She swallowed against the lump in her throat.

"Yes. It's the first hopeful news we've had in months."

"I'm so glad. Tell Olivia I'll be pulling for her."

"Thanks."

"And thanks for your concern. I really appreciate it."

"You stay in touch, okay? Let us know how things are going."

"We will." She handed the phone back to Jack and turned away so he wouldn't see the tears that had sprung to her eyes or how she could explain them to him when she didn't fully understand them herself.

KATHERINE

Kat felt the difference in energy the moment Verner entered the room, as if he, too, had a sense that she was getting stronger, healing, and it hadn't been based on futile hope. Perhaps her latest blood tests had revealed improvement.

She nodded hello, not trusting her voice. She was cautious and on guard around him, saying little, continuing to pretend to be agreeable and that she believed he could still help her, but this role was not natural to her and she feared beneath his piercing eyes that her facade was tissue thin. She forced herself to hold his gaze, hoping it was without guile.

An unfamiliar nurse entered the room and helped her up. Verner opened the door and motioned for two aides to enter, and he pointed toward the bed. Kat froze. Had they somehow discovered she had been hiding pills? One aide went to the head and the other to the foot. They took hold of the frame and began to move it closer to the wall. To her enormous relief, they did not touch the post that contained her Plan Omega.

"Good. Good," Verner said and sent them off. Within minutes they returned carrying an oversize wicker armchair and two cushions. The nurse helped her to the chair. One of the aides left and returned a moment later, this time with a small pedaled contraption that looked like a bike without wheels or seat. He set it in front of Kat.

"I want you to use this several times a day," Verner said. He began to talk, words tumbling out. A breakthrough, he said. A new protocol. He was putting her on a new schedule to start at once. She would continue to be taken to the pool to swim at night. Her diet would be nutrient rich. A new series of injections would begin. She began to demur, remembering what had happened when she had received his injections before. He brushed aside her protests. She would be receiving physical therapy and deep-tissue massage twice a day. Word games would be brought in for her to keep her mind active. And more books. "We will make history. We will not only forestall aging," he said. "We will reverse it."

She heard in his voice all the passion and conviction that had so captivated her five months back when she had arrived for the first time.

And she heard, too, the madness. But what would happen to her if this new protocol failed? She shook off a tremor of fear and forced herself to think clearly. Time was running out.

In the morning, when Rosa appeared with her breakfast tray, Kat smiled and continued her efforts to befriend her. Still unsure how much Spanish Rosa understood, she chatted with her, keeping the subjects neutral and speaking in a soft voice, one she might adopt when comforting a frightened or abused child. She needed an ally, and thus far Rosa was her only possibility.

When the Mayan turned to leave, Kat stopped her. She unclasped the necklace that hung from her neck and gave it to Rosa. The woman recoiled, as if the object in her palm had burned her, and she pushed it back at Kat. But Kat smiled and shook her head, closing Rosa's fingers around the golden *K*. Their eyes met, and Rosa murmured a word Kat didn't understand. But when she left the room, she took Kat's necklace with her.

MADISON

When Maddie appeared on the terrace for breakfast, Jack was already there. She joined him and he motioned for the waiter to bring her coffee. "Sleep well?" he asked.

"Yes. Did you?" In spite of having slept nearly ten hours, she was still tired. Lethargic. She put it down to the dramatic change of climate that was taking a while to become acclimated to. They'd had a dinner at the hotel the night before and then agreed to make it an early evening. Their parting had been awkward. They had lingered for a few moments in the corridor outside their rooms, as if each were waiting for a signal from the other. A sign that never came.

"Out cold," he said. The waiter, different from the one who had served her yesterday, approached with the silver coffee service and handed her a menu. Jack's breakfast was in front of him, a large plate that held salsa and scrambled eggs and sliced avocado. The travel and stress had left her with little appetite, and she ordered only fruit and coffee. Before the server left with her order, she showed him the photo of Kat, told him she was looking for her.

"Ask Ángel," he said, and pointed out to the waterfront to the boy standing by the ticket booth at the pier. "Ángel sees everything that happens in Playa."

"*Gracias,*" she said. When he returned with her breakfast, she nibbled at the fruit and drank the coffee. He had brought her a sweet roll, although she had not ordered it, and she pushed it aside. She glanced out to where the boy, Ángel, stood. She was eager to follow this lead, faint though it was, and waited impatiently for Jack to finish his eggs. He caught her eyes, and although she believed she had concealed her restlessness, he crumpled his napkin and tossed it on the table.

"Let's get going," he said. Together they headed for the ticket booth.

"Buenos días, señorita," Ángel said. He nodded at Jack. *"Señor."*

"Habla inglés?" Maddie asked.

"Sí. You would like to buy a ticket?"

"No."

"You like to scuba, perhaps?" He had the street smarts and quickness of a hustler. "But you must try it. The best reefs in all of Mexico are right here in Playa." He held out a brochure. "Is this your first time in Playa?"

"Yes." She had to admire his determination. Although she judged him to be no more than fifteen or sixteen, he knew the trick of engaging them with a stream of questions, each punctuated with his smile.

"Do you work here every day?" she asked.

"Sí. Every day. You want to buy a ticket to Cozumel?"

"No. But perhaps you can help me with something."

His grin flashed again. *"Sí.* I am Ángel. I can help you with whatever you need. Ask anyone in Playa."

Maddie retrieved the photo of Kat. "Have you seen her? *Mi hermana.*"

He studied the photo carefully. Something flickered in his eyes that Maddie registered as recognition, and she felt a moth-wing flutter of hope. He looked up at her and then down at the picture. *"Muy bella,"* he said.

"Have you seen her? She has visited your village. She stayed here." She pointed to the hotel. "There at the Molcas." He continued to look at the picture. She could almost see his mind at work, figuring an angle.

"Perhaps. *Sí.* Perhaps. I think so. Yes."

She exchanged a glance with Jack and tried to quiet the flutter of hope, even as it grew stronger. Was the boy just trying to please her, or had he actually seen Kat? "When?"

"A few weeks?" He made this a question, as if uncertain.

A few weeks? She clutched Jack's arm and stepped closer to the ticket booth. "Where? Where did you see her?"

He hesitated, as if considering something and then, having decided, pointed down the beach, away from the Hotel Molcas and beyond the shops where, in the distance, was a row of shacks. "There."

Doubt again crept in. Her hand dropped from Jack's arm. Surely Kat would not be staying at one of those places. "You're sure?"

"*Sí.* She went to see the diver. Many people go to him."

"The diver?"

"*Sí.* Víctor. The diver. Go down there, *señorita.* Past the Blue Parrot." He took the brochure from her and pointed to a drawing on the front fold. "Vic's Dive Shop. You go there. He will tell you what you want to know. Tell him Ángel sent you."

"*Gracias.*" Before she could fish change from her tote, Jack was handing two coins to him.

With the quickness of a pickpocket, he took the pesos. "You go see Víctor," he said again.

She clutched the brochure. As they headed off toward the row of shacks, she turned to Jack. "Do you think he really saw Kat?" she asked. Her mouth was dry, and she regretted not bringing the bottle of water from her room.

"Hard to tell," he said. "I'm not sure if he was telling you what he thought you wanted to hear or not. If I had to go by my gut, I'd say this diver might know something."

Two men, clearly Americans, were setting out scuba gear in front of the first shack she passed. She knew the type. They were expatriates, older than she first thought. Hippies who had arrived to sleep in campers on the beach and live the beach life. She had seen men like them in Oaxaca and Guerrero when she'd studied the work of mask makers there right after graduation. The trip had been a graduation gift from Kat. They had traveled together—Kat had been unable to convince her to fly, and Maddie remembered the hours and hours of driving as they'd crossed the continent and down over the border. Kat had never once complained. If she resented Maddie's fear of flying, it never showed. Once again, her sister had been there for her when she needed her. Recalling that and all the ways Kat had supported her, she was grateful to Lonnie for pushing her into this trip. Grateful, too, that Jack had come in support. It was this that made her reach for his hand as they crossed the sand. If he was surprised by this, he did not show it.

As they neared the first shack, she wondered if it was possible that Kat had gotten involved with a man. A vacation romance. Well, what if she had? After all, Kat was an adult. She had never pretended to be a nun. She had a life of her own, a right to do whatever she wanted. Maddie remembered Tom, the trainer in the gym in Georgetown. Perhaps Kat had found another muscular guy to keep her company. Perhaps when she'd heard that Maddie was in love with Jack, she had seen that as an opportunity to start a new life chapter herself. If that was the case, the last thing she would want was to have Maddie showing up. Uninvited. Perhaps unwanted. Maybe Kat wanted more distance between them. More boundaries. Had Maddie misread their relationship? Had she been the one who, out of neediness and dependence, had clung too hard? Had she always been the one to phone Kat, demanding closeness, intruding on Kat's life more than she realized? These thoughts felt so alien. Why would they come to her now? She wondered if it were possible to really know another, or if she had just projected her own needs and desires on what she needed Kat to be.

"Hey," Jack said.

She turned to him. "What?"

"What's going on?"

She realized that at some point when she had been thinking about Kat she had stopped walking and slipped her hand from Jack's. "I just need to think a minute. Okay?"

"Sure," he said. "I'm not going anywhere."

She nearly confided in him, nearly shared the conflicting thoughts that surged through her mind, separating out what she remembered, what she knew to be true, and what she had always imagined or wanted to be so, very nearly asked him if she had been foolish to rush off to Mexico. After all, who had made her Kat's keeper? No one. Certainly not Kat, who hadn't even let her know where she was going. But everything was all entwined. If she had panicked, she knew that part of her reaction had been at her ending the relationship with Jack. Had this entire mission to find Kat been nothing more than a way of escaping from the pain of a broken relationship? She caught her breath as if she had been running. Hadn't that been what she had always done? Run from pain? Run from memories? Run from Jack? None of this could she share with the man standing so patiently at her side.

The sense of purpose that had driven her during the past days drained from her. If they returned to the hotel now, she could be packed and ready to leave in minutes. At this time of year they should be able to get seats on a flight back to Boston.

"Maybe," she finally said. "Maybe Kat doesn't want to be found."

"What do you mean?"

She tried to explain her thoughts, her speculation of why Kat might have a need for time alone, a little independence.

He listened thoughtfully. After a moment, he said, "Why would you think that, Maddie? I obviously don't know Kat, but everything you've told me about her and about your relationship seems the opposite of what you're suggesting."

She stared at the brochure as if the answers to all her questions were contained in the glossy print. Black letters on a yellow background. A photo of a couple outfitted in diving gear. A decorative border of flowers. Orchids. The flowers froze her gaze. She remembered the bone-dry soil in the flowerpots in Kat's home. The dried blossoms on the floor.

And then she remembered the syringe hidden in the bathroom drawer.

"You're right," she said to Jack. "Of course you're right." Whatever she learned about Kat, whatever secrets her sister held, she would deal with them.

The dive shop instantly reinforced the mental picture of an aging hippie that she had formed of its owner. It was a thatched-roof shanty with a half dozen plastic chairs set in the strip of sand in front. Six diving cylinders were propped against the front wall, the paint on each worn off, the steel beneath burnished dull by contact with sand and sea. At the water's edge, a laborer bent over an upturned boat, repairing the bottom with patches of fiberglass. The chemical smell of resin floated down the beach to her. No one else was in sight. As she drew nearer she could hear the man singing, one of those brooding melodies she associated with lost love, regardless of the language. If the man was aware of them, he gave no sign. "Jeez," she said to Jack, "What are we, invisible?" For some reason, this amused him, which only increased her indignation.

"Hola," she called out.

The man looked up and laid the brush atop the resin can. He was taller than most of the native residents she had seen in Playa. There was something about the way he held his body, the set of his shoulders, that told her he was fully aware of his effect on women. For that alone she distrusted him. She was glad that Jack was with her. She waved the brochure Ángel had handed her and spoke slowly. "We are looking for Víctor, the diver."

He smiled, revealing teeth white and even.

"Do you know where I can find him?" she asked, struggling to keep the impatience from her voice.

When he spoke, his voice still held a hint of music. *"Hola,"* he said. "I am Víctor."

Jack stepped forward and held out his hand in greeting. Maddie held back, studying the diver's face, saw in it pride. And beneath that, something it took a moment to interpret. At first, she thought it was loneliness, and then she understood: it was sorrow.

VÍCTOR

Víctor understood much about certain of the foreign women who came to his village. Women of the desperate eyes, he called them. They drank too much and laughed too hard, but despite their forced gaiety he did not judge them harshly. He understood their laughter hid wounds, their drinking filled emptiness. They were not so very different in that way from him. It seemed to him that these women came seeking to find some vision of their destinies. Or perhaps not. Perhaps that was only his romantic imaginings, and they simply came for a vacation.

Still, he felt a kinship with the women. Whatever their reason for coming to Playa, he understood their restlessness. Years before, a similar discontent had caused him to leave this village. For twenty-five years he had traveled until, finally, he grew tired of wandering from one place to another, weary of holding on to the pain he wished to escape, the disappointment of not finding what he sought. After those twenty-five years, he was ready to return to Playa.

He had been born in this village and from the time of his birth until he was fifteen, he had lived in the house of his *abuela*. He was known to everyone as Víctor the Orphan. And later, Víctor the Bastard. Seldom was he called by these names anymore. Now the people of Playa called him Víctor the Diver. But sometimes, inside, he still felt like Víctor the

Orphan. The Bastard. Such a name, even when no longer spoken, was not one easily forgotten.

His *madre* had died when he was four months old. Naturally he held no memory of her face, but as a boy he had discovered two things about her. The first was that she had been beautiful. Her loveliness was a legend in Playa, so much so that even now, all these years later, the old ones still used her as the measure against which to judge all beauty. "The youngest daughter of Hector and María is pretty," they would agree, "but she cannot compare to the loveliness of Consuelo Díaz. Never has there been another such beauty in our village."

If there existed photographs of his *madre*, he had not seen them. There was nothing to validate these claims, but from what others had told him, he held images of what she must have been like, pictures developed in his heart. From old Juan, he learned that his mother's hair was long and thick and as black as a moonless midnight sky. Her eyes, he heard from the *madre* of Carlos Mendes, were as black as her hair. And as shining. Her voice, José Ventura told him, rivaled the song of birds. And her skin—this, too, from José—her skin was smooth like the flesh of a mango. Luis, the fisherman, remembered that her laugh was as light as the flight of the hummingbird. And the scent of her skin, his *abuela* said on the few times he could persuade her to talk of it, her scent could be found deep in the blossom of the vanilla bark. Only one person, his tía Clara, had refused his requests to speak of his mother, her sister. From these pieces he'd gathered from the others, he put together an icon of his *madre*, and wherever he went in the village, whatever his eyes fell on—sky and mango and hummingbird—and whatever familiar smells and sounds he sensed—of birdsong and vanilla blossoms, he recognized some part of her.

This was the other truth he had learned. His *madre* had not been wed when he was born. He'd heard the whispers, but no one would tell him who his *padre* had been. At sixteen, Víctor stood taller than the other men, nearly five foot ten, and from this he concluded that his *padre* must have been an outsider. When he left Playa del Pedro, it was not only to escape the fate of being known as Víctor the Bastard, but to find as well a tall man in whose face he could see traces of his own.

At forty-one, he had returned. His grandmother was gone then, and his only other living relative was his aunt, Tia Clara, the half-mad fortune-teller who wanted nothing to do with him. He built a shack close to the sea, to the blue and green waters that he had missed every day he had been away. He was a strong swimmer, a good laborer. Soon Luis the fisherman offered him a job, and in this way he came to know the reefs along the coast as well as he did the contours of his own heart. He fished and saved, putting away money until he had enough to buy his own boat and some equipment. Then he began to take tourists out in his boat, to show them the magic world of the reefs. To the women, he taught other pleasures. At night, in the cantina or on the moonlit beach, he would sing to them and, sometimes, and only if they wanted, he took them to his bed. During such times he saw their loneliness ease and their desperate eyes soften. But only for a short while, for there was a hunger in them, an emptiness that he could not fill. Just as they could not fill his. Until one day he had met the one who could.

He regarded the couple who stood before him, seeing the quiet strength in the man and the sadness in the woman with the scarred face.

"*Hola,*" she said. "We are looking for a diver named Víctor."

"*Hola,*" he said. She held in her hand a brochure, and he understood that Ángel had sent them to him. "I am Víctor."

The man offered his hand first. "Jack," he said. "This is Madison."

Víctor wiped his hands on a rag and shook both of their hands.

"People call me Maddie," the woman said. At that moment, Kuko scurried from his shelter beneath the overturned boat and darted across the sand. The iguana nearly touched the feet of the *gringa*, and Víctor waited for the inevitable scream. They were so nervous, these women.

But she did not yell. Or even move. He had yet to see her smile. He concluded that she was not like an ordinary *gringa*, and not just because she bore such scars on her face.

"You take people out to the reefs or the island?" the man asked.

"Yes. You are interested?"

"No." The woman reached into her bag and pulled out a picture, which she handed to him. *"Mi hermana,"* she said.

His eyes widened in the shock of recognition as he looked at the photo.

"What?" the woman said, and he knew little had escaped her eyes. He would have to be careful with her.

"Have you seen her?" the man asked. "The boy at the ticket booth believed she might have come here."

He stalled for time. He pretended to study the photo more closely, although he could have closed his eyes and drawn it from memory. "Perhaps I have seen her," he said. Still, he did not return the photo. If it were possible, he would have kept it.

Her face lit with hope. The man beside her studied him, as if searching for truth.

Víctor's mind whirled. Seeing Katherine's picture had shaken him. He had a hundred questions. Where was she? Why had she not returned as she had promised? Had he been a fool to think she shared his feelings? He stalled for more time, time he needed to sort the implications and risks and possible accusations. He wanted no trouble, but he was hungry for news of Katherine. He wanted to know why she had disappeared so suddenly. She had promised to return, and he had believed her. And if he decided to get involved, what should he tell this couple? It was complicated. People were quick to make accusations, to jump to conclusions. What if he had been one of the last people to be with Katherine? What if they gave this information to the police? He had not been in trouble for a long time, but people had memories. Quickly, as if suddenly even holding it implicated him, he passed the photo back to her. He thought quickly and made a decision that satisfied the need to be cautious while at the same time presenting the opportunity to learn more.

"*Señor* Jack," he said. "*Señorita* Madison," he began.

MADISON

"*Señorita*," the diver said. "*Señorita* Madison." He pronounced her name as if each syllable were a word of its own.

"Yes?" Reluctantly, she slipped Kat's photo back in her tote.

"Your sister. Does she like to go to the shops?"

Shops? Kat? Shopping was invented for Kat. She considered it a national sport. "Yes."

"Cozumel." The word came out flat and sure.

"Cozumel?"

"*Sí*, Madison," he said. "Everyone who comes to Playa will go there. For the shopping, and for the diving and snorkeling as well. Have you looked for her there?"

"No." It hadn't occurred to her, but his idea immediately made sense. Wherever she traveled, Kat always returned home with some memento of the trip. Jewelry or art. An article of clothing. Or tales of an adventure. For Kat sought those as eagerly as she did any pottery or watercolor or shawl. It seemed inconceivable that at some point during one of her trips to Playa del Pedro in the past months she wouldn't have taken at least a day trip to the island, if not to shop than for the excursion itself. She turned to Jack. "It's possible," she said.

Víctor again wiped his hands on the rag. She couldn't read his face, and that made her distrustful. "Wait here," he said and disappeared into the shack. He returned moments later with an oversize canvas bag, the once white cloth now yellowed from use and the sea. "I will take you there."

Maddie cast an alarmed glance at Jack. "No. Please. Thank you, but that is not necessary." She immediately understood. It was a slow day, and he saw them as a business opportunity. He wanted them to hire him. She looked back across the distance toward the pier and the ferry docked there. A line was starting to form at the gangplank. Jack reached over and clasped her hand, gave it a quick squeeze. She gathered he intended it as a message, but she didn't know how to interpret it.

Víctor made a sign, as if brushing away a gnat. "It is no bother, Madison." Ma-di-son. "I will go with you." With a finality that brushed away her protests, as if they were agreeing instead of objecting, he set down the canvas bag, tapped the lid on the can of resin, and set the brush in a second can filled with clear liquid. He locked the shack and placed a **Closed** sign on the door.

"What do you think?" Maddie whispered to Jack while the diver was closing up the shack.

"I might be totally off the mark, but I think he might know something he's not telling us. Or isn't ready to tell us. Let's see if we can learn more from him on the ride to the island."

An obese iguana scurried past, back to its place beneath a boat. "I'll be back, Kuko," the diver said, the way one would tell a dog to stay. He started for the pier, and after a moment's hesitation and another whispered consultation, Maddie and Jack followed.

There were two ferries to the island, Víctor explained. A water-jet catamaran and a smaller hull craft. "We will take the slower one," he said. "It is cheaper." Maddie started to argue, but again Jack squeezed her hand and she fell silent. The ferry held a cabin with two rows of seating and more seating on the open deck as well as a bench along one side. They chose the bench. She was glad he was at her side and knew she wouldn't have gone to the island with Víctor if she had been alone. The diver stood, looking out at the horizon, where the relentless azure sky melted into the sea. Maddie recalled the expression she had seen on his face when he had looked at Kat's picture. She stirred, ready to press him, unwilling to wait until they landed on the island.

At that moment, seemingly unmindful of the other passengers, Víctor began to sing, the same sorrowful tune he had been singing when they had approached his shack. Jack winked at her. She settled back on the bench and pulled the guidebook out from her tote, pretending not to know Víctor. Any questions she had would have to wait until they arrived on the island. The horn sounded and she felt the ferry begin to pull away from the pier. Jack leaned back against the rail, closed his eyes, and turned his face to the sun. She opened the guide to read about the island where they were headed.

She'd read only a sentence when she had to close the book. In spite of the calm water, she felt queasy. She swallowed and shut her eyes, which proved a mistake. She opened them quickly. She bent forward, swallowed as the sickness rose in her throat.

"Take a deep breath." The diver was at her side. To her great relief, he had stopped singing.

"I'm fine." She forced the words out, swallowed again, prayed she would not be sick in front of him.

"Are you okay?" Jack asked, his face grave with concern.

She swallowed, tried to nod.

"Deep breaths," the diver repeated.

She felt the color drain from her face, tasted the sourness of sickness in her throat. *Not here,* she thought. Not now. Falsely confident, she had left the Xanax back at the hotel. She heard Jack and the diver conversing in Spanish. Jack nodded at something Víctor said and moved aside to make room for the diver to sit on the bench beside her.

The diver reached for her hand.

"What are you doing?" she hissed and tried to pull away.

"It's okay, Maddie," Jack said. "He's going to make your nausea go away."

Víctor pressed his fingertips into the fleshy pad between her thumb and first finger, held the pressure for a moment of two. Slowly, as he applied the pressure, the nausea, so threatening moments before, faded. "Better?" he asked.

"Yes," she said, surprised. It was as if the sickness had never been. "What did you do? How did you do that?"

"*Mi abuela.* My grandmother." He got up and Jack slid over and reclaimed his spot next to her.

"She taught you that?"

"She was a *curandera*. A healer."

Maddie closed her eyes, testing, but neither the threat of a panic attack nor the nausea returned. She reopened the guidebook, needing to reestablish her composure.

He pointed to the book. "You are interested in knowing about Isla de Cozumel?"

She shrugged. What she was interested in was finding Kat.

"It means the Land of the Swallows. It was sacred to the Maya."

"Really?" Jack sounded genuinely curious.

"It was a ceremonial center where they worshipped *Ixchel*. She was the goddess of fertility and childbirth, the moon and the sea."

"Are there ruins there?" Jack asked. "Temples?"

"One or two. They're small. Not like those in Tulum and Chichén Itzá. Is this your first trip to Mexico? Or perhaps you two came here on your honeymoon?"

Maddie caught Jack's smile and wondered if he was remembering the flight attendant who had also assumed they were honeymooning. "We're not married," she said.

"Just friends," he said.

"Ah, *sí*, friends," Víctor said.

Wild for a change of subject, Maddie said, "I've been to Mexico before. Not to the Yucatán, but to Oaxaca and Guerrero."

"Why there?"

The ferry passed a two-person kayak, leaving it rolling in its wake. "To study the work of the masks made there."

"You have an interest in masks?"

"Yes. I create them. That's what I do."

"In my country," he said, "the magic of the mask makers is powerful."

"You should see Maddie's work," Jack said. "It's magnificent. And brave."

She flushed at his words. "What about you?" she asked Víctor. "Were you born in Playa del Pedro?"

"Yes."

"Do your parents still live there?"

"I did not know my *padre*," he said. "And my *madre* died when I was very young."

"I'm so sorry," Maddie said.

He shrugged. "Tell me, Ma-di-son. Tell me about your sister."

Seeing Jack's nod of encouragement, welcoming the opportunity to pursue the sense that he knew Kat, she put her guidebook back in her tote.

"You say you think she came to Playa?" Víctor said.

"Yes," Maddie said. She searched his face and saw there an intensity that surprised her.

She vowed to be cautious, careful of what she told him.

TIA CLARA

Tia Clara knew there was nothing to comfort her, to ease the sorrow in her heart and the pain of what lay ahead. She stared across the room where the canary sat motionless on the bottom of the wire cage, its head tucked beneath a green wing, as if asleep. For a day it had refused to eat. The fortune-teller couldn't help but wonder whether it was the power of the foreign mask maker that was making the little bird sick. Or was it, at last, her past catching up, as she had always known it would?

Memories tormented her. It had begun earlier, when she had caught sight of Víctor. To her surprise, he had been with the *gringa* and another man. The three of them had been boarding the ferry to Cozumel. Víctor had been smiling at the woman. The sight of him had caused her soul to fill with blackness and had given rise to old memories. How much Víctor looked like his *padre*. And hadn't she and Manny also taken the ferry to Cozumel? Or perhaps not. She could not remember boarding a boat with her husband, and surely that was not something she would forget. She had always distrusted the sea, for it knew everything. If you lost your soul, the water would carry it away. For this reason Tia Clara always stayed away from the open sea. No, she had no memory of the trip, only a familiar sense or sensation as she had watched Víctor walk up the gangplank onto the ferry with the scarred woman. But it had been a long time ago, and this she knew about memory: It was not a straight, flat road. You could not look over your shoulder and see the clear and shimmering view of its truth. Even for her, she who knew so much, it curved and dipped, deceived and held back. Memory, she knew, was only as true as the mind wished to make it.

"Eat," she urged the motionless bird. Molted green feathers littered the floor of the cage. As if she could nourish the bird by feeding herself, she prepared a cup of hot chocolate and a sweet roll she had brought home from Solano's bakery. She broke off a piece of the roll and took a bite and then crumbled a tiny bit. The bird did not move when she opened the cage door and dropped the tiny crumbs at its feet.

While the chocolate was warming, she burned a chunk of copal and tried to console herself by remembering her *madre*'s words. *No hay mal que por bien no venga.* There is nothing bad from which good does not result. Although she knew these words were meant to soothe weaker souls, they could not deny the fact that there existed some evil from which no good could ever come. Still, she repeated the sentence twice. The buzzing of a fly caught her attention. As she watched, it flew closer, over the roll, and, even as the fortune-teller was raising a hand to brush it away, it landed on the edge of the cup of chocolate. Tia Clara sank down on the old wood chair, but the fly did not stir. Even the youngest child knew what this meant. A dead relative had returned. She knew at once whose departed soul had entered her house. It was too late now to alter that which had been. There was no magic that could change the damage of so many years before.

She moved on swollen feet to the shelf above the sink and took down a box. She sprinkled the doorway with salt. She knew evil spirits were persistent, but she hoped this could hold them away so they could do no more damage.

MADISON

The pier at Cozumel was crowded with vessels moored gunwale to gunwale. The ferry slid into its berth. They waited until almost all the others had disembarked before rising from the bench. Víctor tossed his canvas bag out onto the pier while Jack helped Maddie out. At once they were approached by taxi drivers, each shouting above the others, vying for their attention, offering rides to hotels and beaches and tourist sites, but Víctor motioned them away. "First we will have coffee," he said, "and then we will begin with the shops."

She caught Jack's eye and shook her head. She didn't want to waste time and wanted to start canvassing the shops. But Víctor had already claimed a table at a sidewalk café. He was steering the course of the day, and she was unsure how to wrest control back.

Jack reached for her arm. "This is the first café on the way from the pier," he said. "If Kat stopped for coffee or wine while waiting to get a ferry back to Playa, this would be the spot. It's a good place to start."

A good place to start, but to no avail. No one recognized Kat from the photo. Maddie refused anything more than coffee—her stomach held the memory of her earlier nausea—and finished her drink quickly, impatient to begin, but the diver took his time. Finally, unable to wait any longer, she got up. "I'm going to start asking around."

Jack pushed his cup away, threw some pesos on the table, and stood. "I'll join you."

"Me too," Víctor said.

"You finish your coffee," Maddie said. "We'll start on the shops across the *calle*."

The diver ignored this and left the café with them. The streets of San Miguel were laid out in a grid. It was past the high tourist season, but the town was still busy. They began on Avenida Melgar, and then on to Avenida Juarez, stopping at taco shops, a bookstore, T-shirt stores—ubiquitous in every resort town she had ever been to—dive shops and fruit stands and kiosks where sisal baskets were displayed. As they encountered the owners and clerks at each store, she showed Kat's photo while Jack—or occasionally Víctor—spoke to them in Spanish. "If we had another photo of Kat, we could split up and cover more territory," Jack said. Maddie was glad they had only the one picture. She wanted to be the one to search the face of everyone they spoke to, looking for a sign, a fleeting expression, a shadow crossing the eyes, something betraying a flicker of recognition. She wouldn't miss an opportunity to pursue even the slightest interest. She no longer feared appearing rude or pushy. It wouldn't stop her, as it had when she'd approached the old fortune-teller in Playa. After trying the shops, they approached hotels and small guesthouses, but the answer was the same at each. No one recognized Kat.

Disappointment was a stone in her chest. She felt duped that the diver had led her to believe that someone here might have recognized Kat from the picture. They had lost hours in the futile search. He had only wanted their money after all.

Víctor regarded her for a long moment. She had the strong feeling, as she had had on the ferry, that he was debating whether or not to tell her something.

Fueled with her new determination, she asked, "What is it? You seemed so certain that Kat would come here. Was it because you knew her? Just tell me that. Did you see her here? Did you see her on the ferry?"

She was usually good at reading expressions, but even as he held her gaze she was unable to interpret his. Was she seeing fear? Or was he simply annoyed at her questions?

"I'm sorry I could not help you," he said.

"We might as well return to Playa," she said to Jack.

"No. Not yet, Jack. Madison." Ma-di-son. "There is one more place we must go." Without waiting for their reply, he approached one of the taxis and gave the driver directions. He motioned for them to join him.

"Are you up for this?" Jack asked. "You seem really pissed with him."

Maddie walked toward the taxi. "What could one more dead end possibly matter?" She didn't mention her suspicions, nor the fledgling hope that perhaps the diver would now reveal more.

"Where are we going?" Jack asked as he slid in next to Maddie.

"You will see."

The driver left the city center and drove along the coast. Farther from the town, they passed a row of resort hotels, and Maddie wondered if perhaps Kat had stayed at one of them, but the taxi continued without stopping. At last they pulled off the highway. A sign indicated that they were entering Chankanaab Park. The taxi stopped at the edge of the parking area, beside a row of huge kapok trees.

She raised her eyebrows. "What is this place?"

"It has the best snorkeling on Cozumel."

Perhaps not a dead end after all. She remembered how much her sister loved to swim. "You think Kat might have come here?" But if Víctor did not know Kat, how could he have known how she loved swimming? Still, she allowed herself to hold on to that sliver of hope.

Again, she felt him consider his words, deciding what to say. "This is for you," he finally declared, his arm motioning to include them both. "You cannot leave the island without experiencing it."

184

Anger flushed her face. "You brought us here for that? To go snorkeling?"

"Wait until you see. You will be amazed. You cannot leave without trying it." He got out of the taxi.

She turned to Jack. "Tell the driver to take us back to town," she said.

He looked at Víctor, and the two exchanged quick words in Spanish. To her dismay, Jack got out of the cab. He avoided looking at her.

She'd had enough of both of them. "I am not some tourist looking for a good time. I am here to find my sister. If you don't help me, that's fine."

"Don't blame Víctor," Jack said. "Earlier, when you were talking to the clerk in the apparel shop, he mentioned this place, and I thought since we were on the island anyway, you could have one hour of pleasure or relaxation before we left." He shot an apologetic look at Víctor.

The diver's smile disappeared. "If I have offended you, I am sorry, Madison. My only wish was to surprise you, to bring you to this beautiful place so that you will have a lovely memory to take home with you. To ease the *dolor*. The sorrow and sadness you carry in your heart." He set the bag down and walked off, leaving them to talk.

"I am not here for relaxation or fun or whatever the hell you had in mind," she said through clenched teeth. "I'm here to find Kat." The warmth she had been feeling toward Jack disappeared, a wave washing footprints from the sand.

"Look," Jack said. "We have to wait for the afternoon ferry back. Let's just take this moment."

"No."

He opened the canvas tote the diver had set at their feet and took out two masks, snorkels, and two sets of flippers.

"No," she said. "I just want to go back."

He pulled out a faded towel from the bag and then, to the surprise of them both, a black bathing suit.

"He planned this all along. Why else bring the diving gear? That suit? I don't trust him. I think he knows more than he's telling us."

"Like what?"

"I don't know."

"Maybe it's as simple as he said. No matter whether or not you learned anything here about Kat, he wanted us to experience diving here before we leave. He's a diver. It would be natural for him to think that."

She wasn't convinced.

"We're here now. Let's take that lovely memory he wanted us to have."

"I'm not here for lovely memories."

"I saw the changing room over there by the parking lot," Jack said. "By that stand of palm trees." He held out the swimsuit.

She shrank back as if it were a living thing. "I can't. No, I can't."

He looked at her, his gaze lingering on her scarred face. "Water," he said. "Someone once told me that water washes away grief."

"I—I don't swim anymore."

He set the gear down in the shade of a grape tree, placing the black suit on top. Slowly, he pulled his shirt off, stripped off his pants, beneath which he wore only briefs. His eyes did not leave hers, full of challenge. And compassion, for she saw that there, too.

"You keep pushing the good things away, Maddie," he said. "No matter what happens when we return to Playa, if you don't swim here, I think what you'll remember of this day is regret. Always regret at what you have pushed away."

She met his gaze, held it, felt her jaw stiffen in the face of the unspoken challenge. "No," she said. She was remembering how in the first days he had tried to talk her into flying in the small plane with him.

"You're afraid," he said.

She held his gaze. "No," she said. "I'm not."

"Olivia once told me that it's the thing we most fear that we have to face," he said.

"I'm not afraid."

He picked up the suit and handed it to her. They locked eyes, his daring, hers defiant. A flash of the person she had once been, *before*, surfaced. She grabbed the suit from his grasp and stalked off to the changing hut. Even before she stripped off her shift, she regretted her impulsiveness. The suit covered some of her scars but not nearly all. She pictured his eyes challenging her. She tugged on the suit. There was a wall of lockers, and she took the key from the door of one and placed her tote and folded shift in it. The key hung from a thick band of elastic, and she slid it on her wrist like a bracelet. Not giving herself time to change her mind, she walked from the hut to the water's edge where he waited. She tried to stand as tall as he did, but felt shrunken.

He steadied her while she put on the flippers. They did not speak. Wide stone steps led into the water. They were slippery, and when he reached for her hand she resisted only briefly. When they were knee-deep in the water, he showed her how to adjust her mask, submerging it, instructing her to spit on the glass lens, then rinse it. The water was an astonishing turquoise and as warm as she imagined an infant's first bath would be. When she was hip-deep, a neon-blue fish swam by. She sank down into the water, let it capture her hips, waist, breasts, shoulders, and scissor-kicked out deeper until her feet could no longer touch the sea bed. Her chest expanded, as if something held tightly sealed had broken free. She submerged her face and swam deeper, looking down on pocked coral peaks and caverns, shadowy grottoes. She saw Medusa-like sponges and undulating purple sea fans. A school of blue fish suspended like a Calder mobile swam by, winking like Christmas lights. All the while, vibrantly colored fish in gaudy shades of pink and green, blue and black, banded with violet and gold, wove around her, occasionally their fins or tails brushing her legs. This was a world as mysterious and beautiful as the heavens. The ground she had stood on only moments before fell away. How could she have never done this before? *Kat would love this,* she thought. For a moment, panic and guilt shot through her. She should be searching for her sister, not swimming in the sea. And then she remembered that they would have to wait for the ferry back to Playa and pushed the guilt aside.

Jack swam close and took her hand again, a gesture that felt so natural she didn't resist. They swam side by side. Occasionally she would feel a gentle tug, and he would point with his free hand to a fish she might have missed or a mound of coral. He squeezed her fingers and pointed at something below. So unexpected was the sight that it took her a moment for her brain to digest what her eyes were seeing. Perhaps thirty feet below stood a larger-than-life statue of Christ, arms outstretched, the base embedded in the sand. They hovered for a while above it. The figure had grown dark and mossy with ocean growth. After a while they swam on, passing over a half-buried cannon and the curved bones of a sunken fishing boat. Again, he squeezed her fingers. Now they were above a brass Madonna rising from a starfish pedestal. Unlike the statue of Christ, the Madonna had been scrubbed clean and shone like Mayan gold. Someone had tied an offering of red silk blossoms around her strangely amphibian feet. The blowsy flowers swayed and undulated, attracting curious fish who nibbled at the petals before swimming away. Again Maddie felt her heart open, and tears unexpectedly blurred her vision behind the mask.

At last they turned and headed back to the beach. He helped her up the flat rocks that served as steps. Her legs felt shaky from the exertion. She saw the taxi waiting for them in the parking lot. Víctor stood beside it. She took off the flippers and mask, handed them to Jack. "Thank you," she said. To his credit, he did not gloat. When she walked back to the changing hut, she no longer felt shrunken.

Whatever lay ahead, she would carry with her the memories of this day. Of the underwater world achingly beautiful and full of magic. The unexpected vision of the two statues of Christ and the Madonna. She would remember, too, how free it had felt to stand openly with only the black bathing suit for cover, and then enter the water and swim. She felt a renewed sense of strength and determination.

Whatever it took, she would find Kat. She would not give up.

As if he had read her mind, Jack leaned in and said, "It's going to be all right, Maddie." His voice was sure and calm.

She wanted to believe him.

KATHERINE

The sky was moonless, and Kat had only the light of a single tiki torch by the poolside with which to see. She let the robe fall to the ground and entered the water. Nude. There was no one but Verner and Mercer to see her thin body. She stood for a moment, letting the water surround her, and then began to swim. Even wasted, something in her muscles, some vestige of strength, took over. She set out for the far end of the pool. She was growing stronger. She could reach almost the center before she needed to rest. She hung on the lip of the pool and took the opportunity to scan the surroundings. On a previous evening she had seen a shed close to the main house and remembered on her first or second visit she had watched a pool boy retrieve a container of fuel to refill the tiki torches. She did not let her eyes linger there, but she filed away the information.

After a few minutes Verner left. Mercer stayed. Finally, when Kat could swim no longer, Mercer led her back to her room, holding firmly to her arm with the grip that always was separated just one degree from cruel. Kat peered into the shadows of the night but could see no one within earshot, no one who might hear her calls for help. Verner had always been careful in that way. As they made their way back to the concrete building set aside from the main building of the clinic, the sounds of the jungle came to her. Wild sounds she did not recognize. For once she was grateful for the wall that surrounded the clinic. At last, when she was sure she could go no farther, they reached the concrete building. She was weak from the effort of swimming and the walk to and from the pool, but not as fatigued as she had been the time before. As impossible as it seemed, she appeared to be getting better. Perhaps things could be reversed. If one part of the protocol had caused the accelerated aging, couldn't something else do the opposite? Perhaps she would be the miracle Verner had dedicated his life to finding.

Then she remembered the Mexican girl weeping, the harvesting of fetal tissues. Even if Verner had discovered his miracle, at what cost? At what cost?

She knew that nothing, not even her own life, could ever exonerate him for what he had done.

MADISON

She and Jack, as if by mutual agreement, did not talk during the ferry ride back to Playa. At one point she brought the guidebook to where Víctor stood in the bow and asked him if he had any other idea of where she might look for Kat. He considered the horizon, then asked if she had been to the police station. She had told him that information earlier on the ride to the island and was surprised he had forgotten. Perhaps he had not listened as intently as it had appeared.

They arrived back at Playa to a village buzzing with activity. Men stood on ladders hanging strings of lights along the eaves of buildings and looping from poles to poles along the seaside walk. Women and girls were wrapping colorful banners and streamers on anything that stood still.

"What's going on?" Maddie said.

"They are preparing for the fiesta," Víctor said. "For the Masquerade."

"When is that?" Jack asked.

"Tomorrow. It is good you will be here."

Maddie knew of the Mexicans' love of festivals and celebrations. "What is it for?" she asked.

"Originally it was called the Fiesta del San Isidro. He was the patron saint of farmers, and there was a blessing of the seeds and animals. The *padre* still does the blessing, but mainly it is now an excuse to party."

"What happens?" Jack asked.

"There's a masquerade, a parade where everyone wears costumes and masks. And a fishing contest and dancing and fireworks. The festival starts in the morning and lasts until after midnight."

Maddie snorted. Another tourist attraction. Another one of the *memories* they both were so eager for her to take with her when she left. She felt as if the reason they had come to Playa was being pushed into the background.

At the foot of the pier, they said goodbye to the diver and parted ways.

"Well, that was a wasted day," she said to Jack as Víctor walked away.

He gazed at her in silence. "Not entirely wasted," he said.

She didn't answer. Couldn't he understand that if she didn't find Kat, everything was wasted? Nothing—not any snorkeling or festival—would matter if she returned home learning nothing about what had happened to her sister.

"What's the plan now?" he said.

"I need a shower," she said, her voice cool. Now the excursion to Cozumel seemed nothing more than an indulgence. The only real clues she had of where Kat had definitely been were right here in Playa. She headed toward the hotel.

"A shower sounds good," Jack said, his tone so cheerful it annoyed her.

They passed the spot where she had seen the fortune-teller earlier. The table and chair and wooden frame were still there, but the wares that she had seen hanging from the rods were gone. So, too, were the woman and the canary.

"Hold on a sec," Jack said. "I could use something to eat before dinner." He led her into the bakery. The air was thick with the aroma of yeast and honey, sugar and vanilla. A young boy waited behind the counter. "What would you like?" Jack asked her.

"I'm all set," she said. While he purchased a sweet roll, she pointed out the fortune-teller's table. "Where is the woman?" she asked the boy.

"She is gone for *siesta*. She will be back later."

A *siesta*. At the word she felt the lingering heat of the day, mingled with the exertion of swimming at Cozumel, wash over her. A shower would help, and then she would head back out again to resume her canvassing of the shops.

She intended to rest on the bed for only a minute or two, to get a second wind, but she fell asleep almost as soon as she stretched out on the low bed, and when she woke, in the hazy place of half sleep, as if of its own accord her hand reached across the bed for Jack. In spite of her best intentions and the insistence that they were to be no more than friends, there were moments when she was finding it more difficult to hold to this intent.

Her irritation with him faded. Snatches of memory from the day swam before her eyes. The kapok trees, the busy streets of San Miguel. Chankanaab Park. The feeling of sun and water on her body, the fish too beautiful to be real, and the sunken statues. Had the Madonna really had feet of fins, or was that only a slip of memory left from a dream? In the haze of half waking, it all seemed a dream. Had she really stood on a beach in public, revealing her scars? Had she really let Jack lead her into the water? The events of the morning and afternoon seemed a fantasy. Out of that dream came Jack's words. *What you most fear is the thing you must face.*

What did she most fear? The answer came quickly. The loss of Kat. She rose and dressed. Tonight she would go in every bar, every restaurant, talk to every street vendor and waiter and person she encountered. She would return to the police station, exhaust every possibility. If at the end she learned nothing, she would tell Jack it was time to head back to Cancún and get a flight home. If she couldn't find Kat, there was nothing left for her here. If Kat wasn't here, she would have to face that worst fear. The thought added urgency to her step. Determined to stay focused, she passed Jack's room without knocking. She was here to find Kat, not to make more memories with him.

Downstairs, as she walked toward the dining terrace of the hotel, she was overtaken by a roar of female laughter. A group of women wearing T-shirts that said FoB in purple letters on the front were gathering by the bar. By the tenor of the laughter, they had been there for a while. At the center of the group was a blonde with a crown of yellow vanilla flowers on her head. Her shirt read BRIDE. Their gaiety made Maddie feel sharply alone.

She went into three restaurants, each crowded and noisy with voices and music and laughter, as if the fiesta, too eager to wait another day, had already begun. She shoved her way through, showing Kat's photo again and again. At last she came to one café with four tables aligned in front. The sign above the door read MÁSCARA. She knew this word. Masks. Such coincidences were not to be ignored. She went inside.

A tall, fit-looking woman who appeared to be an American in late middle age approached, eying her with curiosity. "How many in your party?" she asked, although it was clear that Maddie was alone.

"Just one," she said.

The woman led her to a table by the window and handed her a menu. "Can I get you something to drink? Our margaritas are famous in Playa."

The idea of tequila made her queasy. On an empty stomach—had she really had nothing since the fruit at breakfast?—it was probably wiser to stay away from anything alcoholic. Then again, wise was not always what was needed. "I'll have a beer," she said.

"Corona or Negra Modelo?"

"If you have the Modelo on tap, I'll take that." She settled back in the chair and felt tightness in her shoulders, a scratchiness of her shirt fabric against her skin, and realized that she had a sunburn from swimming at the park on Cozumel. Again she felt the pang of guilt that she had been snorkeling and—*admit it,* she scolded herself—had allowed the search for Kat to recede for those minutes.

The waitress returned with the beer and set two saucers and a plate of grilled tortilla wedges on the table. She pointed to one of the saucers. "Tomatillo guacamole," she said. "Compliments of the house. And this is *sikil pak*."

Maddie smiled. "Not a clue," she said.

"Pumpkin-seed dip. Try it."

Maddie took the smallest of the wedges and scooped up a small portion of the dip. "Delicious," she announced. She reached into the tote for Kat's picture. The edges were growing slightly dog-eared. She should have protected it with a folder. "I'm looking for my sister. I was wondering if you've seen her."

The waitress took the photo. "Is she here for the fiesta?"

"No. At least I don't think so. She flew here a few weeks ago and hasn't returned home. I haven't heard from her."

The waitress held the photo nearer to her face, examining it closely. "I don't think so," she said. "And I have a pretty good memory for faces. Have you checked with the police?"

"Yes. The State Department had already sent a photo ahead and a missing person alert."

"State Department. Wow, you are really worried."

"Yes."

"I'm sorry. I wish I could help."

Maddie took the photo back. "Me too." She heard the despair in her voice.

"Was she alone?"

"As far as I know."

"Then I definitely would have remembered her. I don't often see women traveling solo," the waitress said.

"Really?" Maddie looked at her more closely, wondering what she was doing in Playa. "How long have you been here?"

"Seven years."

"Seven years? You live here, then?"

"I do now. Originally from Canada. Winnipeg. I came down one year when I couldn't take one more winter of snow and ice."

"And you stayed."

"I did. I fell in love with the place. The people. The music and art. The culture, you know? The pace of life. I kept extending my stay until it became obvious to me that this was where I wanted to live full time. So I bought this place." She extended a hand. "My name's Eve. Short for Evelyn."

"Madison. Though everyone calls me Maddie."

"Welcome to Playa, Maddie. Where are you staying?"

"The Hotel Molcas."

"That's a good place. I know Ramón, the owner. Tell him I said he's to treat you right or he'll have to answer to me." She winked. "We girls have to stick together."

"Thanks, but I'm leaving soon." The taste of failure filled her mouth and she took a sip of beer, as if it could so easily be washed away. "What about your family? Are they here, too?"

"No family." Eve laughed. "I've been happily divorced for twelve years." Two couples entered. She excused herself and went to seat them. Maddie watched her walk away, her stride relaxed. A woman who moved easily.

Even if Kat had decided to make a radical change, as Eve had, there would be no need for secrecy. Maddie's head ached from thinking about it. And from hunger.

The menu was simple. A selection of local dishes. *Sopa de pescado.* Tacos and *ceviche.* Fish *fajitas. Cochinita pibil* and *pollo pibil. Arroz* and *jaibas.* Beside each item was a translation in English. The dips and tortilla had dampened the little appetite she had. She passed on the chicken, pork, and crab dishes and settled on the fish soup.

"Another beer?" Eve asked.

"Better not. I'll have a coffee, though." The jolt of caffeine would give her energy to continue searching the back streets of the village.

Around her, the tables were filling with early diners. She smoothed the edges of Kat's photo and slipped it back into her tote. Her fingers encircled the quartz heart. She held the talisman tightly and closed her eyes briefly. When she opened them, she saw through the window a white van coming into view. She was struck by the anomaly of such a clean white vehicle among the old dusty cars of the village. There were blue letters on the side of the van, and she read them idly. And then with a shock of recognition.

Retirada de la Playa. The words embroidered on the robe in Kat's bathroom in DC.

VÍCTOR

The cantina was crowded and smelled of men and beer and cigarettes and the oily undertone of tequila. Víctor sat in the corner. He knew he should have something to eat and then go home and sleep, but he raised his glass and took a deep swallow. Already, in the short time since he had left the couple at the pier, he had managed to get drunk. Perhaps he should have stuck to beer, but he had needed something stronger, something he wouldn't piss away before it could help him forget. Tomorrow he would have a headache and be unable to dive, but this did not concern him now.

He recalled the image of the woman in the photo Madison had shown him. Katherine. He recalled how at the first sight of her, he had the inexplicable sense that they had met. Later, she had confessed she had felt the same way. It had been a long time since he had lost himself to a woman. He remembered a woman in Texas, a woman with calloused hands from handling horses and eyes that held laughter. Her name had been Suzanna. She had been his last real love, and that had been years ago. She had been married. He raised his hand and signaled that he would have another drink. An arm slid across his back in an easy embrace, and a thick hand gripped his shoulder. It was not his friend Antonio who sat at the bar and knew to leave Víctor alone when he was like this. This was Pedro Gonsalves. He was sweating and his face was red.

"Take it easy, my friend," Pedro said.

Víctor shrugged off the arm. He did not need advice. Someone began to sing. He recognized the voice of José Ventura, and he spat on the floor in disgust. José was a dog who could not sing on key if the angels themselves crept into his mouth. The noise of his off-pitch singing was an insult to the ears.

"Someone should shut him up," he said to Pedro. Even drunk, he could sing better than José.

"You sing," Pedro said.

Juliana Morales left the bar she was tending and sashayed over to José. She took the guitar from him. "Víctor's turn," she said. José gave her a fierce look and slunk into the shadows. She brought the guitar to Víctor. He cradled it in his arms, his hands stroking the worn wood. He took a moment to tune the strings. Even drunk, his ear was truer than the ear of that dog José.

His voice swelled and ebbed, as liquid as the tide, pulling the listeners in. When Víctor lived for a while in Mexico City, he'd worked in a bar, earning more in one night than he did in a week of diving with tourists in Playa. The women told him he looked like the singer Pedro Iglesias. He could have had his choice of any of them. But as he sang, he did not think of them or of the untrue woman in Texas. He thought of the two sisters. The scarred and scared one who was braver than she knew and the other sister, the one of mystery who looked out of the photo and straight into his heart, just as she had the first time they met. The song grew sadder. Many times that day, he had come close to confiding in Madison, but extreme caution had silenced him. Once entangled in a situation, it was not easy to remove oneself. He imagined interviews with the police, pictured the suspicion their faces would wear. It was serious business when an American woman went missing. He knew nothing. There was nothing he could do. He knew no more about where Katherine had gone than her sister did. But would people believe that?

When he finished the song, he put the guitar on the bar and reached for the glass that Juliana pushed toward him.

"Another," a voice called. "Sing us another."

He shook his head. "Please, Víctor," Juliana said. "For me." Already his music had softened her eyes. Another night he might have reached for her, but now he brushed her aside. He stood, wavered, drunker than he had thought.

"Where are you going?" she asked.

He did not answer. As he left the cantina, he heard the sound of laughter. "A woman," Juan Torres was saying in a knowing voice.

"*Sí,*" said Juan Santos. "A woman has taken Víctor to the street of bitterness."

Fuck them, he thought. He staggered toward the sea. The salt air and breeze would clear his head. *Forget the sisters,* he told himself. But then he remembered standing afar and even from that distance being able to see the brave look on the woman's face as she stood revealing her body marked by scars. And the image of her sister, the one who had stirred his frozen heart, swam before his eyes.

There was one person who could help him, one person who knew things no one else could see, but he did not like the idea of going to Tia Clara. He knew the old woman would not welcome him. The grudge between them was long-standing and so entrenched it ran in his blood. He did not know the cause of this ill will, but it had been a part of his life for as long as he could remember. Even when he was a boy, Tia Clara had been cold to him. She had never crushed him to her or stroked his hair or smiled at him as he had seen her do with others. When another boy had cried of a headache, she would touch his brow and wrap halves of split beans to his temples, causing the ache to disappear, but Víctor believed he could be blind with pain from an earache and she would not mix a tea of *manzanilla* or drip the juice of the pita cactus into his ear. But still, he always felt her eyes on him. And if he glanced at her, he could catch her with a look of hate in her black eyes. No. It was unthinkable to go to her now. She would only laugh and turn him away.

Still his feet continued along the sand, taking him toward her, glad now for the many glasses of tequila. Only drunk could he bring himself to beg before Tia Clara.

To ask her what she knew of the woman who had haunted his heart and disappeared.

TIA CLARA

Deep in the center of her bones, Tia Clara was tired. She knew sleep would not bring relief, for it was not weariness of the body alone that drained her. It was her spirit that bore exhaustion with a relentlessness that aged and plagued her. It was the sickness of memory.

She was thinking these things when she heard the pounding on her door. Her hand flew to her chest, felt the rapid beating of her heart beneath her skin. Who could be coming to her door? At this hour and rapping with such fury, such a messenger could only mean misfortune. She crossed the floor and prepared herself to face straight on whatever waited there. Even so, she was unable to control the groan that escaped her when she opened the door and looked into the face of Víctor Díaz.

"Tia Clara," he began.

"What do you want here?"

"Your help," he said.

He was drunk. She saw that at once and knew that without drink he would not have come to stand at her door like a beggar. Years had passed since she had been this close to him, so close she could touch him without extending her arm, but she did not reach out. When she looked into his eyes, eyes so familiar even now after all these years, she felt a sharpness like sticks in her chest.

"You are drunk." Her voice was harsh in an effort to calm the panic that tightened her throat. "You stink of it."

"Por favor," he said, whining on her doorstep like a beaten dog.

Once, perhaps, the sight of his pain might have moved her, but now, looking into his eyes—eyes that reminded her of all that she had once had and all that she had lost so long ago—the old bitterness filled her heart.

"I need your help," he said.

"There is nothing I can do for you." His voice plagued her, as haunting to her ears as his eyes had been. What devil had sent him here to torment her?

"You know things," he said.

"I have nothing for you."

"Not for me. For another. A *norteamericana.* She is looking for her *hermana.*"

"What do you care?" she spat out. "What business is it of yours?"

"I want to help her." She saw this was a half truth, and he still held back why he had come to her.

"You are a fool." She saw in his face the pain of one lost, so like his *padre* it nearly stopped her heart. It was this pain that forced the next words out. "Forget about her. This *gringa* is nothing to you. And the *hermana* she looks for is nothing. She is a foolish woman." Too late, she saw that she had revealed too much and that, even in his drunkenness, Víctor saw this.

"You know about her sister?"

Tia Clara took a step back, suddenly afraid.

"Where is she?"

"I do not know," she said, hoping he was too drunk to detect the lie. "Now go." She closed the door, shutting out the sight of him. She waited, listening for his footsteps to leave, ignoring the sound of his voice calling to her. Eventually he fell silent. She heard him stumble over the pot by the door that held a planting of sage. She crossed back to the wood chair. The fly remained on the rim of the cup. The past, she knew, was not dead. It was not like a door that could be shut and sealed. It remained forever alive with her.

On her wedding day, the village had been surrounded with a rosy light, the edges of which shone with gold. Too happy to sleep, Clara had woken early. Her wedding dress was folded over the back of a chair and glowed in the light of dawn. It was white, with tiny flowers stitched across the bodice. Even her *madre's* disapproval of the groom had not kept her from making the wedding dress. When it was finished, Clara had slipped it on and known that it had made her beautiful. For one day, she would be the most beautiful girl in Playa del Pedro. More beautiful, even, than Consuelo. *Today,* she'd thought as she stared at the garment, *today is the best day of my life.*

The sleeping sounds of her family filled their small *casa.* She tried to foresee what awaited her. Tonight, for the first time in her life, she would not sleep in this house. Tonight she would sleep beside Felipe Manuel Vazquez, the handsome reformed *bandito* who today would become her husband.

It was impossible for Clara to lie still any longer. Before the others awoke, she would go to the forest and ask the talking tree about her future. She slipped from the hammock and ran on bare feet from the house. The grass around the base of the talking tree was flat, trampled by the feet of the villagers who came to seek answers to the questions of their lives. Fearlessly, Clara stood where so many had before her. Birds cawed and sang in the jungle. She heard the words in her head, ready to be spoken. *Tell me about Felipe Manuel Vazquez?* she would ask. *Will we be happy? Will our firstborn be a son? Strong and tall like his father?* She believed that asking the talking tree was only a tradition, and she would receive the answer she already knew in her heart. Who could doubt his love?

At that moment a cloud had passed before the rising sun, casting the jungle into darkness. For that instant the birds had ceased their song. Because of this she ran back to her home before she could give voice to her questions and did not hear the answer she now knew the talking tree would have given her. *One year,* it would have told her. *You and your* bandito *will have one year of happiness.*

And so it was. Exactly one year passed, and the pink and gold shell that had shimmered around the village began to fade, replaced by a somber shade of red. At first, Clara had misread the significance of this and believed the coming of the red fire meant only that the passion she felt for Manny (as she alone called him), and he for her, had grown and deepened, and soon the flower of his seed would take root in her and grow.

When Manny had come to her and revealed his secret, the secret that had caused the delicate color of her universe to darken, she had wept. How could it be so? How could her Manny have fallen in love with Consuelo?

The news had made her sick with fever, but once she regained her strength, because even then she knew she was stronger than he, stronger than Consuelo, she began to plan. It had been a mistake, and she could forgive his weakness. Even if he had left his past behind, he still remained a *bandito* and could not resist the theft of her sister's heart. He was not at fault. Consuelo had bewitched him. Clara began to gather the herbs that would return him to her. One night she slipped her potion into his drink. And she waited. And he came to her and asked forgiveness.

All might have been well had his seed taken root in her belly and not in Consuelo's. And as her sister's belly grew, a corresponding bitterness grew inside Clara's heart. She could not look at Manny without picturing them, their arms and legs entangled, Consuelo's black hair spread across his unfaithful chest. Consuelo's scent—so like the yellow flower of the vanilla plant and the bark of the cinnamon tree—staining his skin. As Consuelo's belly grew, so did the gossip of the villagers. They wondered who had fathered the child. Consuelo, more beautiful than ever, even swollen with child, would not speak of him. And Clara kept the secret. And planned.

After the birth of the child, a beautiful boy—even she had to admit the infant was beautiful—she melted wax and formed it into a candle. She drew figures in the air with its flame and wove her magic, a spell that would make the child grow weak and ill and cause her sister to grow ugly with grief, magic that would free Manny from Consuelo's witchcraft and return him to her bed. And the child did fall sick, and Consuelo did grow thin and worn with worry. It was then that the magic failed Tia Clara and all went wrong. Manny, her Manny, went into the jungle to find the root of the tree that would cure his child. When he didn't return, Clara went looking for him. She found him at the base of the tree, dead from the poison of a snake. When Consuelo learned of Manny's death, she did not weep. The next day she walked into the sea. The villagers, ignorant of the truth, believed that because her infant son was dying, Consuelo had become mad with grief. How else to explain such an act? Only Clara knew the truth. She knew it was not the venom of the snake that had caused the death of her husband, but Clara's own magic, created from the poison of a jealous heart. And such poison had killed her sister as well. Only the infant had escaped to remind her of what she had done.

Tia Clara stared at the canary, unmoving in its cage, its green feathers dull. Soon it, too, would die. Fear moved in her chest, curling like a serpent. Why had Víctor, a man born of the betrayal of the two she had loved most, come to her now? What help did he want of her? For a moment her vision cleared, and she saw the depth of the pain in his heart, but it was nothing compared to the pain she felt when she confronted her own future. Then she glimpsed his future and saw that more pain was waiting for him, but there was more she saw and this caused as much distress as his unhappiness had. She saw a future circled with the rose-gold of love.

If once power was used for evil, could it still be used for good?

Was it too late now for her soul to be saved?

She was an old woman, afraid of dying, but there was one thing she could do. She would go to the hotel and tell the *gringa* mask maker what she knew about her missing sister. She doubted helping the two sisters in this way would balance her own sins that had led to Consuelo's death, but if she could lead Consuelo's son one step closer to his rose-tinged future, perhaps the ghosts that shadowed her days would forgive her.

GRACIELA

There was a commotion in the hall outside her door.

The voices of the doctor and *Señorita* Mercer. A door opening, closing, opening again. She lay still, ready to feign sleep if they should look in on her. She concentrated on the noises in the hall, trying to learn from them what was happening. Had the weeping woman left her room again and collapsed in the hall?

By listening carefully and befriending the Mayan, Rosa, Graciela had come to learn a little more about this place. She learned that she was the only girl there now. Before her there had been two others. She knew, too, that Rosa was afraid of the doctor.

Now she heard footsteps in the corridor and a metallic, familiar noise. She listened to the rhythm of the whirr of wheels. The rolling bed was being pushed down the hall. She stiffened in panic. This was what they had brought to take her to the bad room with the cold table and hard instruments. The room where the doctor with cruel hands touched her.

Were they coming for her again? Icy dread crept up her spine. She held her breath and cupped her hands over her belly, as if that would protect her unborn child.

Perhaps if she were quiet enough, they would forget her. She waited for the door to open and for the two attendants to come into the room. The first time they'd come, she had tried to fight when they had lifted her and set her on the metal table. Remembering how she had been held down, hands clamping down on her mouth so hard she feared she would not be able to breathe, straps quickly pinning her on the table, her strength no match for theirs, she knew that fighting was useless in this place. Her heart beat wildly as she waited for them to come and roll her to the room with the bright lights where the *norteamericano* with the devil face waited for her.

She closed her eyes against the memory of what had happened in that room. The blood they had taken from her arm. The way they had placed her feet in cold metal, exposing her, revealing her shame. And then hands would press against her stomach, and fingers—quick and cruel as his eyes—poked into her private place. Only Ángel had ever touched her there, but his hands had not been like this. His caress had been gentle and teasing until she had been filled with heat and cried out for him with eagerness. But on the cold table she had cried out in terror.

Her fear did not release until the footsteps had passed by her door. If they were not coming for her, where were they going? She tiptoed to the door and pressed her ear against the wood and heard the faint mewing sound of an animal in pain. She wondered who they were taking to the bad room now.

She began to pray to the Virgin, asking that her *padre* come for her. Come to save her from this place of death. She pictured him as he sat next to her on the bench by the sea, his rough hand holding hers. Or behind the wheel of his rusting taxi as he drove a tourist to Cancún. If there was only one passenger, he sometimes allowed her to ride along. So strong was her desire to see him that she could almost feel him coming. The feeling was becoming a certainty. Her *padre* was coming. He was near. Very near.

MADISON

Maddie stared at the lettering on the white van. RETIRADA DE LA PLAYA. How could she have forgotten what now seemed so obvious? The same words that were stitched on the white robe she had seen in Kat's bathroom. The robe, not Kat's credit card statements, had been the first clue.

She felt a quickening beneath her breastbone. She looked around. Evelyn was at the bar pouring a lurid pink drink into two squat glasses. "Eve," she called, her voice urgent, rising above the music. "Eve."

The owner glanced over and held up a finger, signaling she would be over in a minute.

Maddie waited impatiently, keeping an eye on the van, afraid it would drive off before Eve came to her table. She grabbed a pen from her tote and copied the words on the paper mat on the table, mentally urging Eve to hurry.

"What is it, hon? Is something the matter?"

Maddie pointed out the window, where the van had stopped to allow a small group to cross in front of it. As they watched, it started up and lurched forward. "That van," she said. "Do you know anything about it?"

Eve craned her neck to catch sight of the vehicle as it continued by the restaurant. "Oh, sure. The van comes through here several times a week driving guests to and from the airport in Cancún."

"So it belongs to a hotel or resort?"

"No. It's from the place outside of town. I don't know what it is exactly. A spa or a clinic."

"What kind of spa?"

"Or a clinic. Like I said, I'm not exactly sure. I've never been there. And doubt I ever will. It probably costs a fortune to get a massage or treatment there. Places like that are beyond my budget."

"That's all you know?"

"Just about. Occasionally I overhear customers say a few things. Sometimes some of them spend a night or two in the village before they head back home, and they come here to eat." She glanced over at the bar, checked the other tables.

"You said you've overheard them talking. What do they say?"

"Not a lot. Kind of interesting, but twice I've heard women say exactly the identical phrase: 'He works miracles.' That's what made me think it might be more than a high-end spa and was also a place where people got plastic surgery and lipo and all those procedures people chase to stay young."

"Plastic surgery?" Maddie remembered the time Kat had "had a little work done."

"Could be. That's just a guess. Like I said, I don't know exactly. The locals don't know a lot about it. The owner hires help from elsewhere. You know how some places have a mystique about them, and rumors grow because they're so secretive? Some people in Playa think it's a clinic for cancer patients."

"Do you think so?" *Cancer.* Each time she had permitted the idea of Kat being really ill, her heart caught and skipped a beat.

"It's possible. Desperate people have always crossed the border for medicine that isn't legal in the States. I remember reading somewhere that the actor Steve McQueen came to Mexico for injections of medicine extracted from apricot kernels. Can't remember what it was called, but I do know whatever he was getting was illegal to get in the States."

"Laetrile," Maddie said, although she didn't know why she knew this.

Eve returned to the subject at hand. "People who are desperate will try any measure, no matter how far out or dangerous it is."

Maddie remembered the syringe in Kat's bathroom. Was Kat ill after all and receiving treatments not approved or sanctified by the government? "How can I get there?"

"It's outside of the town. A taxi can take you there, but at this hour, you probably won't have any luck."

Now, for the first time since arriving, she had a solid lead. Grounded in real evidence. She cursed herself for overlooking so obvious a clue as the robe in Kat's home. Especially after she'd learned that Kat had flown to Mexico and stayed in this village.

Her first instinct was to return to the hotel and find Jack, tell him what she had learned. Almost immediately she changed her mind. She had a growing certainty that she would find Kat at this clinic or spa or whatever it was and, in fairness to her sister, she would wait until she had learned from Kat herself why she was there. She would keep her sister's secret. If Kat was there for a cosmetic procedure, that was her own business, and she wouldn't want Maddie telling everyone. If it turned out she was ill and had chosen to keep this secret while she pursued the possibility of a cure—wherever it led her—then Maddie would be there for her. As Kat had always been there for her. Urgency overtook her and she wanted to go straight to the clinic, but it was too late to start now. As hard as it was, she corralled her impatience. In the morning she would make her way to Retirada de la Playa.

Her immediate problem was to think of what she would tell Jack, the excuse she could give him that would explain where she was while she went to the clinic without him. By the time she left the restaurant, the streets had become more crowded and now had a heightened sense of celebration. Everyone she passed seemed to be holding a bottle of beer or a drink in a plastic cup.

As she approached the hotel, the sound of the mariachi band, its melding of strings and brass, rolled toward her. People in the streets were rocking to its rhythm. As she drew closer, she saw the men were dressed in ornate black outfits trimmed with gold braid and sequins— except for one of the two trumpet players. She saw with astonishment that it was Jack.

He had not seen her and she hung back, half concealed in the crowd. *How like him,* she thought. *A stranger in the country, in this village, and yet within forty-eight hours he's become part of it. And that's the way he'll always be,* she thought, *open to adventure, open to life.*

It was what he had offered her. And what she had refused. And would continue to refuse.

She could never be what he wanted. Could never be who he thought she was.

TIA CLARA

This was the first time Tia Clara had been inside the walls of the Hotel Molcas—she had never had cause to go. She remembered the time before the hotel had been built, remembered how, even with her gift, she had not foreseen the many changes that would come to Playa. She headed for the lobby, pushing her way through the throng of revelers that filled the terrace, weaving around the waiters who were trying to negotiate the crowds as they made their way to tables while holding trays of food and drink. Although the fiesta and the masquerade parade did not officially begin until the next day, already some of the revelers were wearing masks and behaving with the abandon that such masks so often allowed. Tomorrow, Tia Clara knew, it would be worse.

Luis Castillo stood behind the lobby desk, flashed his gold-edged smile, and listened to her describe the *gringa* with the scarred face, no doubt wondering what the old fortune-teller could possibly want with her. He seemed to almost refuse her request, but in the end, as if afraid of her power, he picked up the desk phone and punched in the number of the guest's room.

Tia Clara had rehearsed what she would tell the *gringa*. She would tell her what she knew about where her sister had gone. She would not tell her what the sea had revealed, only where the woman was. She already regretted coming and, although it had not occurred to her that the woman of masks would not be at the hotel, when the calls to her room went unanswered, she was relieved. She had tried. That had absolved her of her duty. What happened now was no business of hers.

She could not save everybody.

GRACIELA

She woke to the shrill sound of the barking dog. She had again been dreaming of the Mayan girl painted in blue and wreathed in sweet smoke of the copal as she was prepared for the sacrifice to come. But this morning the memory of the dream did not keep her in the grip of its talons. This day she was freed from fear because she remembered that her *padre* was coming for her. As it had been the night before, this knowledge was so powerful and sure she could almost hear the familiar coughing of the taxi's old engine, the rattle of its rusty body. She closed her eyes and felt the closeness of her father.

When she returned home, she would face her *madre*'s anger and disappointment. She would work to earn their forgiveness. She would not lie again with Ángel until they had been wed. Above all, she would never speak to them of this place and the evil that filled the air.

MADISON

Maddie woke early. She was edgy with excitement and anticipation—much as she had felt as a child when she woke on her birthday or the first day of school.

She had expected only stragglers on the streets after the late night—she had woken at two to hear the sounds of pre-fiesta revelry showing no signs of abating—but even now the streets were already coming alive. Men with fishing gear headed toward the pier, and she remembered that the diver Víctor had told them there was a fishing tournament today. Vendors were setting up tables with their wares. Music blared from the loudspeakers above the chapel in the square. Jack was nowhere in sight. She unfolded the note she had found slipped beneath her door when she had returned to her room the night before.

"Tried to find you earlier. I'm going out to get something to eat. I have my cell with me. Call when you get in." She hadn't called him, and once, just as she was falling asleep, the phone in her room had rung, but she hadn't answered. It was easier to withhold the truth when he couldn't hear her voice or see her face. She knew he would insist on going with her and would not understand why she needed to go alone. She slipped down the hall, and when she crossed the lobby she was relieved not to see him. She left a message for him at the desk, telling him she was going to continue to canvass the shops and restaurants she had missed the day before. With luck she would find Kat and would return to Playa by evening.

Evelyn had said the clinic was on the outskirts of the village but hadn't given her an idea of the distance. Eager to get going before Jack appeared, she left the hotel. She stopped a woman sweeping the street in front of the hotel and showed her the paper with the name she had written the night before. "Is this nearby?" she asked.

The woman read the name and looked up at her with an expression she was unable to read.

Maddie pulled out the dictionary and checked the section on useful phrases. "*Qué distancia hay?* Can I walk there, do you think?" She scissored two fingers in the air, mimicking walking.

The woman shook her head.

She checked her dictionary again. "*El camión?* A bus?" She remembered the white van with blue lettering.

"No," the street sweeper said. "A taxi." She pointed out the location of the taxi stand. It was only two blocks from the hotel, by the bakery where Jack had purchased a sweet roll. Near where the fortune-teller sat.

"*Gracias,*" she said.

Two women wearing purple turbans passed her. A young girl in a traditional wedding dress and mantilla hurried by, whether in costume or rushing to a ceremony Maddie could not tell. A man with a basket of cheap masks approached and tried to sell her one. She brushed by him. As if a silent signal had been sounded, more and more people appeared, many fully costumed. A tall man crossed the *calle*, his head and shoulders entirely covered by a papier-mâché horse head. Unbidden, an Oscar Wilde quote came to mind: *Give a man a mask and he will tell you the truth.*

A Pontiac, one whose finest days were a faint and distant memory, was parked along the curb by the bakery. TAXI was hand-lettered on the sides. A man slept in the driver's seat, his snores floating through the window, so robust that they reached her when she was still several yards away. As she approached the driver's door, she could discern, as well, the sour smell of stale alcohol. She looked around, but there was no other taxi in sight. She spied the fortune-teller at her table across the street. Their eyes met for an instant. The old woman was the first to look away.

Maddie crossed to her. "Is there another taxi?"

"No," the fortune-teller said. She offered no more. Her eyes glittered, and Maddie saw in them something close to grief. Or madness. The two, Maddie knew, were closer than people liked to acknowledge. She retrieved the paper with the name of the clinic and placed it on the table in front of the old woman. "You know of this place?" she asked.

The woman looked at the paper and made a furtive gesture, a quick little flick of her hand. Her lips formed a tight line, as if afraid of what might escape.

Maddie waited.

At last, the fortune-teller nodded. *"Sí,"* she said.

Maddie stepped closer. "You do? You know it?"

The hard black eyes stared into hers. *"Su hermana,"* she said.

"My sister?" Her breath caught in her throat, and she pressed her palm against her heart, as if to slow the rapid beating. "My sister is there?"

The old woman nodded and then turned away, her body stiff.

"Wait," Maddie said. "You're saying she's there? My sister is there?" She searched the old woman's face, resisting the urge to grab her arm and shake more information from her. She fumbled through her tote and pulled out a fistful of pesos, but before she could offer them, the old woman pulled back, her face closed and rigid, and Maddie knew she would say no more.

She crossed back to the taxi, reached inside, and jabbed the shoulder of the sleeping man. He woke with a curse and stared at her with bloodshot eyes.

She showed him the paper on which she had written the name of the clinic.

He stared at it and made the sign of the cross.

She ignored the superstitious gesture and pressed him. "Will you take me there?"

He shook his head. Three men carrying instruments—a violin and guitar and something that looked somewhat like a ukulele—walked toward the bakery from the square. She stepped aside to let them pass. As she did so, she glanced toward the hotel and saw Jack. He was walking in her direction but had not yet seen her. She froze in a moment of indecision. She looked over at the fortune-teller, who only stared back with the steely black eyes. She glimpsed the mask vendor, and giving no more time to thought, ducked toward him. She pointed to a full-face mask of a cheetah. "How much?"

"Mucho dinero," he said.

She held out a fistful of pesos. He betrayed a quick moment of surprise that she didn't try to barter and took several of the bills. She had no idea if she was being cheated. She put on the mask. It was made of cheap cardboard and was rough against her skin. She chanced a glance back toward where she had last seen Jack. He was closer now, his eyes scanning the people. When they landed on her she held her breath, but they quickly passed on.

She returned to the taxi stand and held the rest of the pesos toward the driver.

He eyed the money, an avaricious gleam in his red-rimmed eyes. A moment passed when he seemed to be waging an argument with himself; then he nodded and motioned for her to get into the car.

The vehicle was uninviting. The seat was worn and uncomfortable, its upholstery sun-faded and stained, the origins of which Maddie didn't want to consider. The smell of alcohol and mildew pervaded the interior. The inevitable shrine occupied the dashboard and obstructed part of the view. It was composed of dried palm fronds woven into a cross and a tin fan, shaped like a scallop and with holes punched in it in a lacy design, that cradled a figure of the Madonna. The rear passenger window was operated by a crank that no longer worked. Only the idea of Kat waiting for her kept Maddie from getting out of the car.

As they pulled away from the curb, she was aware of the old fortune-teller's eyes following her. They held the potency of either a curse or a blessing, but who could tell? The driver did not give her his name. There was no identifying tag that she could see. For all she knew, the cab wasn't even registered. As soon as they had pulled away from the curb, she pulled off the mask and threw it on the seat. She checked her glossary of phrases. *"Cómo se llama?"* He gave no indication he had heard her, and she surrendered to silence and the discomfort of the ride.

He drove slowly, as if afraid that going any faster might cause a crucial component of the engine to fail or one of the tires to fall off and roll into a ditch. Her excitement morphed into anxiety, and she rethought her decision to not tell Jack exactly where she was going. To choose loyalty to Kat instead.

After a while—it was difficult to estimate time because of the slow speed of the car—the driver turned onto a narrower dirt road, although Maddie had seen no sign. The road ended at an iron-grilled gate, and the driver stopped there. The gate was shut but did not appear secured and only required that someone push it open to afford access to the long drive beyond. There was a crude shelter on the other side of the gate. A guard sat inside but did not move. In the distance, she saw a large *hacienda* that she assumed was the clinic. Or spa. It looked more like the latter. "Can you drive me there?" she asked the driver, motioning for him to continue.

He shook his head, refusing to meet her eyes. She put this down to drunken remorse and took out another clutch of bills from her tote and offered them, but he could not be persuaded to go beyond the gate. She unlatched the door and got out, grabbing her bag but discarding the mask. Even before she had pushed the gate open enough to enter, the taxi had pulled away. She started walking up the drive. As she passed the gatehouse, she checked out the guard, who looked as if he had just awoken, roused, perhaps, by the sound of the taxi. She waited for him to stop her. He was dressed in a uniform and held a rifle slung loosely over one shoulder. She found it unnerving that there would be an armed guard. Was it really so dangerous here? Well, if he was a sentry, he was not one to count on. Even awake, he seemed inattentive to the job. She continued down the drive. As she drew closer to the large, sprawling building, she passed a patio with chaises where three women lazed beneath umbrellas made of palm fronds, reinforcing her initial impression that the place was a spa. Kat was not one of them. Maddie realized she had been preparing herself to encounter patients. Women with heads wrapped in scarfs who belonged to the sisterhood of the hairless. But the three women she saw looked healthy and fit. She shuffled her mental image. Not a clinic then, but a place where well-off women went to rehab or to recover from divorce and prepare for the future they hoped would include another man. She wondered why Kat had chosen this place. What crisis might she be going through that she hadn't shared with her sister?

Inside the *hacienda*, the lobby was immaculate and sparse. Native art adorned the walls. Two carved wooden doors opened to an elegant dining room. A round table in the center held a towering display of fruit. Two of the smaller tables were occupied with women having breakfast.

She turned to the lobby desk, where a woman in a pale blue uniform waited. Maddie clutched her tote to her side. After the crash she had developed a wariness, a heightened sense of danger. The doctors had told her that this was not unusual when one underwent a traumatic incident and that it would probably pass. It was different from the panic attacks. Surer, less frantic. More a knowing than an irrational panic. Ever since she left Playa, this sense of wariness had been with her, first in the taxi and then as she entered the grounds of this place, past the armed and sleeping guard. She had originally planned on asking about Kat as soon as she arrived, but the deep instinct for caution silenced her. It was as innate as the heightened awareness any woman felt when walking alone down a city street at night. Each sense sharpened, alert. Before she could regroup, the woman at the desk addressed her.

"The others arrived last night and are already in the conference room. The morning session is about to begin. You can come back after lunch to register."

As difficult as it was to contain her impatience, to find Kat, or at least learn when she had last been there, her instincts were to conceal her mission for the moment.

"Okay," she said, grateful for the camouflage of a group to disappear into.

MADISON

The conference room was spacious and airy in spite of the low ceiling. A table along one wall held a tray of sectioned melons and a glass dispenser of water in which floated slices of lemon and orange. An array of squat glass tumblers rimmed in blue sat beside it. There were no windows on three of the walls, but an expanse of glass doors on the fourth gave out to a patio and an azure-tiled pool.

Maddie took a seat in the back row, away from the wall of glass, and checked out those who had assembled, scanning faces looking for Kat. She counted fourteen women, several of them thin to the point of scrawniness. There were two men. One woman looked familiar, but Maddie couldn't place her, although she was positive she had seen her before. There was an energy of anticipation in the air. A low buzz of conversation.

"I mortgaged my house to pay for this," said a brunette seated directly in front of her.

"Your first time here?" a woman to the brunette's left asked the speaker.

"Yes. You've been here before?"

"No. But my girlfriend has. She said he's amazing. A miracle worker."

Maddie realized she had been directed to an orientation meeting for new arrivals. Of course Kat would not be attending. She swallowed back her disappointment and started to leave, but then the door in the rear opened and the room fell silent as quickly and cleanly as if a knife had cut off sound. A woman clad in a white doctor's coat strode to the front. Studying her face, Maddie felt a chill. She saw ambition there. And something else. For one odd moment, Maddie pictured the riven mask of Lady Macbeth, the queen whose singular quality was a lack of humanity. A shudder ran through her, so strong the woman at her side whispered, "Are you okay?"

She nodded and resisted the impulse for escape, to distance herself from the spidery effect of the woman, who began to address the group.

"Good morning," she said. "My name is Helen Mercer, and I am the assistant director of Retirada de la Playa. Dr. Verner will be here shortly. Before he arrives, I want to take a minute or two to review some information in addition to that which is in the packet in your rooms. Immediately after this morning's session, we ask that you stop by registration and pick up your individual schedules, which will include the times for your tests and your treatments at the spa. When you have an opening in your schedule, you are free to walk the grounds, use the pool, or take advantage of some of the classes that are available here.

"We ask that you abide by the few regulations. As you've all read in the material you received prior to arrival, alcohol, drugs, and any smoking materials are not allowed on the property."

A dramatic groan went up from several members of the group.

Mercer flashed a falsely sympathetic smile before continuing. "All of our main buildings and the property are available for your use, but the separate building that houses our laboratory and the staff quarters is off-limits. We also request that for your own safety and well-being you stay within the compound."

Creepy. The word sprang to mind. There was definitely something creepy about this place, with its guards and quasi-military rules and regulations, and Maddie couldn't imagine why Kat would have come here.

"Does that mean we can't explore the areas outside?" one of the men asked.

Irritation flashed across Helen Mercer's face. "For your own safety we require that you stay on the grounds at all times. There are feral dogs that sometimes rove in packs—you will hear them at night. Also, as is true in any country, Mexico is not without crime. We have never had a problem here, but we are vigilant in protecting you from falling prey to undesirable persons. Our security team is top-notch."

Maddie thought of the guard sleeping at the gate.

At that moment the door in the rear again opened. Heads swiveled to look at the man entering. All eyes followed him as he walked to the center of a raised platform. He was tall, with the commanding presence of a general or athlete. He wore light tan trousers with pleats that emphasized his trim waist. His hair, just graying at the temples, was thick, and he wore it long and combed back. His eyes were a clear blue and steely. He wore a short-sleeved shirt that revealed muscular arms. There was an aura of vigor and good health around him and the mesmerizing sense of wealth, health, and power. Maddie scanned the gathering, noticing that every eye remained fixed on him. Helen Mercer slipped from the room.

"I am Dr. Paul Verner," he began. "Welcome to Retirada de la Playa. Welcome to a new you. Welcome to the future."

To Maddie, the words were the clichéd phrases of a snake-oil peddler, and she couldn't imagine Kat of all people buying into it, but those gathered leaned forward as if drawn by the power of a vast magnetic pole. He let silence fill the room and took time to make eye contact with every person. When his eyes caught hers, she froze. For one second, quick as lightning, it was as if his mask had slid and she had a glimpse of the ruthlessness that lay beneath the easy charm. As it had when she had seen the true nature of Mercer, a chill ran through her. What a couple they made: he Iago, she Lady Macbeth. His eyes stayed on her for a long moment before moving on; then he returned his attention to the entire group. "Let me ask you this—how long do you want to live?"

The room was silent. No one responded. "How long," he repeated, "do you want to live? Give me a number."

"One hundred!" one of the two men there shouted.

"Only one hundred?" Verner said.

"One hundred and ten," a woman said.

"Okay," Verner said. "Anyone else?"

"One hundred sounds good to me," said the woman who had seemed familiar to Maddie. On hearing her voice, Maddie placed her—she was an actor on a television series. Others joined in, shouting out numbers.

"Good," Verner said. "Now we're getting somewhere. Now we have a goal to aim for."

A husky voice spoke up. "One hundred and ten sounds fine to me, but only if I'm healthy and not warehoused in some nursing home somewhere, propped up in a wheelchair, being spoon-fed applesauce and waiting to die."

There was a murmur of agreement.

"This is possible. I am going to show you that it is not only possible but realistic to live well beyond one hundred and to do so while being active and healthy, to postpone disease and infirmity, to defer degeneration of your physical and mental powers." He paused to let the promise of the words sink in. "The aging that you witness in your world is not inevitable. Aging is not the normal course of events; it is a disease. And like many diseases, it can be cured. I have found the cure."

Again Maddie wondered how Kat could have swallowed Verner's line, and then she was struck with a new thought: Perhaps Kat hadn't bought into it at all. Perhaps she was here investigating the clinic, in search of a story. She looked at Verner, saw him as Kat would have seen him in this new light.

He had them now. He slowed his pace, allowed his voice to drop. "I know you want to hear the specifics of our work here," he said, "but I'll begin by giving you some history." He paused and took a drink of water. "From time immemorial, mankind has been searching for the fountain of youth, a goal as human and as elusive as the ancient alchemists' desire to transform straw into gold. Modern alchemists have continued this pursuit. In 1889, Charles-Édouard Brown-Séquard experimented with injecting extracts of crushed animal testicles into the limbs of his patients." A murmur of repugnance rose, and he waited for it to subside before continuing. Maddie actually felt ill.

"In the 1920s, the Russian Serge Voronoff built on the work of Brown-Séquard and found success by using extracts of monkey glands." Another quick murmur, more restrained this time. "In fact, Voronoff was a brilliant man. His work has never been disproved. Unfortunately, he was never taken seriously by his peers. His work engendered a powerful and negative response among the world's press, an aversion to the idea of being injected with the sex glands of a primate."

A woman in the front row tittered nervously, and Verner smiled. "Don't worry. I have not brought you here to be injected with the testicles of a monkey." There was another spate of laughter, but Maddie, remembering her glimpse of Iago behind the careful facade, did not join in.

"The next pioneer was Paul Niehans, who worked in Switzerland in the 1930s. Among his many hundreds of patients, many of whom survived to their eighties and nineties, were the rich and famous. Their names are familiar to you: Thomas Mann, Pope Pius XII, Somerset Maugham, and the millionaire Bernard Baruch. It is Niehans's work with cellular therapy that is the vanguard of much research today. His discovery of the role of cell therapy, of the use of injected enzymes, is the key to our work here."

In spite of herself, Maddie felt herself being drawn in, fascinated.

"Unfortunately, as most of you are aware, in the United States, cell therapy is prohibited, although it is perfectly legal in other, more enlightened countries. It is regularly practiced in Argentina, France, Belgium, Italy, Holland, Germany, and Great Britain.

"Like most of you here today, I am an American, but I have been forced to come here, exiled to Mexico, to continue my work and to achieve great breakthroughs. Building on the work of Niehans and Voronoff, I have determined precisely how the body ages." He paused to take another sip of water. "And I have learned how to counteract this aging." The room fell still, so silent it was as if everyone feared that drawing a breath would kill the spell, break the promise. Maddie allowed herself to scan their faces but saw no trace of suspicion. Was she the only one in the room who saw the truth of the man?

"If you have already taken the opportunity to look over the reading material we had waiting for you in your rooms, then you know that researchers in the United States have recently stated that if scientific and medical resources were mobilized, aging could be conquered within the decade. Someday, these scientists and geriatricians proclaim, someday the aging process will be chemically controlled. We will have our morning smoothie of chemical cocktails and drink away the prospect of aging as a disease. It sounds exciting, doesn't it?"

Several people voiced their assent.

"But in fact, the researchers and scientists are mistaken."

"They're wrong?" a woman asked.

"Absolutely and totally in error. Not in the promise that the disease of aging can be cured. They are mistaken in their timeline. It is not necessary to wait a decade. Or five years. Or one year. Here, it is happening now. Today."

A wave of reaction swept the room. He walked to the front edge of the platform. "Permit me a little lecture," he began. "A lecture within a lecture, if you will. How do we age?"

"By having birthdays?"

Maddie recognized the voice as that of the man who had announced he wanted to live to one hundred. Verner acknowledged the joke with a slight bow.

"We age," he said, "because around the time we reach our thirties, our bodies begin to decrease production of several essential hormones, hormones that keep our waists thin and our hair thick, our skin supple and smooth. Hormones that allow us the gift of deeper sleep and an active libido." The two women in front of Maddie nudged each other with their elbows, like teenagers in a sex-education class.

He scanned the room to ensure that everyone was following him. "How many of you have heard of metformin? Or nicotinamide riboside? Nobody?" The room was silent.

"You will be hearing more about them this week. Today and tomorrow, each of you will be going through a battery of tests, and from these tests we will determine the precise state of your body's chemistry. We will then be able to put together for each of you an individual prescription, a cocktail, if you will, that will not only prevent aging, but will actually reverse its effects."

His voice, his manner, everything about Verner reminded Mattie of a present-day version of a carnival pitchman. A huckster. A televangelist. If Kat had indeed been here undercover, it must have been a challenge for her to disguise her disdain. And if her disguise had slipped, how had Verner responded? Where was she? For a moment the question was so urgent, Maddie feared she had spoken aloud.

"I want to conduct an experiment," Verner continued in the oily voice. "Unscientific, perhaps, but revealing. Are you ready? With the fingers of your left hand, pinch the skin on the back of your right hand. Hold it for a minute. Now release."

Around the room, each person nipped a pinch of skin then let go, watched the little mound of flesh retract slowly. Maddie kept her hands clasped tightly in her lap, unwilling to play his game. "Once your skin was as tight and taut as that of an infant," Verner said. "As you grew older, as you were exposed to toxins and preservatives, your bodies became damaged and underwent the process we know as aging. Your skin—the first defense again the poisons of what you have ingested and those of the world you inhabit—reveals the extent of this damage."

He leaped down from the platform and crossed to the first row, extended his hand, pinched the flesh, and let it go. Immediately the skin fell flat, no ridge, no time lapse. He went from person to person, repeating the demonstration, occasionally allowing someone else to pinch his skin. When he returned to the platform, he unbuttoned his shirt and slipped it off. His skin was tan and toned, his chest muscles, like those of his arms, well defined. One of the women, the one Maddie had recognized as the television actor, gave a low wolf whistle. Verner bowed to her and smiled. The others laughed. He dropped to the floor and did thirty one-armed push-ups. When he stood he was breathing easily. He put his shirt on and faced them.

"How old do you think I am?"

No one spoke for a moment as they assessed him, the taut skin and toned muscles, the thick hair with just a touch of gray at the temples.

"Thirty-eight?"

"Forty-one?"

"Forty-three?"

He held up his hand to silence them. "As you will see, I am my own best advertisement." He smiled. "For the past twenty years, I have followed my own regimen. Intelligent nutrition, daily exercise, and the Verner hormone treatment." He leaned forward. "I am seventy-eight."

There were gasps of disbelief.

I'd like to have hard proof, Maddie thought. She was sure he was lying. He was not the kind of huckster who ended up in jail for tax evasion or misuse of funds, or one who left a path of infidelity and sex scandals floating in his wake. He reminded her of a charismatic leader who spoke words that left hundreds of followers willingly drinking Kool-Aid in the jungle. She looked at the faces of the people in the room. If they had not been so full of wanting, they might have seen behind his mask.

As surely Kat must have. She was absolutely convinced that Kat had come here as a journalist, and she wondered how she could find her sister without blowing her cover.

Most of all, she wondered where Kat was now.

MADISON

The orientation session ended with a flurry of excitement. Before Verner could step from the platform, a cluster had formed around him. *Like fans at a rock concert,* Maddie thought. No one moved to leave the room. At that moment the rear door opened and Helen Mercer returned, accompanied by the young woman who had manned the reception desk. They crossed to Verner's side, and he bent to listen while Mercer whispered something in his ear. He nodded. The girl looked out over the gathering, scanning each face until her gaze landed on Maddie, and she raised a hand to point at her. Maddie's instinct was to turn away as she continued to be seized by the nearly atavistic need for caution, but she forced herself to be still and meet Verner's eyes. He pushed through the group, apologizing to those waiting to speak to him, and approached her.

"Hello," he said in his smooth huckster voice. "I'm Paul Verner." He held out his hand. Maddie took it but did not offer her name.

"There seems to be some confusion," he said.

Still, she said nothing, not trusting her voice lest it give away her apprehension.

"When you arrived, it was believed that you were a member of the group that arrived last evening."

Maddie nodded. Her mind raced. She needed time to come up with a story, something that wouldn't connect her to Kat, even as she tried to find her.

"That was our mistake. It seems that we were not expecting you."

Keep it simple, she thought. While it seemed preposterous to think that the head of a spa of some repute, surrounded by both staff and guests, would present any actual danger, a growing, nearly feral sense of peril thrummed through her body. She forced a smile. "Actually, I'm on vacation. I was staying in Playa del Pedro, and a woman there told me about this place."

"Really?" An eyebrow raised. "And who was that?"

"Her name is Evelyn. She owns a restaurant. La Máscara."

"I don't know of this place." He smiled apologetically, a smile that did not reach his eyes. "What did she tell you?"

"She said several people have stopped there for a meal after they've been here. She said she's overheard them talking about what good work you do here. From what she said, I wasn't exactly sure if it was a medical clinic or a spa, but I had some time free before I headed back home and decided to come see for myself."

He smiled. "Good word of mouth is always welcome." The room had started to empty, except for a few stragglers who hung at the edges, waiting for a private word with Verner. "And how did you get here from the village?"

"I hired a taxi."

"I see." His eyes searched hers. She forced herself to hold his gaze. "I apologize for all the questions, but we have to be cautious when someone appears unexpectedly."

"Oh?"

"In the past, we've had a reporter or two come here pretending to be a client."

She searched his face for any indication that he was speaking of Kat. "Would that be a problem?"

He flashed his smile, one Maddie was sure he intended to be charmingly apologetic. "Oh, there are always doubters. Those who want to disparage our work. As I said in the meeting, some of our treatments are so advanced that they have yet to be approved in the States."

"Is it true what you said at the session? You've found a way to reverse aging?"

"We have."

"I think I'd like to stay."

"We only take referrals. And forgive me for being frank—" He let his eyes travel over her damaged face. "I don't intend this to be cruel, but we don't do cosmetic surgery."

In spite of his words, Maddie didn't doubt that he was quite capable of deliberate cruelty, and his comments had found their mark. "I was thinking only for a day or two. A chance to recharge. Get rested." She had no intention of actually staying. She would find Kat and then get out.

"Our fee is not insubstantial."

"I'm happy to pay whatever it is."

He stared at her. She was certain he could see through her lies.

He turned to Helen Mercer. "Do we have any rooms available for—" He looked at Maddie. "I'm sorry. I don't know your name."

The feral caution was an electric current, humming through her entire body. "Olivia," she said. "Olivia Moroni." Instantly she regretted the lie. So foolish. One so easily uncovered. They would require a credit card. She was stuck with it now.

"All of our rooms in the main residence are at full occupancy," Mercer said.

"The main residency? But is there any room anywhere? I've come all this way. Even for one night?" She could hear the desperation in her voice. A glance passed between Verner and Mercer, a conversation she was unable to interpret.

"Perhaps we can find a room."

"That would be terrific." What had possessed her to give them a false name? The complications of her lie enveloped her.

"While the staff is preparing a room, why don't I show you around the grounds?"

"That's not necessary. I know you must be busy." She was desperate to be alone, to have the opportunity to investigate. Find Kat. "I'll just wander around myself." She wondered what story Kat had fed them. Had she registered as a client and also given a false name? If Verner had already discovered the real reason Kat was here, had that put her in danger?

"Nonsense," he said, and guided her from the room. She recoiled from his touch and hoped the movement had been too small for him to discern. They began the tour in the main building. He showed her the dining room and gave her a quick peek into the kitchen, where lunch was being prepared. They crossed through the room where the meeting had been held earlier and went out to the pool and spa area. In the distance, across the yards, Maddie noticed the wall constructed of concrete blocks. They continued walking, heading toward a smaller building. A guard passed them. Like the sleeping man in the shelter by the front gate, he held a carbine.

"You have armed guards here?"

"Yes."

"Why is that necessary?"

"For the protection of our guests. As I'm sure Helen told you all in her remarks this morning, Mexico is not always the most hospitable for foreigners. We want everyone to feel perfectly safe here."

"I see." *This place feels inhospitable,* she wanted to say.

"And, of course, we must safeguard the work we do here. Espionage is rampant in the pharmaceutical industry. What we have discovered would be worth billions to them. We have to be alert to the possibility of spies." He gave her a sharp glance. "I'm sure you can understand that."

"Yes," she said. She wondered what he would do if he had learned why Kat was really here. She couldn't shake the belief that Kat had come to investigate what he did. It was the only thing that made sense.

At last he led her across the courtyard. She noticed a building that, like the wall that surrounded the compound, was constructed of concrete blocks. "What is that?"

"Our clinic and laboratory. It's off-limits to guests."

"Thank you." She was eager to explore further but needed to do it alone, without Verner monitoring. The first place she would start was the very building Verner had told her was restricted. "But I'm sure you must be busy. I don't want to keep you from your work."

He turned his searching gaze on her. "Lunch is served at one. After you've eaten and had a chance to get settled, stop by the front desk to register, and then we'll get you scheduled for your lab tests."

She hadn't expected this and scrambled for a plan. "Oh, I won't be here long enough for any tests. Certainly not more than a day."

"That's not a problem. Our on-site lab can fast-track results."

She felt unequal to matching his game, his wits, and couldn't escape the feeling that he had seen right through her from the first. What had she gotten herself into? She was furious with herself for trotting off alone and not telling Jack. The price of pride. She'd been a fool.

He walked her back to the main building. A staff member led her to her room. She closed the door. For an instant the instinct to leave, to just walk out the door and head out to the highway and find a way back to the village, was strong. But if Kat was still here, then Maddie couldn't leave without her. While everything was still fresh in her mind she reviewed the layout of the grounds and buildings, orienting herself. Kat had to be somewhere nearby. She would start by showing her photo to the Mayan woman she had seen sweeping the hall. She dug in the tote and retrieved the photo.

Her thinking was interrupted by a knock at the door. Mercer entered, and Maddie slipped the picture beneath her tote.

"I just spoke with Dr. Verner, and he wants to get you registered immediately."

"I thought I would do that after lunch."

"He wants to get started on your tests."

She tried to think of an excuse but feared that protesting too much would only raise their suspicions. Mercer held the door open, waited. Maddie followed her out. They passed the Mayan sweeping the corridor. At last the woman turned, and Maddie gasped.

Helen Mercer turned. "Is something the matter?" she asked.

"No," Maddie managed. Was it possible she had really seen a golden *K* hanging from a chain around the woman's neck? She looked back toward the Mayan, but she was disappearing behind a door.

The examination room was in the main building, next to the spa. The whole procedure took more than an hour. Every minute felt like an hour, two. Maddie wanted to find the Mayan. Still giving her name as Olivia Moroni, she filled out four pages of forms and questionnaires, a complete listing of her medical history, all conditions, allergies, operations, and medications, including supplements. She did not list the Xanax. Finally, she was directed to change into an examining gown. She was weighed and her height measured. She gave a urine sample. Two vials of blood were taken. Again, as she had with Verner, she protested, saying she would not be staying and would not be signing up for all the clinic offered, but the technicians brushed aside her protests.

When at last they were finished, Maddie nearly ran back to her room. The Mayan was not in sight. Maddie tried the door she had watched her disappear behind, but it was locked. She felt doubt edge in. Could she trust a fleeting glance of what looked to be Kat's necklace from their mother? Was Maddie only seeing what she wanted to see?

Her tote was on top of a short dresser where she had left it. She picked it up, looked for the photo where she had put it earlier when Mercer had come to take her for testing. It wasn't there. She sorted through her tote—wallet, hairbrush, little pouch of makeup—looking for the photo of Kat, but it was not there.

Neither was her passport.

GRACIELA

It was late in the morning when they came for Graciela. When she saw two men, she began to cry. *No pesos.* She didn't want the money they had promised. She only wanted to leave.

The first attendant laughed.

She knew it was futile to struggle. Or cry out. The sense that her *padre* was near, was coming to get her, was fading. Fading. Fading. Fading. So fast it was as if it had never been.

They took her to the room with the bright light and hard table. The *norteamericano* with the eyes of the devil waited for her. Although she knew the futility of it, she began to fight against the hands that pinned her to the table. They fastened the straps. She waited for the needle they would put in her arm, waited for them to fill the tubes with blood, but instead her legs were pulled apart and her feet placed in the stirrups, exposing her again.

She cried out in pain. And then began to scream. The doctor spoke harshly to the woman by his side. Almost immediately she felt the pinch of a needle in her arm. And then her mouth grew dry. She squeezed her eyes shut. Behind her lids, she saw the blue-painted girl from her dreams. *Evil lives in this place,* the girl whispered. Graciela knew this. She knew evil was being done to her.

She tried to cry out. To her *padre.* Her *madre.* To the Virgin Mother. Even to Ángel. No one came to help her. There was a whirling in her head, spinning. From a distance she felt hands, heard noises. The doctor was moving quickly now. A switch was flipped and the soft sound of a pump motor filled the room. She cried out again at the violation. He pulled the machine closer. Began the suctioning.

When she regained consciousness, she was back in her room, bleeding from her place of shame. She had never felt pain like this, and again, as she had when they had taken her, she cried for her *madre*, sobbed as she had when she was only a little girl. Once she thought she saw the Mayan child sitting on the floor in the corner next to the pair of red shoes that had belonged to her *madre*. The child spoke then in a language that Graciela couldn't understand, but the softness of it soothed her.

For an instant she thought she felt her *madre*'s hand on her head, stroking back her hair, but when she opened her eyes she saw the Mayan Rosa, bending over her, crooning an ancient song.

MADISON

She searched the room once more, but her passport and Kat's photo were not there. The foreboding she'd felt since her arrival blossomed into full-blown fear. This was not the panic that could come upon her for no reason; this was grounded in the truth that here there was much to be afraid of. It had been foolish to come alone. Except for Verner's staff, only the taxi driver and the old fortune-teller knew she was here. And, she realized with a shoot of hope, the owner of La Máscara and the clerk at the Molcas. But what had she been thinking not to tell Jack? It had not only been foolish; it had been inconsiderate. Surely by now he must be worried. She was ashamed to recall how angry she had been when he hadn't called to tell her he was safe after the plane had crashed at the airport on the Cape. How she hadn't given him a second chance.

The room offered only a momentary and false haven, and so she forced herself to leave, to find safety with others until she could pass through the gate and escape. Outside, the sunshine, the manicured beds, the groundskeeper bending over and smoothing a stone path with his rake, all seemed surreally normal. She walked toward the long drive of gray sand that led to the gate. She quickened her steps, just short of a trot that would garner attention. As she drew close, the guard, no longer asleep, came out of the shelter, rifle slung across his chest, and stared at her. Her throat closed, and she felt the familiar sweats and palpitations that presaged an attack. *Breathe,* she told herself. *Breathe.* She turned back toward the main building. A small group of women was crossing the grounds, and she hurried to catch up and join them. *Safety in numbers,* she thought, even as she realized this was only another fake refuge. If she was truly in danger, there was no sanctuary on these grounds. And if Verner had learned that Kat was here to investigate, her sister would be in danger, too. Her hands were trembling, and she shoved them in the deep pockets of her slacks, closed her fingers around her talisman, Olivia's quartz heart. It no longer held the power to comfort her.

Unlike the gathering earlier that morning when conversation surged and swelled, the noise in the dining room was muted. She found a chair at the table with the three women she had seen earlier by the pool. *Act normal,* she told herself. She scanned the room, enormously relieved that Verner was absent.

"Quite the morning," the woman sitting on her left said. Maddie recognized her from the orientation session as the one who had said that in order to be there she'd taken out a mortgage on her home. Maddie guessed her to be in her late twenties or early thirties. Her face was flawless, her neck firm. No need to seek youth. She was young. Maddie wondered what reason she could possibly have for coming here, going into debt. What was she searching for? A return to her teenage years? *Jesus,* she thought, *the world has gone mad.*

"Yes," Maddie said. "It was." She was surprised to find her voice was steady. "I thought about walking into Playa, but the guard at the gate wouldn't let me through."

"Oh, Dr. Verner said it wasn't safe to leave. I guess there's a fair amount of crime in this part of Mexico." Her voice was guileless. "I'm Bethany, by the way."

"Madison," she said. "Nice to meet you." Too late, she remembered that she had given her name as Olivia when she'd registered. She glanced around to see if she had been overheard by any of the staff and then realized it no longer mattered. They had her passport. Verner knew her real name.

Bethany said she had come from Houston. She introduced the other women. Ava Dawn and Lynn were from Alabama. Like Bethany, they seemed too young to have the least concern about the ravages of aging. All three were cousins. Their fathers had been brothers. Ava Dawn was divorced; Lynn and Bethany were married. "Our starter marriages," Lynn said with a laugh. They were chatty, with the easy sociability of southern women.

For an instant, Maddie considered telling them the truth. Her sister had come here and was now missing. She looked into their faces, trusting, innocent, excited about Verner and his promises. Would they just put her down as a nutcase? Paranoid. Would they pass on what she told them to Mercer or Verner?

An Mayan server approached bearing a tray. She was not the woman Maddie had seen in the corridor outside her room. She set a bowl of clear soup before each woman. The portions were small.

"Christ," Ava Dawn moaned. "There'd better be a lot more coming, or I'm heading the mutiny."

"Shall we order wine?" asked Lynn.

"I wish," Bethany said. "They toss you out if you bring in any alcohol," she explained to Maddie.

"I told you we should have stashed a bottle in the luggage," Ava Dawn said.

Maddie forced herself to take a spoonful of the broth. She tried to appear attentive to their conversation while considering her next step. She was back to the puzzle that had led her here. Where was Kat? If Verner had discovered she was a reporter, what would he have done? Would he have kept her imprisoned? Even to Maddie, that seemed extreme. He couldn't keep her locked up forever. Could he? Her head ached.

"Yeah," Lynn said. "No alcohol, no tobacco, no sugar, no caffeine."

"Well, I've never been anywhere on the planet where you couldn't find someone to bribe to get a drink if you put your mind and pocketbook to the task," Lynn said.

"You're on," Ava Dawn said. She looked around the dining room, which was filling with women. The two men who had attended the morning session were not there. "And it looks like we might as well add no sex to the list."

"Maybe someone would risk their job to get us a bottle of booze, but I think we're out of luck with drugs," Bethany said.

"Yeah, but speaking of drugs . . . wonder what Dr. Verner pumps us full of?"

Maddie thought of the syringe she'd found in Kat's bathroom. If Kat had taken it from the clinic on an earlier visit, had it been for a piece of evidence, proof of what she had learned? Each question led to another, the mystery composed of layers, beginning with Kat's disappearance. And what she had discovered here . . .

"With all the deprivation we have to endure here, it had better be good," Lynn said.

"I didn't like the sound of the testicles and glands," said Bethany. "That totally creeped me out."

"Listen, I don't care if he stuffs us full of bat shit if it works," Ava Dawn said.

"Three CCs of bat shit."

"One dose of wild bear pee."

"Eye of iguana and nose of newt."

"Do newts have noses?"

Their laughter rose as they began trying to outdo each other, three young and lovely women concocting their brew in a virtual iron cauldron.

Their gaiety and gossipy conversation, the normality and lightness of it, seemed surreal to Maddie. The soup bowls were cleared, replaced by a plate of lightly dressed greens. An idea came to Maddie. In the flurry of clearing one course and serving the next, she leaned toward Bethany. "Listen, I forgot to charge my cell, and now it's completely dead. I was wondering if I could borrow yours after lunch." She smiled in apology. "I promised I'd call home when I got here, and I don't want them to worry."

Bethany looked at her in surprise. "You mean they allowed you to keep your phone? We had to turn ours in when we registered. Something about a firm no-photo policy. I swear, if the man wasn't a genius who absolutely delivers the goods, I wouldn't be here."

"Yeah." Lynn laughed. "He might be a genius, but I gotta say he lands on the high end of the paranoia spectrum."

The hope she had allowed herself faded. She had no way to reach Jack. No way to call the police in Playa. Maddie let the conversation float around her for the rest of the lunch: a piece of white fish that had been broiled and steamed green beans. The dessert was an airy concoction so insubstantial it made the broth they'd been served earlier seem as hearty as gumbo.

When they rose to go, Bethany asked Maddie if she wanted to join them at the pool. She demurred, saying she was tired from the trip and was going to take a nap. She was determined to find the Mayan she had seen in the corridor wearing Kat's necklace.

"See you later, then."

"Thanks, anyway." As she turned to leave the dining room, Helen Mercer approached. She singled Maddie out.

"Dr. Verner asked me to find you. He wants to see you."

Maddie thought of the man's piercing eyes that seemed to see through artifice and wanted more time before she confronted him. She needed to search the grounds and find the Mayan with the necklace. "Maybe later. I'm pretty tired and want a nap."

"This won't take long." Mercer looped her arm in Maddie's and guided her to the building that held Verner's office and the lab. The groundskeeper with the rake nodded in greeting as they passed. A ribbon of laughter floated from the direction of the pool. Maddie slid her free hand into her pocket, clutched the quartz heart.

Mercer knocked on the door before entering. Verner was seated behind the desk, waiting. He did not rise but only nodded toward one of two chairs opposite him, indicating that Maddie should sit. Maddie hesitated, cast a quick glance around the room, and fought the desire to leave. But she would not lose this chance to learn more about Kat. She took one of the chairs, and Mercer sat in the other. His eyes locked on hers, and she forced herself to return the gaze without flinching. Her body tingled with silent alarm. There was a folder on the desktop, and at last he dropped his eyes and referred to the first page.

"We have your test results back," he said.

"Already?"

"As I explained this morning, we have a lab on-site. We can fast-track results."

"Yes."

"Before we review the results, I have a couple of questions." He peered at her. He picked up the top page in the folder. Maddie stared at his hands, the manicured nails. "As I explained this morning, we require referrals for our guests. On occasion we have made an exception, as we did in your case."

She hefted her armor into place and resolved not to let him see how afraid she was that he could see right through her. "I appreciate that."

"To protect ourselves, in such instances we always perform a background check."

She was jolted that they would go to this length to find out about her. And so quickly. She concealed her shock with outrage. "A background check? Really? Why such an invasion of privacy?"

"For our own protection. As I mentioned earlier, we must protect ourselves from espionage. Spies have tried to infiltrate our lab."

He lands on the high end of the paranoia spectrum. But if someone had nothing to hide, why the paranoia? Why the armed guards?

"You gave your name as Olivia Moroni. Is that correct?"

She forced herself to hold his gaze. "Yes."

"From Massachusetts?"

Her mouth went dry. She nodded, not trusting her voice.

"There is some confusion. Our check only turned up one person from Massachusetts with that name. A nineteen-year-old girl who is currently in hospice care. She is dying of cancer." His eyes pinned her. "Do you have cancer?"

"No."

"But you say that you are Olivia Moroni?"

"Yes." She knew he was toying with her. Of course he knew her name. He had her passport.

"Quite a coincidence."

She tried to think of an explanation he would believe. She was saved by a knock on the door. As soon as possible, she would leave. She would walk out the gate. Surely everyone here wasn't in on some grand conspiracy. She would find Jack, and together they would go to the police in Playa. They would contact Detective Miller.

"Come in," Verner said.

A Mayan woman entered. Maddie recognized her as the woman she had seen sweeping the corridor earlier. She couldn't hold back a cry.

"What's wrong?" Verner asked.

"Nothing," she said. It *was* Kat's necklace. Proof that Kat was here. Had been here. She forced herself to look away, holding tight to the chair's inflexible arms.

The Mayan carried a tray that held a plate of biscuits and three glass cups filled with a frothy, dark drink. The rich aroma of chocolate reached Maddie. The woman set the tray on a side table and left.

Mercer stood. She went to the table and retrieved the tray. She served Maddie first, then Verner, before taking the remaining cup and returning to her seat. The biscuit was still warm, as if fresh from the kitchen. Maddie took a bite. It tasted of anise and held a soft, creamy filling that was nearly liquid. She expected the drink to be warm as well, but when she took a sip, it was cool. Beneath the chocolate was a slightly bitter flavor but not unpleasantly so. Very like the chicken *mole* she had eaten long ago on that trip she had taken with Kat to Mexico. Kat. The words pushed against her lips: *Where is my sister?* Perhaps the best course was to stop pretending, to tell him why she was here and demand to know where Kat was.

Verner returned to the folder on his desk and pulled out another paper. "We have the results of your tests."

She wasn't interested in the tests. She folded her hands around the quartz heart. "What I want to know—"

"Our lab is very efficient." He took a swig of the drink. Mercer drank, too. Maddie took another sip, but the bitterness lingered at the back of her throat. She took another bite of the biscuit, hoping it would help wash away the taste, now distinctly unpleasant. She stared into the dark liquid. Was it possible that they had drugged the drink? She set the glass on the desktop. Verner watched her and smiled.

"For the most part," he said, "we found your results to be normal. In fact, your blood profile shows you to be in excellent health. As I said, nothing unexpected."

"For the most part?" Her mind was having trouble keeping up with him.

"You did not tell us."

"Tell you what?"

"That you are expecting."

"Expecting? Expecting what?" Her ears began to ring and sweat dampened her forehead. She had only had two small sips of the drink. They had finished theirs. But they hadn't touched the biscuits.

Verner and Mercer exchanged a glance. "You really don't know?" Verner said.

His words seemed to come from a distance. "Know what?" she managed.

"Your results indicate that you are pregnant, Madison."

She stared in disbelief. "No. No, I'm not." It all came rushing at her in a confusion too complicated to process. She stared at him. His features began to blur. She dropped her gaze to the plate of cookies. Untouched except for the one she had eaten. Then she saw, just as her vision began to swim, a passport book and the photo of Kat that was missing from her tote.

Then the room began to whirl.

KATHERINE

Either they had drugged her food again or her return to a measure of vitality had been brief. She felt weak and ill. Hope, so fleeting and tentative, was gone. There would be no rescue. She would never escape. She would die here, taking with her all the evil secrets of this place she had hoped to reveal to the world.

She pried the cap off the top of the bedpost and carefully retrieved the napkin. She unfolded it to reveal her stash of white pills. She spilled them onto the bed and counted them. Twenty in all. Not as many as she had aimed for but surely enough.

It grieved her to know the pain Maddie would feel: not only that Kat had disappeared but that Maddie would never learn what had happened to her. A loss, complicated by the mystery of the unresolved. Once, years ago, Kat had written an article about MIAs. She had interviewed many families. Wives and parents and siblings. The most difficult thing, they had told her, was never knowing, to be left to always wonder if their loved ones were still alive somewhere or if they were dead. They'd said, each and every one, that it was in many ways worse than if death had been confirmed. At least then you would know, they'd confided. You could go on, freed from the limbo of waiting. She had been foolish to come here without telling anyone. Foolish and vain to chase youth. She had been foolish to trust Verner. Well, it was too late to change any of it, too late to alter history.

From the corridor outside her room, noise reached her. She swept the pills back into the napkin and shoved it under the pillow. She lay back on the bed, closed her eyes. Waited for the door to open, for someone—Verner or Mercer or one of the maids—to enter. Somewhere, a door banged shut.

She must have fallen asleep, because when she woke all was quiet. She drifted off again. She woke to a dream. A young girl was standing by her bed. She was weeping. There was blood on the front of her pajamas. *"¡Ayuda!"* she cried.

Kat reached out, felt the girl's arm, too solid for a dream apparition. The child—for even in the darkness Kat could see that she was young, fourteen or fifteen perhaps—whispered the word between sobs. *"Ayuda."*

Even coming dull-minded from sleep, Kat understood the word. Help. She struggled to sit up. She looked at the girl and, out of the corner of her eye, caught a movement in the shadows of the door.

TIA CLARA

The old ones had been with Tia Clara for several days. She felt their presence everywhere, from the moment of awakening to the last awareness before sleep took her. Even in her sleep they came. But they didn't frighten her. She was surprised to discover that there was a certain comfort to their existence.

She missed the bird. The wire and wood cage was empty, cleared of seeds and crumbs and droppings. She did not wonder what would become of it, nor of any of her belongings. Her many shawls and blankets. Her old deck of cards and the little pink ones she used for the tourists. Or the frame that Felipe had made for her so very long ago in gratitude when she cured his infant son. These things were no longer of concern.

The noises of the fiesta pushed into her home. The intensity of it had been increasing with each hour. Soon the masquerade parade would begin, a riot of color and music and laughter snaking through each *calle* and ending at the square, where the *padre* would bless the seeds, the last remnant of the original fiesta. Another matter of no concern to her.

In the shadows of the room she saw a movement and wondered which of the many souls had come to visit. Only the week before, the specter of the old ones' presence would have held terror for her, but she had learned much in these recent days. All she had been fearing for much of her life no longer held power over her. What would happen would happen. She was powerless to change what was to come, just as she was powerless to alter the past.

She was sitting by the open window, thinking of these things, when a sparrow flew from a nearby tree to land on the sill. The bird was not one of those common to Playa. Its beak was strong with a small curve at the tip, its feathers black, nearly purple. Instinctively Tia Clara moved a hand toward it, as if to offer it a perch. The gesture did not frighten the bird. For one long moment the echo of song of the cicadas passed through the room. The dark sparrow fixed its clever eyes on hers. She felt a flutter in her heart, a quick beating, as if caged inside her own breast an organ as tiny as that of the bird beat a delicate, thin pulse, so insubstantial it seemed impossible to bear the weight of life.

"So you've come for me at last," she said to the bird. Beneath her ribs, the arrhythmia of her heart increased. The creature continued to gaze at her. For a moment Tia Clara's vision clouded. She saw, in a blur, many pictures: the village as it was long ago, before the tourists came; Manny, so strong and handsome and weak; and Consuelo, beautiful Consuelo. She thought of all the passions and pains of the past. All the things they had done in the name of love and the stunning and unforeseen consequences. If she had known, what would she have done differently? Would she have freed Manny and let him go to Consuelo?

The bird spread its wings, as if impatient with the questioning of humans. It tilted its head, withdrew its wings back to its body, and considered a patch of ground and then cocked its head and looked at a branch overhead and the sky.

For years, Tia Clara had thought that when death came for her, it would be presaged by the *zopilotes*. The scavenger bird. She looked again at the dark sparrow and understood this bird was offering her a choice, a chance, and she had only to read the signs to become clear on what to do, but after a lifetime of reading signs she was tired, too tired to read one more, even this one. She turned from the window and a moment later heard the soft rustle as the sparrow flew off. Even then, she did not turn back to see which direction it had taken, the song that would reveal her fate. She would know soon enough. For one brief moment she knew panic. What had she left undone? What was left to repent? It had all passed so quickly, so quickly. All the beauty. All the joys and all the sorrows. Love and betrayal. The sound of the sea rose in her ears.

The old ones grew impatient. It would not be long now.

MADISON

The bed was unfamiliar in its narrowness. Not her bed. Where was she? She worked to ground herself, to wake.

Gradually, she remembered. She was in Mexico. A hotel. She concentrated on remembering the name. Molcas. That was it. The Hotel Molcas. By the water. She was searching for Kat. Jack had come with her.

She sat up. Pale light from the half moon streamed through the skylight. She glanced around at the room, the bare furnishings. Not the hotel, then. The effort to sort it out drained her. She recalled snatches of conversation, of faces. A glimmering Madonna with amphibian feet. A man with a gold-edged tooth. A green-feathered bird in a cage. They became a confusing collage of images. A weathered old woman with two thick white braids. A man with piercing eyes. Whispered words spoken in a language she didn't understand.

Another memory. A man telling her she was having a baby. Another part of the confusing dream. Still, she brought one hand to her belly, cupped it over the soft skin above her pelvis. Her mind refused to work right. To sort out what was part of the dream, to remember where she was. She swallowed, tasted the bitterness of chocolate.

KATHERINE

Kat stared at the girl. In the little light afforded by the moon, she saw the girl's tear-wet face, her blood-spattered gown, and, dropping her gaze farther, the red streaks tracing down the girl's legs, red so dark it seemed nearly black. Even as she wondered what could have happened to the girl, her memory served up the image of the room at the end of the corridor, the machinery, the harvesting of fetal tissue that Verner did there in his mad quest for youth. "Oh, child," she said, trying to conceal her horror. "Oh, child, come here." She opened her arms and embraced her, felt the trembling, a shaking so violent that Kat feared the girl might go into shock. Kat pulled the thin blanket free of her bed and wrapped it about the girl's shoulders. The white pills, so carefully saved and hidden, scattered on the floor.

"Cómo te llamas?" she whispered, and she stroked the girl's hair in an effort to calm her. It did not occur to her to question how she had gotten into the room.

The girl ignored her question and began to pull at Kat's hand, whispering more words in an urgent tone.

"Me llamo Katherine. Kat," she said, and again asked the girl her name. *"Cómo te llamas?"*

"Graciela," the child whispered at last. When Kat did not get up, she began whimpering, pleading, words following one another so fast, Kat couldn't distinguish them.

"Despacio," Kat said. *"Despacio*, Graciela. I can't understand what you are saying."

The girl turned and looked back toward the door, and it was then that a figure moved from the shadows and came into Kat's full view.

VÍCTOR

The celebration spilled toward his shack, but Víctor ignored it. He continued with his work. He had always found it soothing. He continued applying the second coat of resin along the keel of the old boat. Others—Juan Santos, for instance—would settle for a single application, but Víctor had no patience for impatience. Things should be done right. And if a leak was not properly repaired, it was a foolish wasting of time, for it meant more lost days while repairs were made. Kuko basked at his feet. He gazed up at Víctor and gave his slow iguana blink. The diver stood and stretched, arching his back to release the tension of bending over for so long. He looked down the beach toward the center of the village, but the throngs of people, costumed and for the most part drunk, formed a mass so merged it made it impossible to pick out a single individual.

Certainly it was impossible to locate one specific woman in the crowds. He thought of Madison and of her beautiful sister, who, from their first meeting, had seen directly into the truth of his heart. Somehow from the beginning, she had understood his secret self, his loneliness and vulnerability. Unlike other women he had known, she had asked nothing of him. He had wanted to give her everything. Again he searched the horizon, as if by thinking of them he could make either of the sisters appear. Had Madison left the village? Gone back to her home? Or had she accomplished the impossible and found her sister?

He deeply regretted not telling her that he had met Katherine. But how much would he have admitted? Would she have believed him responsible for Katherine's disappearance? Accused him? Taken her suspicions to the police?

But then again, perhaps Madison had not left. He remembered her determination, her conviction that her sister had come to Playa. After a fourth time searching the horizon, he surrendered to the desire that had plagued him since he'd begun work. He set his brush in the cleaning solvent. He carefully poured what remained of the resin into a plastic jug. He remembered the words that Tia Clara had spat at him. "You are a fool," she had said.

"Am I a *tonto*?" he asked the lizard at his feet. "A *pendejo*? A fool?" Kuko regarded him and gave him another lazy blink. Víctor carried the tanks and other diving gear back into his shack and locked the door. Everyone was here today for the fiesta, and there would be no tourists wanting him to take them to see the world beneath the surface of the sea. "A fool," he acknowledged, and headed toward the village.

As he walked past the home of Tia Clara, he did not see her. In fact, he had not seen her since the night he had come to her drunk and full of questions and she had called him a *tonto*. As it had been that night, her door was closed, the windows shuttered. A broken pot sat by the door. Had he fallen over it that night? He believed he did. He would find another. Replace this one. Whether or not the fault belonged to him.

He considered knocking at the door, apologizing for the broken pot, and perhaps again asking her his questions. As he approached, a sparrow, its plumage nearly purple-black, flew to the top of one of the closed shutters and perched. It regarded him with a gaze as steady as that of Kuko. He recognized it as a bird unusual for this place. As he watched, it spread its wings and flew. It dipped once, swooping not a foot from his head, and then soared. It flew straight up, as if its destination lay beyond the clouds, as if heading to heaven itself. He tried to remember what he had heard about the omen of the dark sparrow but could not recall. A chill shot through him. He knocked on Tia Clara's door and, when there was no answer, turned the knob.

The old woman lay on the floor. At first, he believed she was dead and was surprised at his quick tears. And then her eyes opened and she looked at him. He prepared himself for the hate he was used to seeing there.

"Mi sobrino," she whispered. Her eyes were soft.

"Sí," he whispered back, surprising himself with his impulse to comfort the old woman. She was ill, dying, he thought. She had never called him by a familial name or acknowledged their kinship. If it gave her comfort to call him nephew now, he would not correct her. The dying deserved at least kindness. She tried to say more, but he placed his hand on hers, surprised and moved by how insubstantial it was.

She would not be silenced. She rambled on. He struggled to understand, listening while she murmured how even the winds kept secrets, confusing past and present, holding his eyes with hers as if she would never look away. She tightened her hold on his hand, her grip fiercer than he would have thought possible. "Retirada de la Playa," she whispered. He tried to understand what she was trying to tell him but thought it must be a dream or some kind of delirium. She was mistaking him for someone else. She withdrew her hand from his and motioned for him to go. He didn't want to leave her, but she kept repeating it with an urgency that alarmed him. *"Vete. Vete."* Go away. Go away. He tried to lift her, thinking to carry her to a doctor, but she pushed him away, crying out and struggling until he let her go. He found a shawl from where she had left it on a chair and covered her. He promised to send a doctor, but she had closed her eyes and no longer listened.

To his surprise, the doctor was in his office. Víctor had expected the office to be closed and the doctor celebrating with the rest of the village. After being assured that Tia Clara would be cared for, he continued on, returning to the quest that had caused him to leave his work.

For the rest of the distance he looked at the faces of those he passed on the *calle*, as if it were possible to see behind the masks. *Fool,* he told himself as continued on, and again at home as he showered, taking extra care to wash the reek of resin from his hands, his hair. *Fool,* he told himself as he lathered his face and shaved. *Fool,* he told himself as he chose what to wear, settling on loose cotton pants and shirt. *Fool,* he scolded himself as he fastened sandals on his feet. *Fool,* he said as he closed the door and, elbowing his way through the throngs, headed for the Hotel Molcas. A fool to be following a dream that had evaporated before he had even known it. Fool to hold out hope that his brief time with Katherine had meant as much to her as it had to him. Fool to have lost his heart to a woman who could disappear like smoke. He wondered whether she had found another man to love. Still he continued to the hotel. When he caught sight of a face he recognized, he smiled and rushed forward before it was swallowed in the crowd.

KATHERINE

She shrank back from the figure at the door, but she did not relinquish the hand of the girl, Graciela. If it was Verner, she would not let him do more harm to this child. But even as the thought came, she knew its impotence. She was too weak for any battle. She and the girl were both at his mercy. Still, she resolved to fight him with her last ounce of strength. She stood straighter and took a step toward the door, shielding the girl with her body. She felt the white pills crunch beneath her feet, knowing even as she stepped on them that the escape they had once promised was lost to her. Graciela's fingers tightened around hers.

The shape at the door moved out of the shadow and slipped into the room.

"Rosa?" she whispered. Kat hesitated. Would Rosa report them to Verner? Or could she be persuaded to help them? She was afraid to trust anyone in this place.

Rosa beckoned, indicated that she and Graciela should follow. What choice did she have? How much time did she have before Mercer or Verner appeared?

Urgency impelled her to the door. Still clutching the girl's hand, she followed Rosa into the corridor and the unknown. The three paused only a split second before heading to the exit that Kat now knew led to the exterior, the one Verner had taken her through on the nights of the midnight swims. She didn't allow herself to think ahead or consider what they would do once out of the building. She knew the compound was surrounded by a concrete fence and was well guarded by men hired by Verner.

They had almost reached the door when Rosa stopped.

"Come on," Kat said.

But Rosa dug deep into the pocket of her skirt and withdrew a key. She stepped toward another closed door and unlocked it, and she pushed it open. Kat stared into the darkness, giving her eyes time to adjust to the night shadows, and saw the shape of a woman lying on the bed. Was this, like her, another of Verner's failures?

"No," she said. "We can't take anyone else." She and Graciela were weak, and even with Rosa's help, if that was what the Mayan intended, escape would be difficult enough. Taking another with them would surely doom them all. But the Mayan was undeterred. She crossed to the bed, and Kat and the girl went with her, as if the three of them were one.

The woman on the bed moaned and turned her face toward them. Kat froze.

It wasn't possible. How could it be? She took a step closer. And then another. If not for the support of Rosa's arm, she would have fallen. "Maddie?" she whispered. The name no more than a croak. "Maddie, oh God, Maddie, is it really you?"

"Momma," her sister said. And then she started to scream.

MADISON

She remembered. In a wave awash with longing and grief and, at the last, horror, she remembered everything. Her mother was dead. Kat was missing. The clinic. Dr. Verner. His last words to her. He was going to take her baby.

She began to scream.

And then the sound was cut off by a hand clasped over her mouth. She struggled against it, thrashed and fought.

"Maddie," a voice said. "Maddie, stop. It's me. It's Kat."

Kat? Was it possible? She ceased her struggles and turned toward the voice. She looked into her eyes. Kat. But not Kat. Kat older. As if overnight she had aged ten years. Twenty. Gone was the almond-tinged scent she always associated with her sister, replaced by a sour smell.

"Kat?"

She turned to one of the others as if seeking confirmation and saw the Mayan woman who wore Kat's necklace. The other was a young Mexican girl. Who were they, and what was Kat doing with them? And why had Kat given the Mayan their mother's necklace? Her mind spun with questions, but before she could sort them out, Kat was hugging her.

"Jesus, Maddie," her sister said. "What are you doing here? How on earth did you ever find me?"

Maddie reached for her hand. "I did," she said. "I found you."

"Oh, no," Kat said. "You shouldn't have come." Even as she spoke, she wrapped her arms tighter.

"I found you," Maddie said again. She began to weep. "I thought I had lost you."

The young Mexican girl crossed the room and started tugging at Kat.

Kat wiped away her tears. Slid her arm around Maddie's shoulders and helped her sit up. She drew back and stared at her. "You cut your hair," she said.

"Oh, Kat," she said. "Only you would be thinking about hair right now."

Kat gave a crooked smile. "We have to get out of here." Her voice was calm, but Maddie heard the undercurrent of urgency. She remembered Verner, the guards.

"Can you walk?" Kat asked.

"I think so. I was drugged."

"Just hold on to me. And be quiet. I don't know how much time we have."

Maddie stumbled as she rose from the bed. Somehow they reached the door. The silence in the hall was broken only by the shuffle of their feet on the tiles of the corridor. Their labored breathing seemed, to Maddie, as noisy as the shrieking of crows. A murder of crows.

She began to hear sounds from the jungle, feral and eerie. She tried to ignore them. She heard a man's voice. Kat stumbled and fell to one knee. Together the Mayan and the young Mexican girl lifted Kat. The girl's breathing was shallow, and Maddie saw the blood running down her legs.

"Who is the girl?" Maddie whispered.

"Her name is Graciela," Kat said.

"She's bleeding."

"She's been given an abortion," Kat said. "Verner," she added, the one word an explanation.

Maddie's breath froze in her chest. Unaware she was doing so, she curved a hand over her belly as she quickened her steps.

Outside the blue-black sky pressed down. In the distance floated women's laughter. A swooping whoop of delight. Maddie heard the sound of water splashing. The southern cousins. Had they found someone to bribe after all and bring them liquor, or were they just letting loose?

Somehow, slowly moving in the shadows—who was helping whom was not clear—they headed toward the gate. Behind them the noise grew louder. Perhaps in response to the women playing by the pool, a dog began barking in a fit of excitement. The guard came out from the shelter by the gate. They shrank back, but for the moment his attention was focused on the area by the pool, and he did not see them. She wondered how long they would have before the commotion brought someone from the staff, Verner or another guard, to inspect.

"We need a diversion," Kat whispered.

"Like what?" The night air and the shock of seeing Kat helped clear her mind.

"I don't know. Give me a minute to think." Kat turned and looked across the dark grounds, toward the sound of laughter. "Do you think you can make it alone to the *hacienda*?"

"I'm not leaving you here."

"Just for a bit, Maddie."

"Why?" She didn't want to leave Kat.

"I have an idea, but I don't think I have the strength to do it."

Maddie nodded toward the girl and the Mayan, who were huddled off to the side. "What about them?"

"No. I don't think they can do what has to be done."

"Which is?"

"There's a small shed at the rear of the building. I saw a jug of propane there that they use to fill the tiki torches."

"Propane?"

"There won't be anyone in the kitchen at this time of night. You have to get the propane and dump it in the kitchen and set it on fire."

Maddie froze. "No."

"You have to, Maddie. It's the only thing I can think of. If there's a fire it will draw the guards away from the gate."

Maddie pictured flames. Remembered the heat and smells. The pain. "I can't."

"Yes, you can. I know you can."

"I can't, Kat. You have to think of something else."

"There is nothing else. We have to get out of here before they discover we're missing. You can do it, Maddie. I know you can."

Fire. Flames. Heat. Pain.

"Go now, before it's too late. Before they start looking for us."

Heat. Pain. Death.

"There's a wand lighter there, too. I've watched them use it to light the torches."

"I can't do this." A dog barked. A woman laughed.

"You can," Kat whispered. "I know you can. Look what you've already done. You found me."

"I did." Flickering images of her journey to Kat scrolled rapidly through her mind. The flight down, her discovery of the clinic, the many steps it had taken to find Kat. Lastly, oddly, the image of the paper sword Jack had crafted for her came to mind. A warrior, he had called her. An Amazon woman.

"Go," Kat whispered. "We will meet you by the gate. We'll hide there and wait for you."

Fire. Flames.

Maddie turned toward the *hacienda*.

GRACIELA

Graciela crouched in the shadows by the concrete wall. She leaned against Rosa. She could feel the wetness of blood tracing down her thigh, her calf, her foot. She wondered if she was leaving a trail of red on the ground. Pain cut through her belly. She tried not to cry out. She would be brave, as her *abuela* had said. Beside her, Rosa stroked her arm. They tried to be quiet, but once the *gringa* cried out softly. They waited, staring into the darkness, back toward the *hacienda,* straining to see the woman of the scars coming back to them.

At the gatehouse, the guard raised his weapon. *"Hola,"* he called out into the dark. "Who's there?" They shrank farther back and froze against the shadow of a curve in the wall. The scent from a spread of bougainvillea was like a curtain around them. In the distance, the noise from the *hacienda* grew louder still. Lights appeared in windows like eyes opening to the sun.

They waited. The *gringa* who had disappeared into the night did not return. They continued to wait. Still, she did not come. Graciela felt the sister at her side tremble. On her other side, Rosa stood as still as a stone.

MADISON

She crept along the edge of the wall, making her way around the property. The direct route to the *hacienda* would be quicker but would expose her as she crossed the open expanse of the grounds. She tried not to think about what Kat had asked her to do. First, she would get to the propane. As she circled by the pool area, she glimpsed the forms of a half dozen women, some swimming, others sitting on the edge of the concrete surround, dangling their feet in the water. A party in full swing. One of the women turned toward her, and for a long moment Maddie feared she had been seen and the woman would call out for her to join them, revealing her position. Then the woman turned back to the others and Maddie continued, hastening her steps.

The propane was where Kat had said it would be. The cap was fastened tightly, and when she tested it, she was unable to open it. On the second try it turned, releasing the scent of the fuel. At the scent of it, Maddie swallowed back the sickness in her throat and fumbled to recap the jug, but in her haste, the top fell to the floor and rolled beneath a long table. She stared at the open jug, still tasting sickness in her throat. *I can't,* she thought. She turned away and gulped fresh air. She thought of Kat, waiting at the gate. Suppressing a desire to gag, she picked up the jug.

She carried it inside the *hacienda* and to the far side of the kitchen, near the interior wooden door. The liquid sloshed and she felt the chill of it as a splatter hit her leg. This time she was unable to suppress the gagging instinct. The sound echoed in the kitchen. Quickly, afraid if she paused she would give in to the instinct to run, she tilted the jug until the contents spilled out. For a moment, paralyzed, she confused the smell with that of aviation fuel and was back in the moments following the crash. Every instinct screamed at her to flee. Her muscles tensed with the desire. Before she could give in—Kat needed her to do this—she flicked the lighter and tossed it into the pool of fluid.

Swoosh. The explosion, the heat and force of it, knocked her back. Blinded her. For a moment, she was back in the plane, surrounded by fire, and she cried out. She stumbled and felt the edge of a counter slam against her ribs. The fire shot out, a finger of flame fingering out along the floor, spreading up the wall. Her knees gave way, and the hollow ringing that presaged a panic attack echoed in her ears. She remembered the fuel that had spattered on her leg and cried out again. Over the stove an alarm sounded, deafening her. She fought the darkness, the seductive promise of giving in to it. Kat needed her.

Women ran out of the building in a confusion of noise and panic. Maddie felt a flood of adrenaline surge through her body, her heart beating so fiercely she wondered how her chest could contain it, and she again fought hysteria. The noise of the blaze—explosive, crackling, eating air—added to the frenzy of screaming voices. Maddie used the cover of the confusion to dash across the yard and toward the gate. Would they still be there waiting for her? Or had they been discovered? Behind her, the sound of chaos increased. She thought she heard a gunshot.

As she neared the gate, she searched the shadows frantically. Had they been captured? A sob escaped her throat. She stumbled and fell to her knees, forced herself to rise, to continue, to hope.

She saw the girl first. And then Kat. She ran and collapsed in her sister's arms.

The sky behind them was lit by the fire rising to the distant sky, a multicolor display that froze their attention. It took a moment for

Maddie to remember the fiesta in the village. Had it been only that morning that she had left Playa and come to the clinic?

Men were shouting. Smaller beams of light moved about the grounds, across the drive, along the perimeter of the fence, circling and searching.

The four women watched the guard at the gate, waited for him to head for the fire, but he did not leave his post. Maddie's heart fell.

The diversion hadn't worked. There was no way out.

The Mayan tugged at Maddie's arm and motioned that they were to follow her back toward the compound. Maddie shook her head. To go back was to surrender. The Mayan pulled harder at her arm. Kat and Maddie looked at each other.

Maddie shook her head. "I'm not going back."

"We have to trust Rosa," Kat said. Already the Mayan had started back, and Graciela, hesitating only a moment, was following her.

"No," Maddie hissed. "Let them go. We'll stay here and wait for the guard to go join the others. Then we can get through the gate."

Kat turned to look at the guard. He stood at the gatehouse, unmoving. "Rosa got us this far," Kat whispered. "I think we need to go with her."

A second gunshot pierced the air.

"Come on," Kat said. "Before we lose sight of them."

Soundlessly they filed back, sliding along the wall like moving shadows. Soon, Rosa stepped away from the shelter the wall offered and into the open grounds. The screams and crackling of fire and general chaos provided some coverage, but orange flames illuminated the night and presented the constant threat of exposing them. Sparks from the fire rose into the air, mingling with the women's screams. After a while, in the deepest corner of the grounds of Retirada de la Playa, the Mayan walked to a small clearing set off by rocks.

"No," Maddie heard Graciela whimper. "No, Rosa."

There was a short ledge in the clearing and an opening from which came the sound of water.

Graciela began frantically whispering to Kat.

"What is she saying?" Maddie asked.

"I can't make it all out," Kat said. "Something about a blue girl and sacrifice and the *cenote*." As if the girl's fear were contagious, Maddie held back. Rosa urged them toward the sound of water. More lights flashed, moving, searching. Coming closer.

Kat was the first to follow Rosa into the dark opening, a passage made even darker by the contrast with the lights that lit the grounds behind them. She took another step, and then two more. Water lapped at her feet. Maddie followed. The deeper they went, the darker it became. The Mayan had brought them to a cavern. Or a cave. Had she led them here to hide until it was safe to again attempt to escape? Maddie remembered what she had read in the guidebooks about the underground streams and lakes and rivers that flowed beneath the surface of the land. She turned to ask the Mayan if this was where she had led them, but she saw only Kat and Graciela. The girl clung to Kat. The Mayan had slipped away silently, as if all along this was as far as she had planned to lead them. The three of them were on their own. She turned to her sister. "Kat. I think we're at the head of a river. It flows underground, but it will lead somewhere."

"Where?"

"I don't know."

"How far?" Kat's voice was thin, weak, as if getting to this point had taken the last of her strength.

Maddie didn't answer. The water was cold, not like the warm water of the sea that lapped at the shores of the village, or where she had snorkeled with Jack. Kat was already shivering.

"I don't know," Kat said. "I don't think I can do this."

"You have to," Maddie said.

"I can't make it. You go on."

"You have to," Maddie repeated. Now it was her turn to force Kat to be strong. "You can't quit now."

Graciela, too, hung back, refusing to join them in the water. Maddie retraced her steps and took the girl by her hand. It was frigid. Maddie wondered how much blood she had lost. She reached into her pocket and found the quartz heart. "Here," she said to the girl. She turned to Kat. "Tell her it will give her strength." She listened while Kat talked to the girl. Graciela's gaze flicked over Maddie's face, and she curled her slender fingers around the stone. The three walked deeper into the stream.

"Float," she said to Kat. "I'll swim and tow you with me. You take Graciela with you. I'm not sure how much blood she's lost, but I think she's close to being in shock." She swam, pulling Kat along, checking to make sure the girl was with them. Once, she reached out an arm to gauge the width of the stream or river or whatever the Mayan had led them to. She felt coral, the sting of a cut on her hand. She stopped to look back at Graciela, waiting while Kat spoke to her softly in Spanish, her voice encouraging, and then turned her attention ahead. A few feet beyond, a light shone down on the water, forming a cone of illumination. As they swam toward it, she saw it originated from an opening in the limestone overhead. She wondered if the river meandered closer to the fire at the *hacienda* and it was the flames that were lighting the sky. She kept this thought to herself. They rested there a moment, clinging to each other like toddlers abandoned in a pool. The river continued on into the dark, but Maddie was reluctant to leave the circle of light. She shook off this resistance and tightened her hold on Kat. She nodded toward the girl. "How is she doing?"

"She feels pretty hot. Feverish," Kat said. "She needs to rest."

"We have to continue," Maddie said. "We can't stay here."

She pulled Kat into the darkness, felt the tug of Graciela's weight as Kat towed her along. They continued for a while before another faint beam appeared in the ceiling. When they reached it, they saw that ahead the river divided. She looked at Kat for guidance and then to the Mexican girl.

"Toss a coin," Kat said weakly.

"Would if I had one," Maddie replied.

The stream on the left seemed slightly larger, and she started for that. Immediately a hand stopped her. The girl was shaking her head, pointing the other way, saying something insistently.

"What is she saying?" Maddie asked.

"She said we have to go this way," Kat said. "She said the blue girl told her that is the way out."

"The blue girl?" Maddie felt a laugh form in her chest as an edge of hysteria took hold. "Jesus. That's what she said? Again with the blue girl?" She feared the girl was delirious. She looked at the passage she pointed to, which now seemed even smaller, more ominous than the other.

"What do you think?" Kat said. Already, Graciela was heading toward the smaller passage, now taking the lead.

"Oh, what the hell," Maddie said, and followed. None of them really knew what they were doing. At this point, following Graciela was as good a chance as a coin flip. Soon they were again enveloped by the dark. Kat's breathing was more labored now. "You're doing great," Maddie told her.

Maddie's own energy was flagging. She had a flashback to the fire in the *hacienda* kitchen, which had become mixed in her head with the fiery crash that had killed her parents. The frigid water of the river pulled heat from her body. There was only darkness ahead, and she stared into it, trying to see the glimmer of another opening in the ceiling. Her muscles began to lose strength, strained from the effort of towing Kat. She kicked her legs and felt a burning sting as one foot scraped a chunk of coral. It occurred to her again that perhaps the water they had followed did not go beyond the clinic's walled grounds at all but snaked beneath them. She imagined surfacing—eventually they had to surface. What waited ahead?

They heard the bats first. Then they smelled them. Maddie fought back panic as they whirled around her head. Another opening appeared overhead, and now they could see the lace-winged creatures circling around them. A wing brushed her face.

Kat cried out, her arms flailing.

"Stop it," Maddie said, making her voice harsh. "We don't have energy to waste." She was relieved—and surprised—to see the bats didn't seem to bother Graciela at all. But they seemed to have absorbed the last of Kat's will.

"I can't," she mewled.

"You have to. Hold on. We're almost there." Maddie did not know if this was true. How long had they been in the river?

"We're never going to get out of here," Kat cried.

"Don't say that." But Kat's fear was contagious and brought with it a rush of terror. The kernel of the knowledge she held within her, the secret she had barely begun to believe, pushed through. Doggedly, she continued swimming on in the night, just as in her womb, a minute life curled in deeper darkness. If they didn't find their way out of here, Jack would never know.

To push away panic she escaped into imagination, a trick she had learned in the worst days of the burn unit. She envisioned the masks she would create when she returned home. A series that would tell the story of this odyssey. She imagined incorporating elements of everyone who had been a part of the journey, images depicting aspects of evil and goodness, birth and death, hope and despair, fear and faith, greed and redemptive kindness. A series of humankind. These imaginings helped for a while, but eventually they were no match for the river, the darkness, the whimpering of the Mexican girl, the struggle to keep Kat from sinking beneath the surface.

"Tell me, what are you going to do when we get out of here?" she asked Kat.

Kat laughed hollowly. "When did you turn into the family optimist?"

"Come on," Maddie urged. "What's the first thing?"

"After a very hot shower?" Kat said.

"Seriously," Maddie said. "What are you going to do?"

Kat was silent.

"If you tell me, I'll tell you a big secret." Maddie waited. Kat was never able to resist a secret. "A huge one."

Kat stopped swimming. "Does it involve Motorcycle Man?" For a moment she sounded completely like herself.

"Maybe."

In the darkness, they heard the girl's soft crying.

"I'm really afraid she might not make it," Kat whispered, her concern for Graciela blocking out curiosity about Maddie's secret.

"Ask her," Maddie said. "Ask her what she's going to do when we get out of here."

In that way, pushing past fatigue, dodging coral and once or twice slicing exposed flesh, pace slowing, they endured the next while, passing another opening in the river roof. The girl told Kat about returning home to her family, and Kat translated for Maddie. Then Kat told about the article she was going to write, exposing Verner. She said after that she was going to find a man she had met while in Playa, one she believed she would find love with.

Maddie thought of the man in the Georgetown gym. "What's this man's name?" she said. Her voice was more labored now. Her body cold.

"I'll tell you after you tell me what your secret is."

"You were right," Maddie said. "It is about Motorcycle Man." She fell silent, allowing herself a sweet fantasy. A life with Jack. A new life. A profound weariness overtook her. Death seemed not an enemy to be fought, but a release to be sought. She slowed her strokes. "Jack." She said his name aloud. The sorrow of never seeing him again was an actual pain in her body. Now she saw clearly what she had forfeited, the love she had wasted because she had been too cowardly to embrace it. And then, and this was the deepest pain of all, she realized that he would never know she carried his child.

Kat saw light ahead first, not from above now, but straight ahead. "Look," she said. "We're almost there." Maddie took a half dozen strokes and then felt the river bottom strike her foot. She stood. Gathered strength for a moment before reaching out to support Kat and then Graciela. They were all shaking. She saw now how weak they were. Rock outcroppings surrounded the mouth of the river as they emerged from its darkness and stumbled with relief into the soft, moonlit night.

"We made it," Maddie said. "We made it. We're safe."

Almost as soon as she said this, they were pinned by a broad cone of light. Beside her, Kat gave a sob of despair. Graciela fell to the ground. Terrified, Maddie shielded her eyes and tried to focus in the glare after the darkness of the underground river. Then she saw two people coming toward them, freezing them in the light.

VÍCTOR

He shifted his weight. A spring poked up against his thigh. He focused on the road ahead. Since he'd left the village, he had passed only two cars. He hoped not to encounter any *federales*. He knew they patrolled the road at night, and if they stopped him, he would be arrested. Not for drugs or speeding—he was careful to drive beneath the limit—but because he held no license. When he had been unable to find his friend Antonio, he had borrowed the truck from Felipe Leones, the carpenter.

He turned to the man on the truck bench at his side and explained that to speed was to risk being arrested.

"How much further?" Jack asked.

Víctor shrugged. "Do not worry," he said. "We will find them." An explosion of color lit the sky above. "The fireworks," Víctor said. "From the fiesta."

Jack nodded.

"We will find them," Víctor said again. He said this not only to encourage Jack but because he believed it. Ever since he had sat with Tia Clara and she had looked at him and grasped his hand, a sense had enveloped him that he was with the old ones and they would guide him. And hadn't they led him to Jack? And together hadn't they been led to Jorge Portillo and learned that he had driven Madison to Retirada de la Playa? The very name Tia Clara kept whispering. Víctor did not know how far down the highway it was or what they would discover when they arrived, only that he needed to find Katherine.

But that, he knew, was true of life: no way of knowing what was ahead. Always operating blindly and following trails that often diverged, stopping to choose one option at each fork, hoping it was correct but never knowing what might have happened if the decision at the juncture had been different—any more than one could ever have answers to questions that only the dead held.

The road curved and his headlights caught a movement in the field to his right. He eased his foot off the gas. "Probably a wild dog," he said to Jack. "Prowling at night for prey. Or a stray musk hog." Then he saw more movement in the field. Raccoons, then. They could destroy a farmer's field of corn in one night. He switched off the headlights so as not to alarm the animals. He was about to accelerate when Jack grabbed his arm and pointed toward the movement. He made out human figures. If they were part of a drug gang on the way to a meeting, they would be armed. It was best to move on. He scanned the fields on either side of the road and glanced down the road ahead, although with his headlights off he couldn't see far. Within his sight he could see no other vehicles. He should move on, he thought again. Every villager knew the danger of stepping into another's business.

His instincts urged him to return to his journey. Leave behind whatever was happening in the field. He had not lived with only a few scars of history on his body by ignoring common sense. Taking foolish chances. Behaving in foolhardy ways. A stronger sense—beyond whim or curiosity—took hold, and he switched off the ignition. Jack was reaching into the compartment on the dash, groping inside. Looking for what? A weapon? He pulled out a flashlight. *Probably with dead batteries,* Víctor thought, knowing Felipe. Jack tested it. The beam of light lit up the cab.

He opened the door, stepped out onto the road. "Wait," Víctor cautioned. But Jack was already crossing the field. *Don't be stupid,* Víctor told himself. It was idiocy. Again he thought of Tia Clara and the ancestors, and he walked to the edge of the field. Jack shone the light onto the expanse. Coming out of the shadows were three figures. One bent, one erect, and the third supported by the other two. Their faces were obscured by the night. But Víctor could see that they were women. They appeared like figures from a dream. A myth. A story not yet told. *Past, present, and future,* he thought, and snorted at the absurdity of this.

As they drew closer he saw, impossibly, water dripping from their hair, their clothes. Yet they had not come from the direction of the sea. They froze in the circle of the light. Now he was close enough to see their faces. *Not possible,* he thought again. He recognized Graciela first. Called out her name. And then the scarred woman. "Mad-i-son?" he called, the word a question. Before the woman could even respond, Jack had taken off toward her.

Víctor looked at the third woman but did not dare trust what he saw. Overhead, an explosion of colors zigged and zagged and pinwheeled across the sky. In their light, he saw her clearly, and at last believing what his eyes told him, Víctor tore across the field, running to the woman who had won his heart.

MADISON

Maddie stood at the window looking out to where the sun crept toward the western horizon. In the living room below, the others waited. Kat had already gone down, but Maddie wanted time alone before she joined them.

Twice, Lonnie had knocked on the door, checking to see what the delay was. Lonnie, bossy as ever, had taken over the orchestration of the day as if she were totally responsible for it—which, in a way, Maddie had to acknowledge, she was.

The notes of a Haydn trumpet concerto curled up the stairs and across the threshold into her room.

Threshold. The point of beginning.

But at this liminal moment, Maddie was thinking of not just this new beginning and what waited ahead but the past as well and how connected they were, like threads in a tapestry.

She thought of all that had brought her to this moment—all the choices made and the events governed by frivolous chance. The night before that she and Kat had spent together. "Just the two of us," Kat had said.

"Seems funny, doesn't it?" Maddie had said. "For so long we've only had each other and now, look, we're part of a huge family."

"Well, not exactly huge," Kat had said, "but certainly expanding."

Anne D. LeClaire

"If it were possible to change just one thing in your life," Kat had asked at one point during that night, "what would it be? What would you choose?"

Maddie had considered all that had happened—things that for a long time they couldn't talk about, like the fears and secrets they had kept from each other and the other things that only they had shared. The deaths of their parents, the hours they had spent together in the burn unit, the night they'd escaped through the underground river, the horrific media attention during the sideshow of the trials of Verner and Mercer. She thought about how all of it had brought her to this moment. All the pain, loss, and grief. Trust and doubt. Joy and discovery, risk and daring, fear and courage, despair and hope. What single event would she pick out to change? It was an impossible choice.

"Nothing," she said.

"Nothing?" Kat said. "Not even—" Although neither said it aloud, Maddie knew they had both been thinking about their parents and how their absence was so keenly felt on this day.

"No," she said. "Because if we alter one thing, everything would change. It's all of one piece. All of it."

"The good and the bad?" Kat said.

"The good and the bad."

"And we made it. Through it all," Kat said.

"We made it. Yes, we did."

A knock on the door interrupted Maddie's musing. "Okay, Lonnie. Hold your horses. I'm coming."

"It isn't Lonnie. Can I come in?"

Her heart caught and she smiled. "Isn't it bad luck to see the bride before the wedding?"

"I'm not superstitious," Jack said. "Are you?"

In answer, she opened the door.

"Wow." The word was no more than a whisper. "You look—" It took him a moment to find the word. "Awesome," Jack said. "You look awesome."

"Awesome and fat," she said, pressing her hand against her swollen belly.

"Awesome and maternal," he said. "Beautifully maternal."

Below, someone had changed the music from Haydn to a mariachi band.

Maddie laughed. "I guess it's Víctor's turn as deejay." She imagined her new brother-in-law taking control of the room, giving Lonnie a run for her money. *Her new brother-in-law.* Kat and Víctor had been married only a month, and Maddie was still getting used to the idea. "You don't mind?" Kat had asked when she'd told her their plan.

"Why would I mind?" Maddie had said.

"We're getting hitched first," Kat said. "I mean, I don't want to upstage your wedding. And we're only having a small ceremony. It's just that we don't want to wait." Maddie didn't need further explanation. Kat seemed to be responding to the new therapy that had begun to reverse her aging, but as the doctors cautioned, there was no guarantee.

A light ribbon of female gaiety floated up to them. Both recognized the voices. "I love to hear them laugh," Maddie said.

"Mom thinks all this has been the best medicine for Olivia," Jack said. "She and Graciela have been inseparable."

"I know. For a while both Kat and I thought Graciela wouldn't recover."

"Graciela's young. And strong."

"We weren't sure it was the right thing, arranging for her to come here."

"And now? Any doubts now?"

She smiled. "Now I can't imagine life without her here."

The sound of the mariachi band grew louder.

"I think the gang's getting impatient," Jack said.

She hesitated and bit her lip.

"Not getting cold feet, are you?" he said.

"Oh, I think that ship has sailed." The baby moved, and she reached for Jack's hand and pressed it against her belly.

"Active little guy," he said.

"Or girl."

"Guy or girl, it looks like someone else is getting impatient."

She swallowed and blinked back tears. "I wish—I wish they could be here," she whispered.

"I know." He kissed her forehead. "You know what Víctor would say about that?"

She tried to imagine what he would come up with. "What's that?"

"He'd say that they *are* here. He'd say all the ancestors are here."

She closed her eyes, trying to picture their faces. She leaned into the shelter of his arms. "What are they doing?"

"Laughing," Jack said. "No doubt about it. They are laughing and cheering."

"All of them."

"Every one."

She felt it then, filling the room as surely as the music Víctor was playing. Felt the joy and the hope. And the love. All the love circling them. "Then we'd better not keep them waiting," she said.

Together they crossed the threshold.

ACKNOWLEDGMENTS

One again, my gratitude:

To my outstanding agent, Deborah Schneider.

To the entire team at Lake Union: production manager Nicole Pomeroy; the marketing side of the house, which works miracles; and most especially to my brilliant and kickass editors, Alicia Clancy and Tiffany Yates Martin. And if they awarded a Nobel for copyediting, Bill Siever would lead my list of nominees. I feel beyond fortunate to have landed in all of their care.

To my family and friends and members of the team that keeps the vessel afloat, I offer my love and gratitude for sharing the voyage both on and off the page.

ABOUT THE AUTHOR

Photo © 2018 Kim Roderiques

Anne D. LeClaire is the bestselling author of *The Halo Effect*, *Entering Normal*, and *The Lavender Hour*, as well as her critically acclaimed and award-winning memoir, *Listening Below the Noise: The Transformative Power of Silence*. A former op-ed columnist, she's been published in the *New York Times*, the *Boston Globe*, *Redbook*, *Yoga Journal*, and *Yankee Magazine*.

A distinguished fellow at the Ragdale Foundation, she teaches creative-writing workshops around the globe and leads popular seminars and workshops exploring silence, creativity, and deep listening. She has been a visiting lecturer at Mount Holyoke College, the University of Tennessee, and Columbia College and was a featured speaker at the Lincoln Center.

A former reporter, print journalist, radio broadcaster, and private pilot, she is the mother of two and lives with her husband on Cape Cod, where she leads silent retreats, practices yoga, and plays the washboard. For more information, visit the author at www.anneleclaire.com.